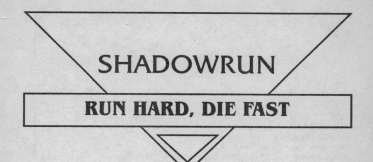

SHADOWRUN

RUN HARD, DIE FAST

Mel Odom

A ROC BOOK

ROC
Published by the Penguin Group
Penguin Putnam Inc., 375 Hudson Street,
New York, New York 10014, U.S.A.
Penguin Books Ltd, 27 Wrights Lane, London W8 5TZ, England
Penguin Books Australia Ltd, Ringwood, Victoria, Australia
Penguin Books Canada Ltd, 10 Alcorn Avenue,
Toronto, Ontario, Canada M4V 3B2
Penguin Books (N.Z.) Ltd, 182–190 Wairau Road,
Auckland 10, New Zealand

Penguin Books Ltd, Registered Offices:
Harmondsworth, Middlesex, England

First published by Roc, an imprint of Dutton NAL, a member of Penguin Putnam Inc.

First Printing, February, 1999
10 9 8 7 6 5 4 3 2 1

Copyright © FASA Corporation, 1999
All rights reserved

Series Editor: Donna Ippolito
Cover art: Luis Royo

RoC REGISTERED TRADEMARK — MARCA REGISTRADA

Dear Matt Dain Odom,

This book is dedicated to you, son, with thanks for sharing your life with me and for introducing me to the rigors of being a wrestling parent! May your world always be as exciting and filled with wonderment as it is now. This book is a toast to that early morning pre-tournament weigh-in filled with Dunkin Donuts, conversation, and just a-borning sun. And to your first pin in the Norman Junior High Duel!

Love,

Dad

Special acknowledgment to Donna Ippolito, one of the finest editors I've worked with, and the person who helped me bring into clearer focus one of the most interesting characters in Shadowrun.

And to Nigel Findley: Argent is your creation, buddy, and I regret that this is the closest I can come to working with you. I think it would have been a blast.

And to the fans of Shadowrun who've written and told me what the shadows mean to them: Se7thSon, Matthew Banning, Buddy Lacey, Robert Doyle, Ron Peterson, Dave, Brandon A. Reed, and STR8EDGBOB! Run fast and true, chummers, or the shadows will get you!

NORTH

CIRCA 2060

TSIMSHIAN

ATHABASKAN COUNCIL

Edmonton

ALGONKIAN-MANITOU COUNCIL

Saskatoon

Vancouver

Calgary

SALISH-SHIDHE COUNCIL

Regina

Pacific Ocean

Seattle

Winnipeg

Spokane

Portland

Salem

Helena

SIOUX NATION

Fargo

Duluth

Butte

Bismarck

Billings

St. Paul
Minneapolis

TIR TAIRNGIRE

Boise

Sheridan

Rapid City

Idaho Falls

Eureka

Reno

Salt Lake City

Cheyenne

Sioux Falls

Des Moines

Provo

Boulder

Denver

Omaha

Kansas City

San Francisco

CALIFORNIA FREE STATE

UTE NATION

Las Vegas

Colorado Springs

Topeka

Bakersfield

Pueblo

Wichita

Santa Barbara
Los Angeles

PUEBLO CORPORATE COUNCIL

Tulsa

San Diego

Santa Fe

Albuquerque

Amarillo

Oklahoma City

Little Rock

Tijuana

Phoenix

Tucson

Roswell

Ft. Worth

Dallas

El Paso

San Angelo

Shreveport

Pacific Ocean

Austin

Houston

San Antonio

Chihuahua

Corpus Christi

AZTLAN

Monterrey

La Paz

Culiacan

Durango

Ciudad Victoria

To Tenochtitlán

AMERICA

CIRCA 2060

Hudson
Bay

Ft. Albany • Waskaganish •

Sept Iles •

Gulf of
St. Lawrence

QUÉBEC

Charlottetown

Thunder
Bay

Fredericton

Québec •

Halifax

Lake
Superior

Sault Ste. Marie
Sudbury Ottawa Montpelier •
Kingston

Montreal • Augusta

Milwaukee

Lake
Michigan

Lansing
Detroit •

Toronto

Albany •
Buffalo •

Concord •
Boston

Hartford •

Chicago • Gary •

Cleveland •

Philadelphia

Newark •
Manhattan •

Indianapolis •

DC •

Springfield •

Cincinnati •

Charleston Richmond •

UNITED CANADIAN AND
AMERICAN STATES (U.C.A.S.)

East
St. Louis •

Louisville •

Roanoke • Norfolk •

Atlantic
Ocean

Nashville •

Durham •
Raleigh •

Knoxville •

Charlotte •

Memphis •

Columbia • Wilmington

Birmingham • Atlanta

CONFEDERATED AMERICAN STATES (C.A.S.)

Jackson •

Montgomery •

Charleston •

Savannah •

Baton
Rouge •

Albany •
Mobile •

Jacksonville •

Orlando •

Gulf of
Mexico

Tampa •

West Palm Beach •

Miami •

Key West •

CARIBBEAN
LEAGUE

Havana •

CUBA

Map of
North America

●	National Capital
Seattle •	City
– – –	International Boundary
——	State Boundary (U.S.A. circa 1990)

Kilometers
0   200   400   600
0   200   400
Miles

Published by Base-Am • Cartographic and Delicatessen
102b w Van Buren Chicago™ • 1312/25 5603 Copyright MMLIII

Prologue

From transcript of conversation with confidential informant, Bonez. Submitted by

Sgt. N. Cooper, Department of
Special Investigation
04:11:23/10-6-60
CC: LTG 2418 (32-0113)

[Note per Cooper: Cap, I know everybody thinks Bonez is a burnout simsense junkie, but the guy is knowledgeable in what goes on in the shadows, a regular fanboy with a serious jones for shadowrunners. Nobody else had a finger on Argent, but Bonez had this.]

"Argent? Sure I've heard of Argent. Frag, anybody who's into the serious end of runners knows about this guy. And yeah, he's one guy. Some of the street guff says he's a clone or something; maybe got five or six of him running around at the same time. Not true.

"Argent is a scary guy. Not 'cause he's one of those sadistic fragging posers that hang out in so many of the flops the shadowfolk have. But when Argent gets down to biz, the hincky guttermeat that goes up against him generally flatlines in messy pyrotechnics if the ops goes bad. Otherwise, Argent's in and out and somebody's slagged before they even know they've been cheated out of their next cardiac bumpety-boom, bumpety-boom.

"Military training? I've heard he had some tours with Fuchi during their Desert Wars. Then he hung it up and went private in the shadows. Had a group they called the

Wrecking Crew. They were a specialty team that handled any kind of project if the credstick was big enough. Very select about what they took on. Argent's got standards. That joker had his flesh and blood arms chopped so he could cyber up. I mean, you know what kind of thinking and self-control that takes? You can have an arm augmented with less trauma. 'Course, then you've only got an augmented arm, not a weapon the way Argent went.

"A few years back, according to a wisp of street buzz I haven't been able to nail down, a run went to squat and two of the Crew got greased in the confusion. Since then, Argent's operated on a smaller scale, only taking on one-man contracts, or two-man if he can fill the bill himself.

"The gen is that Argent lost some of himself when the Wrecking Crew flamed out. Others say that Argent won't just partner with anybody, so that's why he's working lonesome these days. Nobody much is saying either way anyhow 'cause nobody knows.

"I go with the first thought. Every runner I know would give their right nut to work with Argent, and half the cred involved. Argent's a credstick in the slot every time. He's staying small 'cause he wants to.

"Oh, one other word of advice, Cooper: you somehow manage to wind up in Argent's way, get the frag to a new twenty. There's no back-up in the guy, and when he takes something on, his word's his bond. The frag-up that cost the lives of two Crew members? Word I get is that Argent completed the contract anyway. Signed, sealed, and delivered. That's just the kind of joker he is. Real stand-up, you know."

1

"Skyhook, I have your target located."

"Affirmative, Groundwire, bring us onto the target." Argent shifted in the passenger seat of the Hughes WK-2 Stallion helicopter and stared down at the grid of lighted streets through the cool blue polycarbonate glazing of the craft's cockpit bubble.

He was a big man with a squared-off face that looked like it had been cast in bronze. His fair hair was cut in a military flat top that he'd worn for years. He went clean-shaven, and the weak moonlight dusting in from outside the cockpit faded against the camou makeup he wore to blunt his features. Dressed in a dark green one-piece with a combat harness over it, his matte-black finished cyber-arms blended into the overall look.

"Phasing you in, Skyhook," the feminine voice said.

"Copy, Groundwire. GPS coming on-line now." Argent glanced at the Sony Nav-Dat global positioning system mounted amid the helo's control panel. The glowing orange dot that represented the Stallion held its course while a purple triangle took form ahead and to the left. The big man glanced over at the helo pilot.

"I heard," Merkhur stated irritably in his clipped British accent over the helo's commlink. His meat body sagged in the pilot's chair, a vehicle control rig plugged into his right temple under the wild tangle of chestnut hair. Long and lean even for an elf, he looked almost uncomfortable folded into the seat, but the Vehicle Control Rig cyberware made him part of the craft. For all intents and purposes, he was the helo. He saw with its cams, heard with its aud pickups, and even felt the air friction against the helo's skin. He wore traditional Japanese robes, soft cream over brown.

For the moment, the Stallion was covered with the markings of the United Canadian and American States Post Office. The markings were camouflage, though, and a good rain blowing in across Puget Sound would have washed them right off. Argent had known there wouldn't be any rain, and a quick rinse would put the helo back to its original green color, making it harder to trace after the op played out.

The kidnappers had chosen the Lower Queen Anne neighborhood as the dropsite. They couldn't know it, but he was familiar with the area. Much closer to ground zero now, Argent made out the long, winding route of Union Street threading through the sprawl's other thoroughfares.

"If Shaundra Merlini's captors get away," the feminine voice of Groundwire said over the Wiremasters Commlink X, "they'll have plenty of boltholes to rabbit to before you or Lone Star can dig them out. The girl will be dead when she's found."

"I know, Peg," Argent said softly. "But that's not going to happen."

Peg was a decker, one of the best at getting into high-tech systems, and Argent wouldn't have felt as confident without her running the data end of the rescue. He hadn't seen a system yet that she couldn't sleaze her way through given the time. The problem was that in their job there wasn't always time.

This time they'd been lucky. When Victor Merlini had contracted a fixer Argent picked up biz from and explained the situation, mentioning his daughter's amputated thumb as well, Argent decided at once that he'd sign on for the save if he could find a way to get next to the kidnappers. Standing up for an underdog against overwhelming oppressive odds was one of the jobs he took every time.

He'd combed the streets while Peg had ducked through the shadow information alleys of the Matrix linking Seattle's computers and telecom activity. The closest they'd come to identifying the kidnap ring through whispered rumors was to establish a reasonably certain tie to the Alamos 20K hate groups. Neither of them had turned up names of any of the people connected with the kidnap ring.

What Argent was sure of was that Merlini had a right to be fearful for his daughter. Argent's research had turned up seven people in the Seattle-based shipping industry who'd lost family members in the last handful of months.

Merlini's family physician had also supplied a tissue sample from the girl, allowing Argent to hire two street mages and a snake shaman to help him look for Shaundra. Escadero, the snake shaman, had gotten the closest to finding the girl.

While in an induced trance, slithering through the maybes of what might come to pass regarding Shaundra Merlini's future, Escadero had spotted the young woman in a van in the Lower Queen Anne District. But the foretelling vision wasn't always accurate, as Escadero had pointed out.

Tonight, it had proven on the mark. And one of the three mages now astrally searching for Shaundra Merlini in Lower Queen Anne using the tissue sample had found her and relayed the information to Peg. It had been a long shot, but it was all Argent had left to play. Lone Star had covered all the conventional routes.

The Stallion skimmed the canyons of corporate skyscrapers, apartment buildings, and shopping complexes, staying barely five meters above the uneven skyline, juking sideways as Merkhur controlled it. The rigger handled the craft with smooth confidence, using some of the buildings for cover as they swooped toward Union Street.

"Groundwire," Argent said over the commlink. "Can you paint the target?"

"I'm collating data now." As always Peg sounded cool and assured.

Argent released the catches on the door, letting the wind whip into the cockpit. Holding onto the door with one hand, he checked his gear with the other, running his palm over the twin Smartlink Level II outfitted Ingram Super Mach 100s riding in crossed bands over his hips. A Smartlink Level II equipped Savalette Guardian was synthleathered in a jackass shoulder rig under his left arm as backup in case the Ingrams didn't quite turn the trick. And he had a monofilament whip tucked away in his boot if things turned truly fragged.

"Skyhook," Peg called, "stand by for targeting."

"Get to it." Argent activated the circuitry in his cyber-eyes and brought the thermographic utility on-line in his right eye. Immediately, the sprawl below took on a new look as the thermographic vision picked up heat patterns rather than conventional sight. The signals coming through both his eyes was confusing, but he was used to going monocular when he needed to. It affected his depth perception, but mostly only at distances, and that was why the eye was also equipped with a range-finder to compensate. He carried a lot of cybernetics in his body, but all of it was user-friendly, top-of-the-line deltaware, some of it barely out of the prototype stage. His contacts put him next to a lot of gear that wasn't on the market, and he spent the money for the upgrades.

Another moment passed, then an oval pale lavender light lit up the top of a charcoal-colored Ares Roadmaster cargo vehicle. The lavender light was the result of thermal imaging projected by a drone locked into a pattern above the target vehicle. The drone, a stripped-down, highly illegal Lone Star Strato-9 surveillance model knock-off engineered by black marketeers in Singapore, had been leased from an outlaw rigger for the night's op.

"Skyhook, your target has been painted," Peg declared. Operating from information she'd gathered from the mages, she'd managed to ID the vehicle.

"Affirmative," Argent said. "Skyhook sees the paint. Merkhur?"

"Got it, got it, mate. I'm not exactly sleeping at the post, you know." The helo lost altitude rapidly, streaking for the Roadmaster.

Unaware, the Roadmaster cruised easily through the streets, negotiating the intersections without getting hung up. It was coming up on the Seattle Aquarium, crossing Ninth Avenue.

Argent shifted, opening the helo's door more. He stepped out into the chill wind blowing in from Elliott Bay. Traffic whisked by less than ten meters below as the helo closed rapidly on its prey.

With the cargo door open, the wind slammed into the helo's cockpit, throwing its aerodynamics off. Merkhur struggled with the controls, forcing the Stallion to stay on course.

"Lower," Argent ordered.

"Mate," Merkhur protested, "you're about pushing this old lady's limits."

Argent didn't have any sympathy. His thoughts were on the young woman in the speeding van, and on her father. Corp exec though he was, and used to a daily grind of high-pressure deals and bargaining, Victor Merlini had barely made it through the telecom interview Argent had insisted on.

The Roadmaster pulled into the right lane again. Argent marked the next intersection as Boren Avenue, and Union Street curved back to the left, straightening out now. From what Peg had learned in the Lone Star files, the ransom dropsite hadn't been announced to Merlini yet. Peg had confirmed that with a call to the young woman's father.

In each of the previous cases, the kidnappers had stayed on the move with their hostage, allowing them to have contact with a second group of kidnappers. With all the cards in their hands, the kidnappers downloaded the ransom money through a telecom-equipped deck without having to produce the hostage. The third kidnapping had resulted in the hostage getting chilled while on-line with her husband, and the kidnappers had disappeared without a trace.

The only chance Shaundra Merlini had of getting out of the situation alive was if someone could get to her before the ransom changed hands.

"Skyhook," Peg called out. "The call has been made."

Argent logged the time on his retinal clock, advanced it two minutes, then started counting down. None of the other ransom transfers had taken more than two minutes. At the end of that time, the hostages had been executed, their bodies thrown out into the streets.

Merkhur straightened the Stallion again, bringing it closer to the Roadmaster. Now that the kidnapper's vehicle had reached the part of Union Street that ran independent of the other side streets and had a higher speed limit, it sped up.

A minute flashed by as Merkhur worked to get the helo over the Roadmaster. Out in traffic now, Argent watched the way the vehicle moved, then noticed the two dark blue Ford Americars running blocker and flanker for the bigger vehicle.

It wasn't a total surprise to Argent, but it did make things more complicated. He spoke over the commlink. "They've got cars running cover for the Roadmaster, Merkhur."

"I see them. But there's no way they won't see us coming if they're alert."

The retinal clock was down to fifty-two seconds. "Then we're going to have to do this quick."

"I know. I'm ready to start my final approach."

"Go." Argent clambered down the side of the helo until he was at the landing gear. He handled his weight easily, maintaining holds with the cyberhands. The cyberarms more than doubled his original strength and weren't as prone to fatigue.

The Stallion dove like a hunting hawk, curving gracefully through the area toward the Roadmaster. Merkhur handled his craft expertly, matching the helo's speed with the cargo vehicle. Dropping into position over the Roadmaster, he maintained a distance of less than three meters.

Virulent red tracer fire streaked through the night around Argent, pinging off the armored sides of the Stallion. He glanced down and saw gunners from the rear car firing up at the helo.

Over the speeding Roadmaster now, Argent released his hold on the Stallion's landing gear and dropped.

2

Falling free of the helo and no longer part of its forward momentum, Argent became prey for the vicious wind. It buffeted him for an instant, pushing him like a kite. Then he flailed, regaining control over his body with difficulty.

When both his feet missed the Roadmaster, he accessed the circuitry in his left cyberhand and switched on the electro-magnets. He arced his body and slammed his hand against the top of the cargo vehicle. The magnetic field created by the electricity juicing the cyberhand pulled his palm and fingers against the metal vehicle roof, snugging them tight. Even then, it took a moment for his fall to stop, his hand dragging toward the edge, shrilling noisily.

Argent found purchase with his feet and hauled one of the Ingram Super 100s free of synthleather. Bracing himself, the sound of the engine behind him suddenly racing, he brought the Ingram up and twisted around.

The car behind the Roadmaster sped up, lurching forward. A man leaned out of the passenger window and brought up a machine pistol. The pistol's red aiming laser flicked across Argent and the Roadmaster, then ejected brass glinted as the bullets ripped free of the vicious muzzle. The dulled *thwocks* of the rounds striking the back of the cargo vehicle rattled over the noise of the traffic.

With the smartlink operational, Argent's cybered eyes became gunsights. Cross hairs appeared in his vision, tracking the Ingram's sweep. He caressed the trigger, expertly unleashing a three-round burst that decapitated his attacker.

The headless corpse writhed in pain and reflex, tumbling back inside the Americar. Blood filmed the inside of the windshield in haphazard streaks.

Alarmed by his dead companion, the driver swerved, reaching out with one hand to block the corpse from falling onto him. The Americar veered sharply into oncoming traffic, drawing a series of hostile horn bleats, then came roaring back at the rear of the Roadmaster again.

Argent shifted the Ingram and squeezed off four sustained bursts that emptied the machine pistol's 60-round, high-density clip. The max amount of rounds that could be fired from the machine pistol in a burst was fifteen. The initial burst starred the Americar's bulletproof windshield on the driver's side, covering it over with cracks and limiting the driver's vision. The second and third, aimed toward the pavement in front of the car to take advantage of the ricochet potential from the hard surface, chopped the front tires to bits. The last burst sprayed across the Americar's front grill, puncturing the radiator and punching into the engine block.

Fire surged from under the Americar's hood, trailing black smoke. The car lost ground, rocking out of control.

Above, the Stallion climbed rapidly into the air, without so much as a fare-thee-well from Merkhur. The comm-link remained silent, with even Peg quiet on the sidelines. Argent felt alone in that instant, missing his dead team mates from the Wrecking Crew as much as he ever had. If Hawk and Toshi had survived the run against the Fort Lewis ISP facility Dirk Montgomery had contracted them for . . . but he checked his thinking, getting back to the biz at hand.

Holstering the empty Ingram, he turned his attention to the maglock holding the cargo vehicle's rear doors closed. He straightened his free hand, then popped the retractable punching dagger free of his wrist. The triangular blade extended nearly ten centimeters beyond his fingertips. He rocketed his arm forward, shearing into the plastisteel door. He retracted the blade and shoved his fingers through the opening, ripping it larger.

Equipped with sensors sensitive enough to allow him to read Braille if he needed to, the cybernetic interface linking Argent's meat body to his bodyware also gave him the choice of how much sensation came charging back through his nervous system. He'd chosen to feel only the impact of his hand driving through the doors, nothing that his mind could have comprehended as pain.

Although his arm was joined to a flesh and blood body with a reinforced spine and joint and other structural supports, he still didn't possess the leverage to throw cars around the way street sams did on the trid action shows. With his cyberware, his already considerable strength did double. And the grip in his hand, depending on leverage, was incredible, like the jaws of a vise.

He closed his hand around the locking mechanism holding the door closed. One quick squeeze later, all that remained of the lock was a handful of metallic and ceramic splinters.

The shriek of the collapsing lock was still in his ears when Argent pulled the door open and stepped into the back of the Roadmaster. Bullets smashed into the kevlar covering his chest.

Five men occupied the vehicle's cargo space, dressed in nondescript coveralls that Argent assumed disguised the street clothes worn under them. Shaundra Merlini, blond and disheveled, her left hand wrapped in a heavy pad of blood-spotted gauze, sat tied to one of the built-in cargo securing hooks on the side wall. She wore the same chartreuse Vashon Island skirt-suit that she'd been wearing when she'd been abducted. Her father had shown Argent a pic from the sec cam loop of her departure. Her head swiveled weakly in the big samurai's direction, a scream parting her lips.

One of the young woman's kidnappers rushed toward her with a monofilament knife glinting in his fist. Argent sprinted to intercept the man wielding the knife. To his left, one of the other men broke into a reflexive offensive move that was so smooth it told Argent immediately the man was equipped with a move-by-wire cybernetic system. The man's hand flashed for a Colt Manhunter snugged up under his left arm.

Letting his own reflexes take over, guided by experience and his own move-by-wire system, Argent shifted points of attack. The move-by-wire system kept the individual equipped with it in a constant state of readiness, almost like a seizure, but resulting motion was simple, direct, and unbelievably fast to anyone who didn't have it. The only drawback was the slight tremors Argent experienced when his muscles were relaxed—an unfortunate side effect.

Argent watched the kidnapper's Manhunter pull free of the holster before the man with the knife could take one more running step toward the defenseless young woman. Argent accessed the BrightLight system built into his left eye and triggered the Flash-pak.

The sudden glare of the intensely bright light strobing from the samurai's eye filled the Roadmaster's cargo space. No matter what kind of cybered eyes any of the kidnappers had, Argent knew the Flash-pak was going to have an effect. His own vision, however, remained unaffected.

In the brief flicker of confusion that followed, Argent closed on the man holding the knife. The joker had staggered, hammered by the painful intensity of the Flash-pak, stopping short of his intended prey. Ripping the Guardian free of his shoulder holster, the big street samurai brought the pistol up. The smartgun link built into the handle of the weapon transferred information through Argent's hand, allowing his move-by-wire system to incorporate all the specifics of the weapon in a nanosecond.

Squeezing off his first shot, Argent put the round into the move-by-wire equipped kidnapper's gunhand. The heavy-caliber bullet split the hand open, reducing it to metal splinters. He'd had to aim for the weapon because geeking the kidnapper might not have stopped his cybersystems from flatlining the young woman.

Unable to take another clear shot and not wanting any more bullets whizzing around in the back of the cargo vehicle than necessary, Argent concentrated on the knife man. He stiffened the fingers of his free hand and shot them into the man's throat, driving the tips through flesh to the spinal column.

The kidnapper's charge broke into a loose collapse

of limbs. Catching the dead man still a meter short of Shaundra Merlini, Argent wheeled with the man's body before him, holding the corpse up to use it as a shield to defend the woman.

Bullets thudded into the dead man's back.

At a glance, Argent saw that the shots came from one of the other surviving kidnappers. The heavily cybered man had moved from his position, lost for a moment in the confusion of bodies shifting in the Roadmaster's cargo space. Targeting the shooter, Argent placed a single round between the man's eyes that voided his brain pan in a glistening rush.

A shadow flicked into motion at the periphery of Argent's vision, followed immediately by a foul collection of curses. The Merlini woman screamed behind him, her voice sounding lost and pathetic. She was still under the blinding effects of the Flash-pak, totally panicked.

Before he could bring the Guardian around to face the new threat, the razored joker dropped an arm like an iron bar across Argent's wrist, knocking the corpse from his grip. Without wasted motion, the razorboy shoved the mangled remains of his hand at Argent's face.

3

Argent twisted, narrowly avoiding the knot of shrapnel the razorboy's arm had become. He shoved the Guardian's blunt snout into his opponent's wide mouth, breaking teeth, then pulled the trigger. Even move-by-wire reflexes couldn't avoid the bullet that blew through the back of the gillette's skull.

The dead man stumbled back, propelled by the large-caliber round.

Even before the corpse could fall, Argent moved on the remaining two kidnappers. A backhanded blow took down the man on the left, the metal cyberhand shredding flesh to the bone with the impact.

The last man set himself up in a martial arts kata, his arms whipping around as he positioned himself for Argent's attack. He gave a yell, meeting the street samurai halfway with a front snapkick that snaked through Argent's defenses.

The kick collided with Argent's face, popping his head back. Pain flared through his face, but he forced it out of his mind, automatically grabbing his attacker's foot with his left hand before the man could pull it back to safety. Argent brought his other hand across, defending against a flurry of punches, then smashed the Guardian down on the knee of the captured leg.

Bone crunched, and Argent's enhanced hearing picked up the sound of reinforcing ceramics and metals in the man's joint architecture giving way as well. The kidnapper screamed in pain but tried to continue the fight. He reached, bending from the waist. Razors popped free of his fingers, licking for Argent's eyes.

Argent held onto the mangled leg, twisting to gain leverage and to keep his opponent off balance. The man yelled, but swiped the finger razors again. Lifting the Guardian, Argent squeezed off a round that impacted in the center of the man's face. He dropped the corpse and turned his attention to the door shutting the cargo space off from the Roadmaster's front cab.

The door opened easily at his touch, but the way the Roadmaster swerved let him know the driver was aware that things had gone to hell in the cargo section. As Argent moved into the cramped cab area, the kidnapper riding shotgun fired his Manhunter from point-blank range.

Only Argent's reflexes, honed from dozens of battles, and the move-by-wire system saved him. He dodged to one side, his free hand arcing out to grab the pistol barrel.

Before another round could be fired, he squeezed his hand, smashing the barrel together.

The kidnapper pulled the trigger anyway, not knowing the damage that had been done to his weapon. The Man-hunter exploded, blowing the slide backward into the man's face and turning it into a mask of blood.

Shoving his way into the cab, Argent brushed aside the driver's attempt to aim a pistol at him, causing the man to fire a round through the windshield. Argent squeezed off two rounds into the wounded man's face to make sure he was down, then turned his attention to the driver.

The Roadmaster rushed through the streets of Lower Queen Anne, drawing a number of frustrated and angry horn blasts from other vehicles. The driver pulled on the wheel hard, ramming the Roadmaster into a Metro Tran-sit bus, driving the bigger vehicle onto the sidewalk along Union Street. Scattered pockets of the sprawl's night life ran for their lives as the bus and Roadmaster fought for control. The bus plowed through a small group of um-brella tables at an open-air Thai restaurant. Luckily, the diners all got to safety. Some of them even put a few shots through the Roadmaster's windshield. It was no real surprise, Argent reflected grimly. In the Lower Queen Anne District a chummer watched his or her hoop as a full-time job.

Clenching his fist in the driver's coverall, Argent lifted the man from behind the wheel and swung him toward the pistol-blasted windshield. Already weakened from the bullets that had struck it, the windshield gave way at once.

The driver tried to grab a secure hold as he slid over the Roadmaster's blunt nose, but failed. He dropped in front of the big cargo vehicle as Argent holstered the Guardian and slid into the seat.

The street samurai fought the wheel for control, pull-ing away from the bus. There was only one more tick of resistance as the wheels rolled over the kidnapper. Reaching down to the gear shift lever between the seats, Argent shifted into a lower gear, then put his foot heavier on the accelerator, controlling the vehicle.

Activating the commlink, he said, "Groundwire."

Peg came back on-line at once, a calming influence inside his busy mind. "Here, Skyhook."

Argent scanned the line of traffic ahead of him and in the oncoming lanes. "There was another vehicle running blocker." The other Americar was no longer in front of him.

"The second car is coming up beside you," Peg replied coolly. She was tied into the action by the drone over the scene, scanning the vid it relayed. "It dropped back as you were getting control of the Roadmaster."

Argent glanced in the side mirror, recognizing the other Americar at once from the autofire flaming from two of the windows. "Got it," he said. "Can you contact Lone Star?"

"I've already alerted them," Peg answered. "And given them the specifics of who you are and what's going on. Estimated time of arrival is seventeen seconds. They have a unit en route."

Driving expertly, Argent used the traffic against his pursuers, filling the middle of Union Street when the flow of traffic backed off. He watched the digital readout of his retinal clock as it counted down, then noticed the fat shape of the Chrysler-Nissan G12A hovercraft in front of him as it plowed through traffic with full light bars blazing to announce its presence.

Heavily armored and distinctly marked, the Lone Star SWAT unit looked like a mechanized predator on the prowl. Traffic readily made room for it, cringing to the sides of Union Street as the whirling light peeled away the layers of neon spilling from the various businesses lining both sides of the thoroughfare. Lone Star's SWAT teams had a reputation for getting a job done quickly in spite of unfavorable conditions.

Argent glanced in the side mirror, watching the Americar swing out wide behind him, intent on overtaking the Roadmaster. This time, the street samurai let the vehicle come, knowing the SWAT unit had to be locked onto the Americar.

The hovercraft sped down Union Street, scarcely more than fifty meters away. Guns mounted on firm points on the G12A glinted against the hide of black armor. A Victory rotary assault cannon kept a low profile above the black-lensed glass of the hovercraft's windshield.

Gunfire raked the Roadmaster's side in a sudden drumming din. Argent hunkered down low behind the steering wheel, dodging a car in front of him that had come to a full stop. He edged to the left, keeping the attention of the men in the Americar, watching as the hovercraft settled in the middle of Union Street atop its cushion of air.

He recognized all the telltales of the hovercraft's gunners, knowing they'd locked onto their target. Without warning, he hit the brakes and pulled the steering wheel hard right. Since the cargo area was virtually empty, making the back end of the Roadmaster light, the vehicle fishtailed, the back end coming around like it was racing the front end.

Argent had timed the move well enough that the Roadmaster's heavier bulk caught the Americar from behind, batting it forward and to the left. The Americar driver fought his vehicle for control. The men inside the car were close enough for Argent to see. As he continued shutting the Roadmaster down, he watched the men's faces swivel toward the waiting Lone Star hovercraft.

A micro-tick later, as soon as the Americar was clear of the Roadmaster, the SWAT craft's rotary cannon opened up with a thunderous roar. A full salvo of five cannon rounds slammed into the Americar, reducing it to a tumbling ball of fire and wreckage that pummeled the side of a coffin hotel, shedding bits of flaming scrap.

Miraculously, the hotel wall held. Fire washed over the windows when the Americar exploded in a heated rush.

Argent knew most of the hotel's guests shunted away in their small, stacked cubicles with the simsense rigs or gooned on the what-me-worry of their choice wouldn't even have registered the impact. The Roadmaster quivered to a halt.

Sliding from behind the wheel, Argent returned to the compartment area of the vehicle. Shaundra Merlini wept openly, her mouth working continuously. Tenderly, he freed her from the restraints, then picked her up in his arms. She folded in on herself like a child, arms crossed, her chin tucked down on top of her hands.

Carrying the young woman's weight easily, Argent strode to the back of the Roadmaster. "You're going to be okay," he told her in a soft voice. "Your father sent me to bring you home. And I'm going to see that done. No one else is going to hurt you. That's a promise."

She pressed against his chest, shivering.

Argent held her and forced himself to keep his distance, didn't allow himself to think of all the things she'd been through since she'd been taken. Success in his line of work all too often resulted only in keeping a bad situation from getting worse, not by saving the weak and the innocent from what they'd already experienced. He couldn't change history; only influence the future. A soldier learned where the lines were between what was possible and what wasn't. Personal involvement had gotten too many good men dead, and he knew that from experience.

The SWAT members ringed the Roadmaster, pointing their rifles and pistols at Argent. He remained standing when he was ordered, then told them to contact Victor Merlini to check on his involvement.

"Argent," Peg called over the commlink.

That surprised him. This deep into an op, without knowing whether they could put a handle on all the elements,

Peg knew better than to break the communication black-out. He waited as the SWAT members came for him. One of the first things they would do was slap a headjammer on him to block out whatever internal commlinks he might have.

"I knew you'd want to know," Peg went. "I just received a message from Brynnmawr."

And that act, Argent knew, was even more dangerous than staring down the muzzles of a dozen adrenaline-charged Lone Star SWAT members. Brynnmawr was part of his past, one of a number of pasts.

Only Brynnmawr was more dangerous than all others put together. If everything had gone right, Argent knew he'd never have heard from the man again. Even as Shaundra Merlini was taken from his arms and containment manacles were snapped around his wrists, he couldn't help wondering what had gone wrong and who had been flatlined.

Or who was going to be.

4

[Chip file: Argent
[Personal log and review file: Classified]
Security access: ******—22:43:43/10-9-60]

BEGIN UPLOAD

Location: Everett Safe House

Lone Star didn't try to detain me long. Or if they did, they didn't get to. Victor Merlini saw to that. An exec with his kind of power and political clout is going to get what he wants. Of course, if things had turned out differently with his daughter, I'd probably still be buried deep in the slammer. I kept a realistic view of the world.

After I got away from the Star, after I cleared Victor Merlini's Toyota Elite limo with a certified credstick in the amount we'd agreed on, I took a half-dozen cabs to the rented doss in Everett that I had waiting. At least, almost there; I walked the last three klicks after being let out at the main gates to the Federated Everett Boeing Facility on 84th Street SW.

Merkhur had disappeared before any of the Star flyboys could run him to ground. A quick wash in one of the units down near the docks in Elliott Bay and he was as gone as they got. He'd gotten paid half his fee up front, and Peg had transferred the other half to the bank he was using once I'd dropped from the helo. The biz I do is by the numbers and on time. I even paid up front for the drone he left behind so there'd be no hard feelings.

The Everett doss wasn't home; it was just a flop, a place to go to ground. When I pulled the kind of high-profile shadowrun the Merlini kidnapping turned out to be, I stayed away from my homeground for a couple days, maybe even a couple weeks. Sometimes the trouble I took on had a habit of following me around for a time.

Everett was a good location for cooling out, and the doss itself was a few blocks down from Casino Corner, the only red-light zone in the district. I took the four flights of stairs up to the doss because the elevators didn't work. The bruising I'd taken during the Merlini recovery burned with a slow flame across my chest, tightening up over my ribs.

A wave of stale, humid air slapped me in the face as I stepped into the room, like the liquid stench from a jungle soldier's athlete's foot gone near to gangrenous rot. I dropped the duffel on the sway-backed bed and got serious about the room's security.

I took a scrambler-equipped Sony telecom from my

duffel and plugged it into the wall outlet. Once it was operational, I tapped in the codes for the MishiMoshi commlink program and the Roller Coaster relocate program Peg had installed in the unit and let them run along with the self-driven compatibility diagnostics. Even if anyone out there happened to be listening and managed to trace the call, they'd show the origination point as being down in Tir Tairngire, and no one in Seattle was going to traipse down into the elflands easily.

Reaching into the duffel again, I dug out the battery-operated motion detector wand set. The monofilament ends of the wands sank into the floor without a problem. They extended sectionally to a height of under one meter, hidden in the shadows draped across the room, covering the door and the window. When they were switched on, an overlapping field of fire surrounded the interior of the room, including me. If anything moved in that area, a high-pitched warning screech would sound that my cyber-enhanced hearing would detect.

Lights flashed across the front of the telecom as the programs cycled through. When they finished, I punched in the LTG code that Peg was using this half-hour.

She came on at once. "I was getting worried. You're calling later than I thought you would."

I gazed at the blank face of the telecom even though I knew she wouldn't broadcast vid. Peg didn't like people to see her. Fourteen years ago, when she was sixteen, she'd had an accident on her bike. She'd lost.

When she came out of surgery, barely alive, she'd been a quadriplegic, with the injury so high up her spinal cord that cyberlimbs were never going to be an option. Even before then, from the bits and pieces I'd been able to put together about her life over the years, she hadn't had a good relationship with her parents. They'd liked her even less as an invalid.

After awhile, her parents wanted to put her in a clinic, get her out from under foot. It had been a hard decision for a sixteen-year-old kid to make, but she'd agreed. For a price.

Peg had always been good with computers. In return for accepting the exile to the quad clinic, they'd paid for her first datajack. She took to the Matrix immediately, spending hours every day in there, learning from anyone who would teach her, hoping to find skills that would allow her to live her life on her own terms instead of being dependent.

She'd hoped to get enough education that a corp would hire her. Maybe she would have made it. Except that she discovered shadowrunners. Slipping through black IC on datasteals gave her an adrenaline rush like nothing else.

In all the years I'd worked with her, I'd only seen her once. Then she was being kept in a clinic in San Francisco. I didn't know for sure where she was now. At the time I'd seen her, the paralysis had wasted her body away, leaning it down to skin over bone, putting premature gray in the thick red hair she wore cut short.

But I never felt sorry for her. If I had, she would have known about it and been gone. A woman like Peg, you accept her on her terms or else.

I shifted on the bed, feeling myself grow tense. "What's the skinny on Brynnmawr?"

"He wants to meet with you."

"Where?" I tried to figure out how old Brynnmawr must be. He'd looked ancient when I'd first met him, a frail old man who'd proven to have a mind as sharp as a monofilament edge.

"In the Matrix," Peg answered. "I can take you there."

"Did Brynnmawr say what this was about?" I asked.

"No."

I heard the frustration in her voice, knew she was taking my reluctance to talk personally.

"Who is this joker?" she asked. "I ran him through every database I know. I turned up zilch."

I wasn't surprised. Of course, Brynnmawr wasn't his

real name. I didn't know his real name, so he was one up
on me, which I never had liked.

"A man we're going to have to deal with." I opened the
duffel again and pulled out the trode rig. Lying in my
hand, the rig looked like the latticework of a helmet waiting to be finished. I pulled the rig into place on my head,
then inserted the plug into the telecom beside the bed,
shifting to make myself feel comfortable.

Without another word, Peg reached out for me and
yanked me into the Matrix, funneling my conscious mind
through the trode rig.

I didn't go willingly. I never did.

UPLOAD TO CONTINUE

5

"Sorry to keep you waiting, but I had something working
that couldn't be put on hold." Richard Villiers walked
through a seemingly solid wall. Actually, holos covered
the room's three separate exits, and those exits moved,
creating new corridors to other sections of the NovaTech
executive suite and making it harder for anyone to pene-
trate any further into the rooms. None of the doors were
opened except by Villiers himself. Once inside the suite,
Villiers's guests were essentially prisoners. Villiers was
dark and handsome, and moved with grace and razor-
edged self-confidence. The pin-striped Vashon Island
three-piece suit draped him like it had been surgically fit.
"This unscheduled visit *is* about Sencio?"

"Yes." Miles Lanier was a tall man with an average
build, his chestnut hair styled to look like he was a week
late for his next appointment. He looked ten years younger

than he was, old enough to demand automatic respect, but appearing young enough that someone who didn't know him might make the mistake of thinking he wasn't as good as he was. The dark maroon Armanté evening suit fit him well.

As Villiers's security head, he knew that the biz they were doing, trying to shape NovaTech up from the gutted remains of Fuchi Industrial Electronics, required huge risks and tremendous forethought. Until the recent dissolution of the three entities that had made up Fuchi, Villiers had been viewed by the other megacorps as a gifted player in the economic market. Now he worked to recoup that image, and increase his holdings. "It appears she's gotten a message out."

"To who?"

"I don't know," Lanier replied. "I've got agents in the field trying to find out."

"But it wasn't us?" Villiers asked.

"No."

The NovaTech CEO gave a half smile. "Then I guess we've about worn out the trust she had in us."

Lanier shrugged. "The only chance she has of getting out is us."

"I saw your reports this morning. Ironaxe hasn't given up pursuit of Sencio and her team."

"Ironaxe has taken this piece of industrial espionage personally."

"A pity. And after all the bribes were in place with his staff, too."

Some of those bribes, Lanier knew, were in the form of blackmail. Extortion always carried more weight than a credstick. "We knew at the outset that Sencio and her team might be compromised."

"We did," Villiers agreed. His face showed concern. "But she didn't. She may choose to hold this corporation at fault. Sencio can be a vindictive individual."

Lanier knew that was a definite understatement. Coupled with that was that fact that if Clay Ironaxe managed to capture Sencio alive, the woman could be a death sentence for them both. And for the fledgling NovaTech corporation.

6

Clay Ironaxe switched his commlink over to the frequency his team was using, then curled his left fist around the butt of the Seco LD-120 combat pistol. When his palm made contact with the smartgun link, his cybersystems came on-line. Cross hairs formed in his vision as he scanned the Albuquerque sprawl from the safety of the metallic silver Rolls Royce Phaeton limousine.

At something less than ten minutes after midnight, the plex's red light district was still in full swing. A mixture of corpgeeks and execs socialized on the wild side, while the night predators went to work.

The address was in Martinez Town, east of Highway 47. The limo rigger handled the expensive luxury vehicle with accomplished ease, propelling it off Grand Avenue NE onto John Street.

Ironaxe watched the dimmed lights of Saint Joseph's Medical Center coming up on the right as they headed north. The hospital stood as one of the few remaining bastions of civilization in the area.

When the Treaty of Denver settled the dispute between the North American federal governments and the Native American Nations, part of the agreement had been to force any non-natives to leave the region. Albuquerque had become a business force to be reckoned with in the Southwest before the Awakening and the Ghost Dance, and many of the non-natives had been defiant about being forced out.

The fighting had spilled out into the streets, and Martinez Town had been one of the hardest hit. When the dispute was finally settled, no one had cared enough to rebuild the areas of the sprawl that didn't directly contribute to profits. Martinez Town, like a number of other areas, had ended up with nothing except a ghetto of broken buildings filled with squatters, native and non-native, as well as metahumanity of both kinds.

The area had also picked up a contingent of low-rent mercenaries who fought for all sides in the border skirmishes between other members of NAN and UCAS. Base camps for shadowrunners tackling the corporations scattered across the Pueblo Corporate Council lands were built and shifted as quickly as rats' nests.

Clay Ironaxe was on a rat-killing spree tonight.

He shifted in the back of the Phaeton, a big broad man more than two meters tall and a meter across at the shoulders. The battle-hardened kevlar body armor fit him well, covered with brightly colored war paint that striped his arms, legs, and chest. More paint covered his broad, blocky face, teasing the flesh with highlights in white that turned his features into a skullface with black eye hollows. A beaten gold circlet with engraved Zuñi markings held his long black hair back, funneling it down his back.

"Maybe we'll get lucky and the woman will be there," Aaron Bearstalker said beside him. He was a big man as well, though still dwarfed by his employer and friend. Like Ironaxe, he wore kevlar body armor bearing the war marks of the Ashiwi, their people. He cradled an Ares Alpha Combat Gun loosely, the blued steel of the battle rifle looking oily in the dim glare that filtered in from the street.

Ironaxe shook his head. He'd had his fortune read in the sand that day, and the portents indicated that his quest for honor was not going to be easily won. "No, but perhaps Korrin will know where we may find her."

The Phaeton rolled to a stop at the end of the cul-de-sac where the present section of John Street ended. The luxury car's headlights knifed through the dark shadows surrounding the collection of shattered warehouses and apartment buildings. Train tracks gleamed white-silver to the west, only occasionally noticeable through the few open areas.

"I've got movement," one of the men in the front seats called out. The others immediately echoed him.

Ironaxe watched the squatters flee. As a general rule, they were thin and wiry, dressed in rags collected from refuse bins. But some of them brandished weapons as they retreated.

"The man we're hunting won't run," Ironaxe said. He let himself out of the Rolls Royce ahead of the others. They followed his lead, spreading out in a loose perimeter that maintained overlapping fields of fire.

7

[Chip file: Argent
Security access: ******—23:13:24/10-9-60]

UPLOAD CONTINUED

Location: Everett Safehouse

Everything went black, and stillness filled the world I'd entered. I've never found another experience so perfect or so complete as the Matrix.

Then color entered that perfect blackness, shooting

streamers of bright reds, greens, golds, purples, a plethora
of prismatic incandescence that resembled tracer fire.
The streamers created a grid around us, over us, and below us, connecting dozens of different icons to each other
in convoluted patterns. The horizon in any direction was
so far off it looked like the world twisted and funneled
into a tight knot.

Instinctively, I tried to move, to center myself. But I
couldn't. The trode rig was a hitcher device, enabling me
to enter the Matrix and interact with Peg, but not to interact with the Matrix itself. It was like being wrapped in a
cocoon.

"Easy," Peg said. "I'm here." Her voice came from
somewhere that my mind identified as being to my left.
Actually, there was no left because I had no body.

Mentally, I pulled back and dropped into parade rest.
I'd learned to hold that position for hours if I needed to,
and it was even easier in the Matrix because gravity didn't
exist.

Without warning, the glowing colored lines began whipping past as we gained momentum. Peg controlled our
movements, thrusting us through a hundred different land-
scapes in an eyeblink. Our destination became immediately apparent: a lambent green glass tower corkscrewed
into a chunk of gigantic tree roots that were twisted together and slithered like snakes.

"Now, there's a pretty picture," Peg commented.

Her revulsion dripped in her words. "It fits Brynnmawr," I told her. "Just so you know what you're getting
into."

She lifted an arm, perfectly proportioned and translucent, glowing from an inner blue fire. Peg's persona, the
way she saw herself in the Matrix, resembled a liquid being, totally feminine with unrestrained curves. Her eyes
were pits of stormy blue fire, her lips tight and full, rolling waves held in restraint. Her blue-black hair cascaded
around her shoulders. She went nude, but the translucent

body she chose somehow didn't look naked. She'd had other personas over the years I'd known her, but this was the one she chose when she went into situations where the outcome wasn't something she could readily control. It was battledress, a flaunting of confidence and self, a mentality I totally understood.

A blaze of dark violet light jumped from Peg's fingertip when she pointed, stopping meters short of touching the twisted snarl of roots at the base of the corkscrew tower. Some of the roots unwrapped from the base of the tower and shot out at us. Peg pulled us back, then formed flat shields of glowing gold and green that fit against her palms, no bigger than a buckler used by a Roman legionary. The roots bounced off her shields, then withered and died, leaving a trail of gray ash scattered across the black. A moment later a breeze gusted up and blew it away.

"The node's surrounded by IC," she said. Her persona voice fit her image in the Matrix, husky and full. "I could possibly get through it, but it would take time."

"Just knock," I said. "If Brynnmawr's expecting us, he'll let us in."

"If it's not a trap."

Attacks in the Matrix could also be lethal. A decker took his or her life in hand every time he or she went online. That world was full of predators and minefields. I knew that from military experience as well as what I'd learned from deckers I'd worked with.

"No," I told Peg. "If Brynnmawr had wanted me flatlined, he wouldn't have gone to the trouble of leaving a message."

"It was a way of finding you."

"Going through the drop gave me control," I pointed out to her. "I could have ignored the message."

"But he knew you wouldn't."

I considered that, realizing that Peg knew me as well as Brynnmawr. Almost as well. Brynnmawr was a big reason I'd become the person I was, a big reason why I thought the way I thought. "Maybe." I used Peg's eyes and stared hard into the core of twisted roots.

"You still want to go in?" she asked.

"Yes." There could be no other choice, not and remain true to my convictions. I held a certain amount of fear of Brynnmawr, but I refused to knuckle under to it. He was a man, and men died. Sometimes.

"Give me a minute," Peg requested.

I waited, watching as a console appeared in the black ether before us. Peg's translucent blue hands glided across the buttons and dials, making adjustments.

"I'm building us an escape route," she explained. "In case this meet doesn't go as friendly as you think it will." She continued working as she spoke. "When Brynnmawr tagged the message drop, he tripped three separate trace programs I had set up on that drop. None of them got me Brynnmawr's real-world twenty, but one of them got in far enough to let me know he keeps a line open to the Wall Street stock exchange."

I listened to her, letting her talk because I had some thinking to do myself. Brynnmawr's interest in me brought up a lot of speculation, none of it with a foundation that I could reason.

"A lot of people keep lines of communication open to the East Coast Stock Exchange," Peg said. "They have to look after all that money. And, usually, you can bet you're going to hit some of the deadliest black IC ever designed if you try to follow them up. Assuming you get through the Stock Exchange Matrix defenses, which is as near an impossibility as I've ever found. But that black IC is set up to intercept improper incoming datastreams, not outgoing."

The root system below the corkscrewed green glass tower writhed restlessly, and I could almost feel eyes scanning me.

"There," Peg said. "That program should be enough to

allow us to sleaze out if things start going to slot." The console folded swiftly in front of her, reducing in size until it became a tiny red button. She closed her hand over it, hiding it from sight. "Ready?"

"Yeah."

Peg fired another purple beam from her fingertip. The roots engaged again, wiggling toward us. "Do you have a password?" she asked.

"Prodigal," I answered. Brynnmawr had a wicked sense of humor. Everything about him was wicked. I just didn't see it when I was younger.

Abruptly, the roots stopped their approach. In concert, the section in front of us opened, becoming an ebony maw.

"Well?" Peg prompted.

"Go," I told her.

She spread her arms, the button she'd created still tight in her fist. Then she flew into the mouth. The roots closed the opening behind us.

UPLOAD TO CONTINUE

8

Ironaxe took the lead, running across the open space and skirting the remains of the convenience store. A rusted sign that announced WALKER'S STUFFER SHACK stuck up from the pile of debris. The roaring of the nature spirits and the intermittent blasts of autofire were almost deafening.

It took a moment for him to spot the stone steps leading to an underground apartment area below the building across from the Stuffer Shack. He raced down them at once, pausing at the bottom only long enough to kick the door off the hinges.

The small dwelling under the apartment building was small and neat, furnished haphazardly and barren of personal effects.

Tall but seriously underweight, Korrin was an ork, possessing the broad nose and thin lips of his kind. His elongated ears tapered to points, matching the disarray of bottom fangs that thrust up from his lower jaw. Bushy hair sprouting from the top of his head nearly covered his eyes. He wore a one-piece coverall with a patch over the left breast that advertised KIMIKO'S DOMESTIC SERVICE.

Korrin raised a Fichetti Tiffani Needler and closed his eyes when he fired. The small needle rounds hardly made any noise, but they thumped into the wall behind Ironaxe with explosive detonations that left pockmarks ten centimeters across.

Ironaxe avoided the needler. He slapped the Fichetti from Korrin's hand, then reached out and grabbed a fistful of the man's shirt. He pulled Korrin close, shoving the LD-120's barrel under the ork's left eye.

"Breathe wrong," Ironaxe promised, "and I'll wipe your brainpan."

Korrin swallowed hard but didn't move. "I'll talk. You don't have to do anything to me." He cringed as Bearstalker moved in closer, sweeping the apartment with the combat rifle.

"You helped a woman two days ago," Ironaxe said. "Talk to me about her, browncone, and you get to live. Lie to me and you die. You scan me?"

"Yeah. Sure. What's not to understand?"

"You know the woman I'm talking about?" Ironaxe asked.

Korrin hesitated.

Holding the man by the lapels of his coverall, Ironaxe

slammed Korrin into the wall inside the open door. The
man's breath exploded from his lungs.

"Do you know the woman I'm talking about?" Ironaxe
repeated. He kept the ork pressed up against the wall.

"Yeah. Her name was Sencio. Andi Sencio."

9

[Chip file: Argent
Security access: ******—23:17:52/10-9-60]

UPLOAD CONTINUED

Location: Everett Safehouse

A night-draped cemetery formed around Peg and me,
complete with grave markers that looked like tablets
with rounded shoulders, and stones marked with winged
cherubs nearly three meters tall. Thick woods stood beyond a tall wrought iron fence. Through the gaps in the
fence, I thought I could make out the yellow and red glow
of predator's eyes. But it might have been laser spotter
scopes. In Peg's persona, I didn't have access to all the
cyberware I carry so I couldn't zoom in on their positions. That's one of the main things I hated about the Matrix. It stripped away so much of what made me who I
was these days.

>*This place is schizzed,*< Peg said. >*Even for a meet-
ing place, this would only slot a nutter's chip-dreams.*<
Her eyes locked on a grave marker nearby that towered
over us. Cut from an azure stone, the statue featured a
tentacled monstrosity atop it, a pair of wicked hooks at
the end of each tentacle.

She talked to me over the private frequency she'd set up through the commlink built into my headware. That way we could speak between ourselves as well as through the commlink open on the Matrix construct.

Rows and rows of grave markers spread out over the rolling hills under the pecan trees. A pale crescent of moon peered out from behind scudding clouds overhead.

"Argent?"

I recognized Brynnmawr's voice at once. There was always something about the timbre that made it stand out from anyone else's. Or maybe he'd conditioned me to respond to his voice. I never knew.

"Yes, sir," I said, and Peg projected my voice into the construct. She turned and we looked at Brynnmawr.

Slightly less than two meters tall, he was above average height and built compactly. Short-clipped gray hair covered his face, and hard black eyes gleamed under a widow's peak. His Vashon Island suit was simply cut, with a bowstring tie at his throat. He looked like an undertaker, like I always saw him, and the appearance was deliberate. But he was younger than I remembered, thanks to the Matrix persona he was using.

Brynnmawr stopped in front of us. Uncertainty gleamed in his bright eyes, something I'd *never* seen in his eyes before. "How do I know it's you?"

"Prodigal, sir," I told him after a moment's hesitation. "Who else would know our password?"

He shook his head. "You can never tell, my boy. They know so much more than I ever thought they would."

"It's me, sir," I said gently. And it felt uncomfortable, because I'd never talked that way to him before.

He smiled. "You look more like your friend, I guess."

>*I can fix that,* < Peg told me.

In my field of vision, her translucent blue body changed. In seconds, I was looking down at my own arms, my own body instead of her persona. But those limbs moved as Peg made them, not me.

Brynnmawr nodded. "It's good to see you, my boy."

I held my own counsel. Brynnmawr knew I didn't respond in any other way than honestly.

"Walk with me," he said, choosing a well-trodden path through the gravestones.

I tried to fall into step beside him, but couldn't. It was Peg who moved the persona even though it looked like me. >*Walk beside him,*< I told her privately. >*To the right and one step behind.*<

She did it without asking why. Maybe she understood it was deference or maybe she was simply fascinated by him. Brynnmawr had that effect on many people, and some of the most responsive were female.

"How have you been, my boy?" Brynnmawr asked.

"Well, sir," I replied.

"I don't get much news of you here."

"You shouldn't, sir," I said, "as long as I do my job right."

Brynnmawr led the way through the gravestones, idly reaching out to touch some of them and inspect them, though I was certain he was intimate with them all.

>*Why can't we read the grave markers?*< I asked Peg.

>*They're covered in IC,*< she replied. >*I could try, but there's no telling what security measures I might set off.*<

>*Don't,*< I told her. I knew the kinds of deadly surprises Brynnmawr could devise.

>*Good choice,*< she said.

"You're still a shadowrunner," Brynnmawr observed.

"It pays the bills, sir."

He laughed then, that thin sibilant sound that few people had ever heard. "You were so much more than that, my boy. Probably the best I'd ever seen at your chosen field of work."

I felt uncomfortable. I'd never talked over my past with any of the Wrecking Crew. And of them, Peg would have probably been the least understanding. But I'd been young, and my view of the world was very encapsulated, handed to me by the man walking beside me.

"We're not here to discuss that," I said. "Nor are we entirely alone, sir."

"I realize that," Brynnmawr snapped. "I'm quite capable of keeping secrets." His response sounded practiced, filled with more than casual anger.

But there was something in the way he said it that convinced me he had forgotten Peg was there. That was something I wasn't used to. Brynnmawr never forgot anything. His vengeance was a legendary force in the right circles, enough to give men nightmares.

"Why did you ask me to come here, sir?"

"I'm doing a favor for a friend," he replied.

I was surprised when I felt a small ache that I wasn't there by Brynnmawr's own choice. Still, it wasn't too surprising, given the relationship I'd had with him. Teacher and student had come as close to father and son as any I'd ever had. Only betrayal could have ever broken us apart. And I'd known that at the moment I'd betrayed him.

"Who, sir?"

"Andi Sencio," he answered.

That name sent my mind spinning because it carried almost as much regret as Brynnmawr's. It just went to show that history was cyclical. The past was always intertwined with the present, always with us.

"She's in a lot of trouble, my boy," Brynnmawr said.

Given the fact that she had contacted me through Brynnmawr, I knew Andi's situation was highly understated.

UPLOAD TO CONTINUE

10

"Are you certain Andi Sencio got a message out?" Richard Villiers asked.

Miles Lanier nodded. "Yes. The security unit I've placed around what we believe to be her current position in Pueblo found a jury-rigged satellite dish she used to bounce a laser burst transmission off a satellite to access the Pueblo LTG. Once in the Matrix for that brief period, she had access to several options. Till her position was overrun."

Villiers appeared to give that some thought. "Your people had no chance to intercept the message?"

"No. Nakatomi had a group in the area as well. I've discovered that Pendleton Frost, the double-agent Nakatomi put in Sencio's group, also managed to deliver DNA samples to Nakatomi." And that was what had kept Sencio and her group from using conventional commlinks. Wherever they were hiding, it was proof—so far—against the mage-commanded watchers Nakatomi and Villiers had searching the area.

"Before Sencio flatlined him."

"Yes. I don't know if Frost gave the DNA samples to Ironaxe, but my people are telling me he's definitely the guy who tipped Ironaxe off that something was wrong with LegacyTrax."

LegacyTrax had been the Trojan horse Villiers had used to trap Ironaxe and render his corporation vulnerable to Sencio's shadow ops team. Though incredibly savvy in biz, Ironaxe had a weakness for the lore of his people.

LegacyTrax had a history of ferreting out such information. They'd asked for, and received, access to Ironaxe's huge library on the subject, then winnowed their way into VaulTek itself. The op had been going smoothly—until Nakatomi's double-agent stepped in and gave Sencio away.

"Our people weren't expecting the crudeness of the communications effort," Lanier went on. "They spotted it in the commlink traps they'd set up in the Pueblo LTGs to monitor activity, but in burst mode. It was gone before they could nail it down. No one's used that kind of technology in decades. Ironaxe's men closed on the team that sent it and succeeded in killing one of them. Sencio and another man escaped."

"Did Ironaxe intercept it?"

"I don't know," Lanier answered honestly. "But probably not. If he had, he'd have been in your face by now. And Nakatomi's waiting in the wings to make this deal if you get blown out of the water." Shikei Nakatomi, until last year, had been one of the three top men in Fuchi. Now the man headed up the Fuchi Asia remnants, and had bought the four million shares of Renraku Computer Systems that Lanier had sold to the Zurich-Orbital Gemeinschaft Bank, aligning his corp with Renraku. Or positioning himself to take it over, depending on which line of thinking was followed. Nakatomi was also Richard Villiers' mortal enemy. One of them, Lanier amended silently.

"You said the burst transmission was traced. Where?"

"To a geosynchronous satellite over North America. We haven't been able to discover who owns it." And that alone, Lanier knew, meant a lot. Villiers himself had masterminded shadow ops that no one had ever penetrated. The LegacyTrax op had run smoothly for months before being discovered. Even now, no one could assign blame for what had happened. Unless they could catch Sencio. "All of our attempts to break through the IC covering the system have been blocked. Two deckers are dead from dump shock after being forcibly ejected from the system, and another is in a coma. Even then, the chances are that the message has been relayed and no longer exists within the satellite's subsystems."

"A satellite buried that far back and that deeply," Villiers said, "suggests another megacorp."

"Or the military," Lanier said. "They have unlisted satellites. And they were the last to stop using the burst transmission sequencing." Security was one area where he excelled over Villiers. He also had the determination and resolve to take chances himself, and kill those who got in his way. Villiers was good with stock and bonds, but Lanier had grown to adulthood with a gun and a knife in his hands.

"Sencio was in the military, wasn't she?"

"UCAS special forces," Lanier confirmed. "All of that information is highly classified."

"If Ironaxe gets his hands on Sencio, things could go badly for us down there. The advances in Matrix security VaultTek has come up with will buy NovaTech weeks or months against anything shadowrunner teams can put together. Not to mention the worth of a merger with a major player in the Pueblo Corporate Council."

"The possibility also exists that we weren't able to download everything Sencio and her team got from Vaul-Tek," Lanier pointed out.

"I know. I try to keep that in mind. But every breath that woman takes is a menace to NovaTech."

"I could send the secondary team in now," Lanier said, "but I'd like to wait on that. There's a wild card that could still show up on the table."

"Whoever Sencio contacted?"

Lanier nodded. "We may be able to use that."

"Need I point out," Villiers asked, "that person may be an even bigger threat than either Nakatomi or Ironaxe?"

"Maybe," Lanier admitted. "But that other party could

also turn out to be a smokescreen we can use. Or it could be another resource that could be tapped in our favor."

Villiers nodded his agreement. "Keep me in the loop, Miles. I'm depending on you."

And Lanier knew that was true. There was no one Villiers had ever trusted more. He wasn't about to let his friend down.

11

"How you did you know Sencio?" Ironaxe demanded, his cyberhand tight on the ork's thin shoulder.

"I did a couple tours in the Desert Wars with her," Korrin said. "Both of us were with Fuchi then. You don't forget chummers you fought with."

"What did she want with you?" Ironaxe asked.

"Out. She wanted out of the Pueblo Corporate Council lands, omae. She'd heard I was connected in Pueblo, but I couldn't help her." Korrin shivered again and shook his head. "I'm small-time. She was asking too much."

"She's still in Pueblo?"

Korrin nodded. "As of this morning. Unless she found someone who could get her out."

Ironaxe glared into the ork's weak eyes. "If she contacts you again, you'll let me know."

"Sure, sure. The minute I hear from her."

Pushing the man away, Ironaxe gestured to Bearstalker to follow him out. Outside, he made his way back to the Phaeton limousine, then dropped into the back seat. He accessed his commlink and broke off the engagement.

The rigger powered the big luxury vehicle up smoothly and rocketed them away, heading back to Highway 47.

"This Andi Sencio won't be in contact with Korrin

again," Bearstalker said. "Not if she's as good as she's proven so far."

"I know."

"Have you gotten any closer to finding out who actually owns LegacyTrax?"

Ironaxe shook his head. "No. The corporation's real ownership is buried in holding companies and shell corporations. Whoever hid it knew what they were doing. My people have followed a dozen different trails so far." Someone had done their research well; first by finding out his interest in his people's history, and second by discovering his business with LegacyTrax.

LegacyTrax was a small operation that specialized in locating information about Amerindian culture. The only other major players in the field of locating magical artifacts from different cultures that had come to light since the Awakening were the Atlantean Foundation, the Draco Foundation, and Aztechnology. The first two were headed by people close to Dunkelzahn before the great dragon was assassinated. Of them all, LegacyTrax's initial findings seemed the most promising. Now, Ironaxe had to wonder if even that was a lie.

"Did you find out if Villiers was actually using their services?"

"Yes. One of our deckers who built the back door into LegacyTrax's mainframes after security in the corp had been breached found files on Villiers."

"What was he looking for?"

"That's secured," Ironaxe replied. "Apparently he never risked his own corp's security integrity."

"He was already working with LegacyTrax at the time they found you," Bearstalker said.

"It gave us something in common, I thought," Ironaxe replied. "Though I still don't know for sure if he was aware that I was involved with them. Now, the possibility exists that I was set up by Villiers. And if I find that to be true, not only will I shut down the mergers he was wanting to do with VaulTek, but I'll do my best to smash that fledgling corporation of his."

The commlink buzzed for his attention and he opened the phone connection. "Mr. Ironaxe," a woman said smoothly, "I have Shikei Nakatomi of Fuchi Asia on the line for you."

"Patch it to the car," Ironaxe said. The Phaeton was equipped with a satellite uplink. He cleared the commlink and waited for the limo's commlink to come on-line. "Nakatomi," he told Bearstalker.

"Now that's fragging interesting," Bearstalker said.

Ironaxe couldn't help but agree. Then the uplink juiced to life, enabling the transmission.

12

[Chip file: Argent
Security access: ******—23:24:02/10-9-60]

UPLOAD CONTINUED

Location: Everett Safehouse

"What kind of trouble is Andi Sencio in, sir?" I asked.

Brynnmawr stood before me, gazing off at the rows of tombstones, cherubs, and monsters. "I don't know the specifics, my boy. Only that she needed me to contact you."

>*Who's Sencio?*< Peg asked.

>*Not now,*< I told her, knowing full well she'd run Sencio's name in case the meeting with Brynnmawr went to drek. Whatever Peg found, if anything, wouldn't tie Sencio to me, though. Brynnmawr had provided both of

us—and others—complete security packs that had effectively erased anyone we'd ever been the day we walked
away from him. Not all of them had gotten to keep on
walking. We had.

Her contacting Brynnmawr through the private satellite and construct were guaranteed to be one of the safest
routes of communication. He knew too many secrets to
live, but he knew them about too many people for any of
them to ever kill him. One of the reasons he'd had people
like Andi and I working for him was because we were
good enough to become faceless ciphers in every dangerous game he played.

"Why you, sir?" I asked.

"Did she know where you were or how to get in touch
with you discreetly?"

"I don't know, sir." And I didn't. Andi and I had parted
ways years ago.

"She knew I'd be able to get in touch with you."

I remained silent, trying to sort through all the emotions that ran rampant inside me. That was another of the
reasons I didn't like the Matrix much: it put nearly everything down on a tactile level. Or maybe that was just because Peg got everything that way and my experiences
were filtered through hers.

"I keep an eye on you," Brynnmawr said. "I can't see
everything, my boy, so don't worry about that. But I know
about some things, like the message drop I used tonight.
You haven't changed much, you know."

"I've changed, sir," I argued, keeping my tone light,
but needing to say it all the same.

"Only your frame of reference," Brynnmawr accused.
"You're still the boy I remember. Why else do you insist
only on taking shadowruns that are on the side of what
you consider to be of moral good?"

>*Because,*< Peg put in, >*you're basically a good
chummer doing a dirty biz. If we didn't do the work we*

*do, a lot more people would be in more trouble than we
found them in.<*

I didn't say anything to either of them. They both had
their opinions, and I didn't agree with either's assessment. I was what I was, what I'd spent all of my life
learning to be. I knew where my boundaries were, what I
would and wouldn't do.

"When you were younger," Brynnmawr admitted, "I
used that idealism that is so ingrained in you to my advantage. Do you know what you are, Argent?"

He'd never called me by my given name since he'd
renamed me Argent. I sometimes wondered if he'd forgotten it. I returned his level gaze and kept my mouth shut.

"You're a believer," he declared. "Maybe one of the
last true believers I've ever met in my life. You believed
in me. You believed in the work that I had you doing. You
believed you could make a difference in all the cruel in-
justice that I set you up against day after day. And when
you found out I was lying to you, you still believed you
could make that difference. That's why you betrayed me."

If I'd been under my own power instead of lodged
there in Peg's persona, I'd have walked away from him
then. I felt a pressure on my chest back in the real world,
suddenly aware of my meat body.

"Follow me only a little longer," Brynnmawr said.
He turned and continued down the paths through the
graveyard.

When I wanted to do nothing more than walk away
from him, Peg got us in step with him. I didn't trust my
voice to speak with her, and I needed to wait to find out
what had happened to Andi.

"They never trusted me after you left quite the way
they had before," Brynnmawr said. His voice sounded
suddenly old and hollow. "I continued with my caseload
and taking charge of field assignments for years. Ironi-
cally, I was relieved of duty the same year you lost your
team mates."

"This has nothing to do with why I'm here, sir." No way did I want to discuss Toshi and Hawk with him. They were a part of my history, *not* his.

"It has everything to do with it," he snapped, growing impatient with me. "The trouble that Sencio's in isn't simple or she wouldn't have contacted me. You can't afford to be at any less than your best if you go to help her."

"I haven't said that I would yet, sir. Like I said, things have changed."

"Not that about you, Argent. Never that. You'll never stop believing in the things you believe in."

"I think you're wrong about that, sir," I said, maybe a little more harshly than I intended. "Once I believed in you. Now I don't."

His left eye flickered just a tick, but he never broke eye contact with me. "But you're here, aren't you, my boy?" he asked softly.

"Only for a short time, sir. If you want to continue playing cat-and-mouse games, I'll find Andi on my own." I called out silently to Peg. >*Get ready to get us out of here.*<

>*Say the word. This guy really creeps me out.*<

"We're a lot alike now, you and I," Brynnmawr said. "After your betrayal, I couldn't trust anyone the way I'd trusted you. I gave you much more of myself than I'd intended. And when you walked away, there was quite a lot I didn't get back."

"That went for both of us, sir."

He shook his head. "Not true. You had your friends. I had no one."

"Sir," I said, "you chose that life."

"Not hardly, my boy. I feel that it chose me." Brynnmawr gestured to the graveyard around him. "This is my prison. My body is failing me, but they insist on keeping me alive. Too many of them are afraid that the secrets I know will come tumbling out of the hiding places where

I've stored them." He waved at the gravesites. "Do you know what lies buried in these?"

"No, sir."

He grinned, baring the white shark's grin. "My sins," he answered. "Memories of everything I'd ever done. Atrocities piled upon atrocities. And every now and again when I walk through this prison they've left me in, one of those atrocities will rise up out of the grave and try to kill me."

>*Oh drek,*< Peg whispered. >*They've trapped him in here with this?*<

She sounded like she couldn't believe it. I did; I knew some of the people Brynnmawr had been responsible to.

"They also make me hungry, part of the programming, you see, to remind me that I am not king of my own castle anymore." Reaching up, he plucked a pecan from the branch above him, then held it out for me to inspect.

Even in the moonlight, I could see that it looked like an ordinary pecan, paper-shelled and slightly bigger and longer than my thumb.

"Think about it, my boy," Brynnmawr said. "Think about where the roots of these pecan trees grow."

I did think about it, and I forced myself to be cold about it. Peg made retching noises inside my head.

"Those roots dig down into those graves," he went on, "and they suck out everything inside to make these nuts. All the dead that I laid to rest, or caused to be laid to rest. With the programming in this place, I have to eat the pecans." His voice broke. "I'm feeding on my own sins here, and I can't stop."

"What can I do?" I asked.

He looked at me strangely, then broke into laughter, convulsing so hard that he had to sit down on one of the grave markers. "See, Argent, you haven't changed at all. You *still* believe that you can do something about everything."

I didn't know how to take his reaction, so I remained quiet.

>*He's insane,*< Peg stated. >*But you can't blame him.*<

"Don't you see how humorous this all is?" Brynnmawr asked. "I'm trapped in this prison because I believed I could do anything I wanted, and you're trapped by your own fears after losing Toshi and Hawk. I'm afraid to die, and you're afraid to live."

"I live just fine, sir," I told him.

"And you work alone," Brynnmawr said, "except for that bedridden slitch that feeds off your heart and legs."

>*That son-of-a-slitch,*< Peg grated.

"I'm leaving now, sir," I told him. "I've taken all of this I intend to."

"Go," Brynnmawr said. "But you ask yourself who else could have told it to you like this, to your face? You've got to put those dead men behind you, get back to being what you were before it gets you flatlined. If you're not ready for this, I'm sending you to your death. Believe it or not, my boy, but I don't want any more of your blood on my hands."

"Where can I find Andi?"

Brynnmawr pushed himself up from the grave marker and dusted off his suit. "She's set up a contact with a Mr. Johnson in CalFree State. In Los Angeles. A simsense tavern down in East Hollywood called Lookers. He'll have all the details you need."

"How do I find him?"

"He'll find you. Sencio gave him a holo of you, and a password. She said you'd know it when you hear it."

"Thank you, sir."

He looked at me. "You're going, aren't you?"

"I don't see that I have a choice, sir. She asked."

"Even though the two of you haven't seen each other in years."

"Yes, sir."

"Do you realize how dit-brained that is?"

"You relayed the message, sir," I pointed out. "That possibly isn't one of the safest moves you've made."

"No, but my jailers are quite protective." He crossed over to me and put a hand on my shoulder. "Take care of yourself, my boy, and if you should get the chance—" He stopped speaking.

"Yes, sir?" I inquired.

"Nothing," he said gruffly. "Just don't get your fragging hoop spiked while you're out there. I taught you better than that. Don't be a drekking embarrassment to me." Without another word, he turned and walked away, threading his way through the gravestones.

>*Get us out of here,*< I told Peg.

She pressed the concealed panicbutton in her hand. My senses blurred as we shot through the airspace above the graveyard, the markers dwindling down to black pinpoints behind us.

"If you're going after this Sencio person," she said as we skidded along one of the Matrix's gridlines and came out of the East Coast Stock Exchange without being noticed by the security IC, "maybe you should tell me about her."

"I'll think about it," I replied, knowing her statement revealed that she hadn't found out a single fact about Andi. If that was the case, if Andi had conducted her biz so well, I knew the problems she'd be facing would be large, nasty ones.

END UPLOAD

13

At the other end of the satellite uplink beaming into Clay Ironaxe's Phaeton limousine, Shikei Nakatomi sat at the big desk Ironaxe had come to associate with the Fuchi Asia CEO. He was smooth and elegant, round-faced, with his black and silver hair carefully combed back. His narrow black tie was knotted precisely. Behind him was a holo of a cherry tree in full bloom.

"Ironaxe-*san*," Nakatomi stated in his precise English, "please pardon the interruption I have caused. I know it is quite late there. I was hoping to make the job of tracking down your betrayer somewhat easier."

"I have the woman's name now." Only a few days ago, Nakatomi had given Ironaxe the information about the team of shadowrunners operating inside LegacyTrax. Despite that, Ironaxe knew the man had held onto the information for longer than that. Maybe even long enough to have made a difference.

"*Hai.* As do we. Only moments ago, we discovered her identity as well: Andrea Louise Sencio."

Ironaxe forced himself to remain poker-faced. "I'm listening."

"Very good," Nakatomi nodded happily. "As you know, I have recently made some business commitments to Renraku."

Four million shares of Renraku wasn't what Ironaxe would have called a commitment; it was more like a blood oath. Using that much liquid capital to buy up the shares back in April must have tapped the Fuchi Asian banks for a time. Perhaps the corp was still reeling from the effects. Anytime liquid assets were used up, it impacted directly on research and development, the area where most liquid capital was spent, and was demanded. Not many people wanted to buy into or finance a *maybe,* and Ironaxe knew that first-hand.

"Without going into detail concerning your internal security problems," Nakatomi went on, "I contacted some of the sec chiefs in Renraku and sent them a holo of the woman." Sencio, if that was her name, and her team had been caught on security cams while fleeing the Legacy-Trax offices. The sec cam footage had immediately been impounded by Ironaxe's sec teams. Evidently Nakatomi had a decker who'd gotten to them. "The Renraku security staff confirmed three of the shadowrunners' identities. The other two men worked with Sencio in sensitive areas for Renraku over five years ago."

"But they weren't working for Renraku when they hit the mainframes at LegacyTrax," Bearstalker sneered.

"No." Nakatomi remained quiet after he gave his answer. His eyes remained locked on Ironaxe's.

Ironaxe knew full well that Nakatomi wasn't above lying. "What have you found out about her?" he asked.

"She was with the military at one point," Nakatomi went on. "During another part of her career, it has been confirmed that she worked for Richard Villiers during the Desert Wars."

"That tie is damning," Ironaxe said. "Because if she worked for Villiers at that time, it also means she was working for Fuchi. And you."

"I had no contact with her."

"Can you prove that?" Bearstalker asked.

"Unfortunately, no. I have only my word to offer you."

"And that's worth about as much as a degaussed credstick," Bearstalker said harshly.

"Agreed." Nakatomi's voice reflected no rancor.

Ironaxe was impressed by the man's restraint.

"There is, however," Nakatomi went on, "one more chit that I have to offer. Earlier today, Sencio and her people were able to get a message out of Albuquerque. I'm sure you were aware of it."

"Yes," Ironaxe admitted. Their taps on the Pueblo LTGs had spotted the illegal message blasting through the grids the moment it was released.

"One is beyond my reach, having arrived at a satellite in geosynchronous orbit with the earth that I can't get to. My people were successful in tracking the second to California Free State." Nakatomi leaned back in his chair, looking satisfied with himself. "You'll find that Richard Villiers has been duplicitous with you. I've only treated you fairly. Your business means much to me. I've taken the liberty of ordering a team into the area. When they apprehend the person or persons who are in receipt of this message, I'll be happy to turn them over to you. As you know, Amerindians aren't always welcome in Cal-Free. And I do have teams already inside the nation. I could have them moving in a couple hours if you will allow me."

What Nakatomi said was true, and Ironaxe knew it. When the NAN had split away, splintering the North American countries and states, then had kicked out all the non-natives at gunpoint, they'd made no friends in the other nations. Also, he didn't have a team ready for insertion into CalFree.

"I'd like them alive if I can get them," Ironaxe said finally, knowing there was no way to keep Nakatomi out of the mix. Watching the man's actions might help, though.

"It shall be done." The uplink broke and the commlink vid faded to black.

"So who do you trust? Villiers or Nakatomi?" Bearstalker asked.

Ironaxe relaxed in the plush seat as the Phaeton shot up the ramp leading them to Highway 47. "Neither. But both will have stories to tell as they war against each other. In that confusion, the truth will come out. And when I find out who betrayed me, they'll come to know true regret." It was a promise he meant to keep. No one threatened what was his and lived.

14

Argent booked a seat on one of the evening suborbitals from Sea-Tac International Airport and landed at Long Beach International in California Free State before 10 p.m. In order to get the security clearances he needed to get through the airport enforcement arm with all his cyberware, Peg set up an interview with Affiliated Artists for the next day, leaving him today free to make the meet with the Johnson at Lookers.

The interview regarding Affiliated Artists was legitimate. One of the execs at the media studios had been trying to contract Argent for a shadowrun over the last three weeks. The run entailed "freeing" a talent from AA's rival, Amalgamated Studios. The talent happened to be a dwarf named Klingsteidt who was quickly becoming one of the best F/X guys in the biz. AA was currently experiencing a boom in the simflick industry, involving real life actors doing their own stunts instead of simsense reproductions. In fact, three current productions had a body count attached to them that was boosting ticket sales.

The contact person at AA had no problem arranging free passes for Argent and the two people he'd hired to come with him. AA was a multi-billion-dollar biz and carried considerable corporate clout in the economic arena. Politicos still liked to rub shoulders with the simstars as well.

Argent passed through the doors of the circular tunnel leading from the suborbital to the airport gate. He'd gotten no sleep at all after last night's visit to Brynnmawr. Thoughts of Andi Sencio had plagued his mind, memories of how things had been and how they'd gotten to be. And wondering if she was still alive now.

"Mr. Erskine?"

Swiveling his head, Argent spotted a young elf in bottle-green chauffeur's livery holding up a sign that said MR. ERSKINE. "Yes?" Argent said, coming around to square up with the elf. Argent wore a steel-gray Vashon Island business suit, cut stylish but conservative by the local standards. Gray synthleather gloves concealed the cyberhands. A pair of gray wraparound Corona "Private Eye" Computer Display glasses completed the look and gave him access to the computer datafeed Peg could provide over the glasses and the commlink chipped inside his head. His deltaware commlink had an add-on spur that allowed him to jack it into the Coronas for Peg's use.

Passersby kept on their appointed paths, chatting and hurrying to their destinations. Out in the center of the long corridor connecting the gates, moving sidewalks rolled steadily in either direction, passing the shops that lined both sides.

"Mr. Hornberg sent me," the young elf said. "From the studio. He thought maybe you'd appreciate the use of a car while you're with us."

"Do you have identification?" Argent asked.

The elf hesitated, seemingly caught off-guard by the question. He reached into his jacket and brought out a credstick. "Sure. Here."

Argent took the credstick and crossed over to the ticket booth. While he slotted the stick into the public reader/transfer system, Argent also accessed his headlink and called Peg. She was there even before the transfer/reader had time to *ping* up a reply. "Run Shamura, Tobin. Get back to me." He spelled the name, speaking quietly, then added the SIN.

Shamura took his credstick back and pocketed it uncertainly. "Is everything all right?"

"I'd like to see the car," Argent said.

"Sure, Mr. Erskine."

Argent fell in a half-step behind the nervous chauffeur and opened another channel on the commlink. The bright lights of a Stuffer Shack blazed out into the dimmer recesses of the airport corridor. "Beedle," he said, calling for one of the two-member team he'd hired in Everett that morning. The pair cost plenty, but they were worth it. And they'd arrived in CalFree on the same flight so they could provide security for him, as well as handle the meet with the Mr. Johnson later.

"Here," Beedle's voice croaked over the commlink.

"Talk to me." Argent kept his gaze sweeping the corridor ahead of him. With its crowds and constant movement, he knew from experience that an airport was a good place for an assassination as long as the wetware specialist kept a low profile. And a weapon didn't have to be anything high-tech. He'd once known an assassin who'd only had one finger augmented, turning it into a dart pistol that held one shot. That one shot contained cyanide and killed almost instantly. Most of her victims had never met her.

"The driver's mundane," Beedle replied, verifying that he'd checked the scene out on the astral and with detect spells at his access. "No Art, and no cyber. That guy's one hundred percent flesh and blood. But I gotta tell you, the sec systems in this place are wiz. I've ferreted out cyber systems hidden in the walls, but only because the magic barrier has been breached before. And you don't even want to know about the wards the sec mages have put over the property."

"Good enough." Argent followed Shamura through sliding glass doors past a McHugh's and a Sloppie stand.

Beedle was a street mage, one of the best Argent had ever seen, and one of the few he would trust on a run.

Human and thin, barely above medium height, with a long nose and close-set eyes below a razored shock of dark brown hair, Beedle hardly ever drew a second glance. But mages who assensed him registered him on their personal radar because he carried a lot of power.

"Telma," Argent prompted.

"Telma reads you, Thunder-Walker," the sultry voice answered. "Your escort is unescorted. He and you make two. And two is the magic number."

Telma Stinnett was a professional bodyguard with an impressive record. She hadn't gone in for augmentation, choosing to remain flesh and blood entirely so she could better fit into the social calendar of her upper crust employers, as well as pass all their security ware. Besides mastering most of the known martial art forms, she knew everything worth knowing about small arms and close combat.

Shamura led Argent to an escalator that took them down into the private loading area below. Sec teams patrolled the area with vigilance, guns plainly visible on their belts. The chauffeur's and Argent's sec clearance chips were scanned at the entry gate. The passes Hornberg of AA had arranged allowed access to the heavily guarded floor.

Ever since the Great Quake of 2028 had hit and wiped out Los Angeles, Long Beach had become the most secure airport in the area. Besides the augmented muscle on hand and the hi-tech equipment, mages also contributed to the defenses covering the area.

"I've got that information," Peg called back.

"Show me," Argent responded, following the young man through the final gates and out onto the concourse. The interior was dimly lit for privacy, with pools of light staggered systematically through the underground parking garage.

The right lens of the Corona wrap-arounds grayed over, becoming slightly opaque. Argent could still see through it by concentrating on the images on the other side of the lens, but he was also able to see the display Peg juiced through the computer display connected to his commlink.

"Shamura, Tobin," Peg intoned as front and right profile images of the chauffeur formed on the lens, "checks out. He's licensed and bonded, and employed by Affiliated Artists. His length of service is slightly more than eight months in that capacity, which is actually enough to qualify him as someone considered to be a long-time employee." The front and profile views blurred into a single three-dimensional image that rotated on an axis.

"Any records?" Argent asked.

"Shamura's been noosed for DWI and DUI, but that's been four years ago. There were a couple shop-lifting charges at about the same time. Evidently he's cleaned up his act."

Data streamed across the right lens of the Corona. Argent stared through it at the bottle-green Toyota Elite limousine as Shamura opened one of the rear doors. "End transmission," he told Peg. So far, so good.

15

Dropping his valise on the bed, Argent scanned the hotel suite Affiliated Artists had reserved in the Erskine name. They hadn't spared the expense. The decor was the epitome of affluence and decadence. The theme for this one was 1940s, with the large, bulky furniture and Salvador Dali prints of the time on the walls. Unfortunately, that opulence also provided for a number of hiding places for aud and vid snoops.

He checked his retina clock. It was 10:21:43, giving him something over an hour to make the rendezvous at Lookers. By that time, Beedle and Telma should have everything in place at the tavern. He'd briefed them on the meet before the flight to CalFree. Peg had provided the floor plans and a place to pick up the necessary hardware.

Accessing the commlink hardwired inside his skull, Argent called Peg. "I'm ready to set up and bring the Parabyte on-line." He thumbprinted the maglocks on the valise, releasing the catches. He worked coolly, taking the Parabyte out of its case. It was small, no longer than five centimeters to a side, and thinner than his forefinger. Trodes stuck out near the top, and they were formatted to slip directly into a telecom's circuit grid. He used a small electric screwdriver to remove the suite's telecom case as the unit sat on the nightstand beside the bed. The telecom case came off and he laid it to one side. He studied the interfaces left open for his inspection. Lights winked red, green, blue, and amber as current flowed through the connections, keeping the telecom ready to access the Matrix. "Power up the Parabyte and get it on-line."

"I'm bringing the Parabyte on-line now and taking over the telecom LTG there."

Argent watched as the lights on the telecom blinked in syncopation. The cycle was familiar. He'd used it with other Mr. Johnsons in the past.

The Parabyte was only one of the contributions Peg had made to the Wrecking Crew over the years. The device, when hooked in, took over the transmission and reception of the frequency at the LTG, then shunted the signal through the main switchboards of a given arena. If the signal was tracked back, Peg would know it and could cut the trace off before it reached any destination except the Parabyte's location. With it in place, she could also

spin out communications lines, splitting them and sending them to more than one commlink.

"You've got a green light at that end," Peg stated.
"Standing by to access the other units."

Argent watched the screen closely. From her deck, Peg
carefully blended all the incoming telecom signals. Using
the hotel suite telecom line, she created a web in the local
communications grid, then masked it with a Passport 55
deception utility she'd layered in for that purpose.

Five small windows opened across the telecom screen,
leaving a sixth space blank. Two of them showed views
inside the tavern Argent knew to be Lookers. The other
three showed exterior street scenes covering three sides
of the tavern.

Four stories tall, Lookers stood like a staggered giant
amid the clutter of L.A.'s El Infierno neighborhood. Argent was familiar with the area from past assignments.
"Where's the fourth exterior cam?" he asked.

"Couldn't get that one in place," Telma answered from
the bar where she was positioned. "I used two broken
telecom lines and a patch into a security cam at a convenience store to get what we have, but there wasn't access
to the fourth side."

The cams she'd used were fish-eye cams, no longer
than Argent's forefinger and smaller in diameter. They
were designed to plug into telecom lines and transmit vid
and aud. The aud pickups left a lot to be desired because
they couldn't always cut out the undercurrent of noise.

Argent didn't like the idea of leaving the west wall out
of the complete picture, but there wasn't anything to be
done for it. He studied the views open to him, memoriz-
ing the layout of the tavern and the surrounding streets.
Terrain was everything to a soldier.

"Argent," Peg called, "let's see if the Coronas are on-
line through your headware."

Taking the sunglasses out of his pocket, Argent slid

them on, making the connection to his commlink so Peg could start feeding him data. "Go."

"Processing," Peg responded. "With the smaller area of the lens, you won't be able to see all of the individual frames at one time the way you can on the telecom there."

"Understood. Can you change them as I need them?" Argent studied the views of the different screens as they flipped through a steady cycle. He viewed the streets and the tavern's gathering late night crowd. Lookers definitely didn't bring in the high rollers.

"I've got them set up on voice command," Peg answered. "As you can see them on the screen there, they are views one through five. Memorize their sequence and call them out to bring them up on display."

Argent quickly checked the voice command, noting the smooth way each scene was replaced by the other. The image inside the tavern showed Beedle lounging at one of the tables making interlocking circles on a napkin with the bottom of a sweating glass. The mage fit in with the rough crowd. Where Argent had expected Telma to stick out, though, he was only slightly surprised to see that she had set herself up as a street hustler. She sat at a table near the back, fanning out cards from a Tarot deck. Three spectators watched her flip the cards, prompting her with questions and dropping nuyen notes on the table. She'd gone high-profile, knowing she was going to be noticed, and blending in as a huckster that no one wanted to make eye contact with if they wanted to hang onto their money.

The operation was as complete as Argent could make it. The Affiliated Artists cover was still intact, and he had the zone wired for vid and aud.

Twenty-seven minutes remained before the meet. He removed the Ingram Super Mach 100s from the valise and snugged them under the suit jacket. It had been cut well enough to conceal the snubbed machine pistols. Extra magazines for the pistols hooked onto the specially made belt he wore, at his back and out of casual sight.

He closed the valise and triggered the release of the powerful acid trapped inside the lining. His cyber fingers left no prints and AA would do their best to clean up after him for deniability if anything went wrong today. Equipped with an auto-destruct, the Parabyte on the suite's telecom was gone as soon as Peg triggered the proper sequence. Argent concentrated on his breathing as he quit the room, keeping the memories at bay while he centered himself. Life and death was measured in those heartbeats.

16

The ork cab driver braked his wheezing vehicle at the curb twenty meters from the El Infierno district's main gate. "Sorry, chummer," the cabbie said, shaking his head. "This is as far as I go. El Infierno's more like a demilitarized zone than a part of this city."

Argent looked at the massive open gate ahead. The night-darkened street continued, but not much traffic went. The stone wall encompassing El Infierno branched in both directions. Homeless people nestled against the base of the wall in plastiboard shacks shivering in the breeze.

Words carved into the stone above the main gate announced: "Abandon hope, all ye who enter here." Despite the mortaring jobs that had been done over the years, bullet holes and grenade scars showed through. More war had taken place than repair.

"This is fine." Argent slotted his credstick into the cab's reader, added a tip, then climbed out of the cab and

crossed the street. There were no guards on the gate into
El Infierno. Guards weren't put there until the rest of the
city was ready to keep the locals in.

El Infierno had a history of trouble. Even as far back
as the 1990s, the area had been filled with violence;
gang wars and drive-by shootings. In the early 21st cen-
tury, the violence had been stepped up by the addition of
yakuza and Korean Seoulpa Rings filtering into the area
and adding to the turf war. Then VITAS II, cousin to the
virulent strain that had depopulated so much of the earth,
hit and the National Guard was called in to liberate the
stockpiles of anti-VITAS serum that were on hand. After
the virus had been eliminated, a major war for real estate
was fought in the area. The walls had gone up to section
off the neighborhoods that hadn't been taken over. When
the L.A. city government, already granted free city sta-
tus, realized how many losses it was going to incur in the
effort to try to take the rest of the neighborhoods, they
cut their losses. As a result, El Infierno festered and fed
off the rest of L.A. like an infected boil that no one dared
lance for fear of unleashing all the poisons into the other
communities.

Six blocks of buildings that had been battered and broken, and gutted by fires stretched out behind Argent. The
populace showed a higher percentage of metas versus
human norms than the overall demographics of the Cal-
Free State published. Prejudice, Argent had found in his
dealing around the world, was established and enforced
by wealth.

Taking a left at East Alondra Street, Argent strode under a withered canopy of sun-faded synthcotton, past the
collection of empty fruit and water stands. A pawn shop
across the street blared out hot salsa music from a public
address system in an attempt to draw paying customers.
All of the buildings more than two stories tall were generally filled with squatters or gangers. Both groups were

transitory, one fleeing retribution and the other seeking new market areas.

Lookers towered above the buildings around it, topping out at four stories. A hand-painted sign hung out front, the letters big and bold in bright crimson. The two windows facing the street had been shattered, then coated with spray-on acrylic to hold the pieces in place. Electrostatically charged chalk held the day's specials on the acrylic in day-glo blue.

A Latino troll yabo guarded the bar's main entrance, carrying a chopped-down Defiance T-50 shotgun in one hand. Bandoliers of ammo crossed his chest.

"There's a cover charge, chummer," the yabo stated around the thick nicostick in his mouth. He released a cloud of blue-gray smoke.

Argent slotted his credstick, noting the way the yabo's eyes flickered to the reader.

"Mr. Smith," the yabo read.

Argent gave him a small smile. "You can all me John."

"Yeah, well, get this *Mr. Smith:* I don't put up with no trouble in my place." The ork lifted the shotgun meaningfully.

"I'm not here for trouble."

"You decide you are," the ork warned, "and we dole out double portions around here."

"Got a regular buffet, right?" Argent gave the ork a cold smile, then stepped on into the tavern.

The tavern was dimly lit, the effort beaten into docile submission by the clouds of nicosticks and reefer. Several small tables and booths covered the floor space as well as booths to the left of the long bar and in the back. Over the bar, two trids were tuned to World Sports Broadcasting's "Combat Bike Heat XXVII." The signal to the trids was pirated, Argent knew, because WSB was a premium pay-channel. Most of the tavern's customers were quiet, but some of them shouted encouragement to the recorded version of the competition.

Argent felt eyes on him as he stepped up to the bar.

"Want something?" the laconic elven bartender asked. Slender and pale, a bar towel thrown over one shoulder, the bartender glanced up over the noteputer he was working on.

"Water," Argent said. Water was in short supply in all of CalFree State, but not nearly so much as in El Infierno. Some gangers regularly hijacked water delivery trucks and brought it back into the district to sell there, or to resell to the original owners.

"Got some stuff in from Denver." The elven bartender pulled the bottled water from the chiller racks behind the bar and named the price.

After slotting his credstick, Argent took the bottle and sat at the corner of the bar furthest from the tavern's main door. Speaking softly, he started the sec-cam images cycling through the right lens of the Coronas. Neither Beedle nor Telma paid any attention to him.

There were a few passersby. Most of them looked like they were just getting started with the night, cruising the broken streets outside. Only a handful of vehicles passed by. Four of them looked like they were on their last legs, springs and shocks worn, and belching from black market fuel.

Argent's stomach tensed when a silver and crimson Chrysler-Nissan Jackrabbit pulled to a stop in front of Lookers. Two Korean men got out, dressed in black suits and wraparound black sunglasses.

Argent knew from the way they walked and the cut of their suits that both were armed. He kept his hands on the table, trusting his speed and reflexes to keep him out of harm's way if the drek hit the fan.

The men were young and cocky, talking easily between themselves in Korean as they entered the tavern. Some of the men seated at the bar left their seats to make room. The yabo at the door let them pass without a word.

They spoke briefly with the bartender, who disappeared behind the bar for a moment.

Argent tagged them then, knowing they must have been representatives from a local Seoulpa ring. The Korean crime families had a lock on some of the areas within El Infierno.

One of the Seoulpa soldiers stared at Argent, his obsidian gaze totally unreadable.

"Chemistry," Telma said inside Argent's head. "He just doesn't like you."

Argent didn't comment. He knew the look, and what made the man respond to him. He returned the man's stare in full measure.

The second Korean took the gray plastisteel case the elven bartender offered. The man tapped his partner on the shoulder and nodded toward the door. They left together, without another word.

"Bag man," Peg said over the commlink. "Picking up the protection fee."

Argent silently agreed. He froze the cam view on the Coronas and watched the image of the Jackrabbit speed down the street.

"Tense," Beedle said with a forced lightness in his tone. "One of those guys was carrying some heavy ju-ju."

Uncapping his water, Argent took a long drink. The liquid tasted clear and clean, totally out of place with the dirt and foulness that seemed to cling to the air in El Infierno.

"Why would Sencio choose this place?" Peg asked over the commlink. "She should know you'd stick out in a place like this."

Argent knew she was watching him, patched in through the sec-cams tied to the telecom back at the hotel suite. Even if things went right, he planned on finding another place to stay than the hotel. "Exactly. I'll stick out and whoever's hunting her will stick out as well. If it's someone who can't afford to get identified, they may pass up the meet. If it's not, I'll scan them up close and personal."

A rental car with a misfiring engine stuttered to a stop in front of the tavern. The driver stayed put, fingers drumming nervously on the steering wheel.

Watching the man, Argent knew it was the Johnson. He alerted Beedle and Telma, then waited.

Somewhat reluctantly, the Johnson pushed himself out of the car. Slim and twenty-something, the man looked like he'd traveled far and hard. He wore a brown turtleneck and synthdenim jeans that had seen better days, covered by a mid-thigh khaki jacket. Stubble covered his chiseled lower face under the long chestnut hair that trailed down to his shoulders. Blue lensed Whitelaw sunglasses walled his gaze off from scrutiny.

The way the man moved surprised Argent. It was a gliding stride that the big warrior had seen in a number of martial arts masters, but never in one so young. He entered through the door without hesitation once he got underway.

"Beedle?" Argent asked quietly over the commlink.

"Don't know," the street mage answered. "I'm getting some fragged up readings when I assense him. But he's flesh and blood."

"Is he augmented?"

"No. Flesh and blood through and through."

As the Johnson closed on him, Argent felt a tightness in his chest. The nape of his neck prickled in silent warning.

"He moves too cleanly for someone not razored," Telma said. "He's been trained, but I don't recognize the style. From the cut of his jacket, he's carrying a pistol at the back of his belt."

Argent had already picked up the weapon. "Peg?"

"I can't get a scan on him," she answered. "The vid acts like it's on the blink when I try to scan an image and save it. I can't check if there's a legitimate ID out on him."

Turning slowly, Argent faced the approaching man.

The man stopped more than an arm's length away, then scanned the tavern. "Jesus, what a dive."

Argent didn't comment, waiting.

"You're Argent," the man said. "The lady who contacted me said you'd have a password." His face remained cool and dispassionate under the blue lenses of the Whitelaws.

"Not without prompting, Mr. Johnson," Argent replied. "You've had more contact with her than I have."

"Mr. Johnson?" A smile that could have been called cruel twisted his lips. "Call me Chandler."

Argent spread his hands. "Buy you a drink?"

Chandler waved a hand around the tavern, taking in the clientele. "You and me, we're set up as a regular sideshow here. We're so wiz we could sell tickets."

"There was a purpose for that."

"Figured that. Should have turned the job down flat, but I'll admit it got my curiosity up. There's not many things that'll do that these days." Chandler pulled a chair out and sat across the table from Argent. "She said you had a name in common."

Argent answered without hesitation. "Iron Albatross." The name was a reference to the CAS/GD Battle Tank they'd used during an exfiltration during the Desert Wars. It was the first time they'd met, the first time they'd nearly lost their lives together. The heavy cav unit had earned its name during the operation.

"That's the name," Chandler agreed. "Let's get down to biz."

17

"Have you got a team in there?"

Miles Lanier glanced up from his office console as Richard Villiers strode into the room. Villiers had changed clothes, but Lanier doubted that his friend had slept.

"Insertion's taking place now," Lanier said.

"How are you handling it?"

Tapping the keyboard, Lanier booted the image he was viewing on the flat screen into the holo projector built into the right side of his desk. The image took on three dimensions, forming the buildings of downtown El Infierno in miniature landscape.

"L.A.?" Villiers asked in surprise, reading the data-string hanging in the air under the holo. He sat in one of the plush chairs in front of the desk.

Lanier took pride in his office primarily because it put the world at his fingertips. As long as a spy drone was in position like the one out in El Infierno, or other measures had been taken, he could almost be there.

"El Infierno," Lanier corrected, taking a laser pointer from his desk drawer.

"Do you know who the contact is yet?"

Lanier nodded. "We've got the go-between." He used the keyboard to shift the downtown scene to an image of a young man with long chestnut hair. "His name's Vincent Chandler. He's licensed as a private investigator in CalFree. Chandler's also an oddity."

"How so?"

"For starters, he's supposed to be forty-seven years

old. That holo doesn't show it. And a joker we ran the information down with said there's been this rumor that Chandler once took on a case for Lofwyr."

"Can this man be bought?"

"Not from what I understand. When Chandler takes on a case, he sticks with it. Before I interfered, I thought it might be better to know who he was meeting." Lanier switched the holos again, going back to the street scene of El Infierno. He flicked the laser pointer on and placed a purple dot over the tallest building among those shown. "We've got two of our best armed surveillance drones on-site and in the air. Commlinks are being managed through one of the geosynchronous satellites we have over Seattle. L.A. is well within its broadcast range."

"Have you identified whomever Chandler is meeting?"

"No." Lanier moved the laser pointer to indicate a building to the right of Lookers. "We also followed Nakatomi's people into the area."

"Nakatomi. Not Ironaxe?"

Lanier nodded.

Villiers stroked his jawline thoughtfully. "Nakatomi must have convinced Ironaxe to let him handle things in CalFree."

"Nakatomi does have a number of people in the area," Lanier commented. "He'd stand a better chance of getting one of his teams in close quickly."

"Evidently he talked Ironaxe into that as well. It doesn't surprise me, though. Ironaxe is going to see how far he can trust Nakatomi. He wants to make a deal with one of us. If he can keep his defenses up. Where's your team?"

"Setting up a commlink relay station in this building." Lanier flashed the pointer on the building. His attention was drawn to the monitor. The surveillance team across the street had set up on Lookers. Their cams came on-line, filling the screen with three different views of the tavern. "We've got the contact in El Infierno. There's Chandler." He flicked the laser pointer on the private eye.

Chandler sat at a table across from a man.

Villiers tapped the keyboard and sharpened the image, bringing both men into focus. "You say Nakatomi has fielded a team into the area?"

Lanier nodded. "They're there now." He used the laser pointer, putting four purple dots on men along the perimeter of the tavern on one of the other views provided. As he watched, a white Federated-Boeing Commuter 2050 tilt-wing plane appeared on the holo. Equipped with vertical take-off and landing capabilities, the Commuter locked into position above the street, and dropped altitude.

"Do you recognize the man with Chandler?" Villiers asked.

"Argent," Lanier said. "He's a guy you tend not to forget."

"Surprising that Sencio would reach out to him," Villiers commented.

"She didn't have a lot of choices," Lanier pointed out. "She knew we'd already hung her out to dry."

A cargo door on the Commuter opened, revealing men in red riot armor. They threw lines out the door, then stepped over the side and slid down the street.

"Does Chandler have a mobile telecom listing?" Villiers asked.

Lanier nodded.

"You've got the LTG?"

"Of course."

Villiers's eyes glittered as he watched the Nakatomi sec force drop into the street. "Call him. Tell him you'll give him a million nuyen for whatever he's about to turn over to Argent."

"I don't think he will," Lanier said.

"It would be more to our benefit if he didn't," Villiers stated. "Be sure he knows who made the offer."

"And if he tells Argent?" Lanier asked.

"I want Argent to know I'm involved," Villiers said. "He worked for me once, remember? Maybe with enough pressure, it can happen again."

Lanier glanced at the holo, watching the action unfold. He reached for the telecom headset built into the desk. The unit was heavily encrypted so the signal couldn't be easily accessed. "You're assuming Argent's going to live through that drekstorm descending on him."

"I'd put money on it," Villiers said. "Argent's not a man who's easy to flatline."

18

Clay Ironaxe watched Nakatomi's sec force deploy from the Commuter 2050 in El Infierno. Tense, he stood in his VaulTek office in Albuquerque in front of the holo-display, unable to sit. The furniture reflected his cultural heritage, big and blocky, made of timbers hewn from land that he owned, that his father and his father's father had owned before him. Designs made of colored sand were etched into each piece, telling histories and mythologies of his people.

More sand paintings covered the walls, along with ceremonial weapons warriors in his tribe had carried into a dozen different battles over the generations. Ceramic pots and kachina dolls filled niches, and a totem to his chosen deity, Wolf, stood in one corner. The four faces on the totem were all incarnations of Wolf, brilliantly painted. Mixed in with the cultural artwork, Ironaxe had also added some original paintings of the Southwest by Georgia O'Keefe.

"We have identified the man the courier was meeting with," Nakatomi announced.

"Who is he?" Ironaxe asked.

Another bubble opened on the holo, showing an oval view of the interior of the tavern. Two men sat at a table. Ironaxe recognized one of them as the CalFree private investigator Nakatomi's people had originally identified and his own sec staff had verified.

"His name is Argent," Nakatomi said. "At least, that's the only name my people have been able to find for him. He's a shadowrunner."

Ironaxe looked at Bearstalker, who immediately relayed the name by intercom.

"By all accounts," Nakatomi said, "Argent is a very dangerous man. I'm not sure if we can take him alive."

"I'd prefer it," Ironaxe said without inflection. "I want the woman's location, and I want to make certain who employed her."

Nakatomi hesitated, frowning slightly. "My teams will do what they can." He broke the connection.

Ironaxe waited, feeling the tension build. So many things were out of his hands.

19

Chandler folded the portable telecom and dropped it into a jacket pocket. "Now that," he said, "was interesting." He smiled, honestly amused.

Argent waited, not asking the obvious question.

"Andi Sencio offered me ten thousand nuyen to deliver this package of hers," Chandler said. "An amount she said you'd be willing to pay."

"I am," Argent replied.

"I took her job on faith, not knowing if I was even going to be able to cover my fuel cost on this one, let alone turn a profit." Chandler tapped the pocket that contained the portable telecom. "Now I'm offered a million nuyen for it."

"If he tries," Telma promised, "he won't make it out the door."

Argent had Telma in his view over Chandler's shoulder. "So how are you going to play it out?"

"I hired on at a price," Chandler said. "I stay hired. You heard me tell him I'd think about it."

"Yeah."

Chandler relaxed on the other side of the table, spreading his arms out to claim the booth completely. "That was to buy you time, not me. The joker told me he was Miles Lanier, making the offer on behalf of Richard Villiers. I'm guessing that was more of a message for you than for me."

"You're guessing right," Argent replied.

"So how do you want to handle it?"

"Keep thinking about it." Argent took his credstick from inside his jacket. "You and I have some unfinished biz."

"The chip, you mean?" Chandler gave him a blank blue-lensed stare. "The message I got from Sencio was recorded. It hit my telecom service and stayed there. I didn't have an opportunity to talk to her. But she sounded like she was in deep drek. And if names like Lanier and Villiers are going to be tossed around so casually, I have reason to believe she is in deep drek."

Argent waited getting a feel for the man's motivations. "You want to know what my intentions are."

"Sounds kind of archaic when you put it that way, but yeah."

"That's none of your biz."

Chandler shrugged expansively and grinned coldly. "Call me old-fashioned."

"Give me a green light," Beedle said over the comm-link, "and he goes to sleep before he knows what hit him."

"What if you don't like the answer I give you?" Argent asked.

"Then I breeze," Chandler replied, "and see if I can get the lady some help elsewhere. You come across as a real hard guy. You might not be concerned enough about how she's going to turn out after all this."

"Do you know where she's at?" Argent asked.

Chandler shook his head. "The download was en-crypted, but I know people who've got resources that are on the cutting edge of wiz. I've got a few favors I can call in. It might take some time, but I'd get it broken."

"She might be dead by then."

"She might be dead if I give you the information."

Argent closed his hand over the credstick. Chandler didn't even glance at it. Money wasn't his motivation.

"He's for real," Peg said inside Argent's skull. "I ran his file. CalFree Lone Star and the Better Corp Bureau have data on him. He plays fast and loose with the rules, and has come close to losing his license, but he has a reputation for sticking by his clients."

"The message was for me," Argent said.

"Yeah, and I keep wondering about that. If the mes-sage was for you, why not send it to you?"

"Because it wasn't safe to. It might have been intercepted."

"Yet she sent you a message to have you meet me here."

"The source she used to get to me wasn't one she'd want to trust."

"But you did," Chandler pointed out.

"No. She knew I wouldn't ignore the message. There was a possibility that it wouldn't have been passed on. What would you have done if I hadn't been here today?"

"Looked you up."

"It would have been harder than you think. And by then, it might have been too late."

Chandler decided to try another tack. "What's your relationship with the lady?"

Argent got the impression that the eyes behind the blue lenses never ceased in their effort to size him up. "We were friends."

"Were?"

"We went our separate ways years ago."

"But she put out the call for you."

"All of which indicates to me," Argent said, "that she can't trust anyone around her now. That's more reason for me to move quickly on whatever info you have."

Chandler leaned forward again, and this time he had a datachip folded in one hand. "For the moment," he said in a calm, measured tone, "I want you to hang onto your ten thousand nuyen. When this situation resolves itself, I want to hear from the lady. You can send me my fee then."

"If this thing gets totally fragged up," Argent said, "this could be your only chance to collect your fee."

Chandler's smile was mirthless. "Then somebody else will owe it to me. I'll make sure I collect. I don't like leaving unfinished biz."

Moved by the man's commitment to his work and to his view of himself, Argent offered his hand. "Another time, maybe."

"Turns out you ever need an investigator, Argent, I'm listed." Chandler took the hand and squeezed with surprising strength. "Maybe I can toss some work your way, now that I've got a feel for the biz you're in."

"I'll leave you a number where you can reach me."

The investigator handed the datachip across, safely sealed in a gel Pro-Tek pouch.

As Argent took the datachip, Peg's voice blared inside

his head. >*Get out of there! A sec force in a Commuter just pulled into the air space above the building!*<

Wheeling around, Argent spotted the first of the shock troops descending rappelling lines that undoubtedly came from the VTOL craft hanging above the streets. He slid the sleeve back on his left arm, then flipped open a storage compartment built into the cybernetic limb where the disk would be protected. He pushed himself out of the booth, unlimbering the Ingram Super Mach 100s. The smartlinks zapped into his nervous system, putting dual cross hairs in his vision, one blue and the other red.

A hail of bullets shattered the big window overlooking the street. A handful of them smashed to painful stops against the body armor worked into Argent's suit. Beside him, Chandler went down, literally blown apart by the heavy-caliber rounds.

20

Argent leveled both Ingram Super Machs before him, taking cover behind the wall to one side of the window. The vicious little machine pistols balanced in his metal hands, and the recoil was negligible as he squeezed off controlled bursts through the shattered plastiglass of the tavern. The smartlink connections kept him on target.

The first wave of blackclad shocktroops ignored the autofire. Then a handful of them went down, bloody holes ripped through their armor. Two explosions jarred the surrounding area, brief flashes of light illuminating the night.

Expecting company of the worst sort if the meet got slotted, Argent had selected his ammunition with mass destruction in mind. Instead of hardball rounds, he'd loaded the Machs with EXAmmo explosive armor-piercing rounds.

The survivors went to cover, ducking behind parked and abandoned cars.

Argent used more deliberate aim and took out another of the attackers. "Do you have any idea who they belong to?" he asked Peg over the commlink. He wheeled behind the window frame and ejected the spent clips from the Ingrams. Tucking one after the other under his arm after reloading, he had both weapons fully recharged in less than three seconds.

"I'm running the Commuter's serial number now," Peg replied.

The tavern's patrons had joined in the fight, armed to the teeth. Judging from the shouted curses, most of them believed the attack came from the Los Angeles City Authority. Instead of having one or two targets, the arriving hard crew suddenly faced nearly two dozen armed citizens in the tavern equipped with a razor-edged paranoia.

Argent also knew that if the men and women in the tavern realized *he* was actually the target they'd get down to some serious negotiating with the yabos outside. He glanced across the room and spotted Telma in motion.

She laid down a pattern of fire with her pistol that picked off two men beating feet for the doorway. "Staying here is not an option," she said over the commlink. "Whoever put this into play may also have enough pull with the Cal-Free National Guard to get them in as backup."

"We go up," Argent said. His satlink connection through the Corona glasses to the mini-cams revealed that ground units had arrived at the scene as well. They fanned out behind and along the sides of the building, creating an armed perimeter.

"And get trapped like rats at the top of this building?" Beedle asked. He gestured at the street outside. In response, a three-meter wide section of the pavement suddenly erupted. The earth beneath the concrete rose up a meter and a half and shoved itself forward in a ripple that ran nearly six meters before collapsing. The secguards that occupied positions in its path were flung around like sparks jumping from a malfunctioning static-charged dust sweeper.

"They've got the building surrounded," Argent replied.

"So fragging quick?" Beedle asked in disbelief.

"Yes."

A high-caliber round caught the troll bouncer in the head and punched him free from his position near the open door. As he stumbled back, struggling to retain his footing, a dozen more rounds smacked into him, driving him backward. His corpse slammed into the bar counter and left a bloody swath on the synthwood as it slumped to the floor. Other bullets chipped away the synthwood surface, revealing the ceramic plating beneath.

Keeping the mini-cams cycling on the right lens of the Coronas, Argent watched as some of the attack team infiltrated the building. Once inside, they disappeared from view.

"The helicopter belongs to Asian Fuchi," Peg reported. "By way of four shell companies in the area. The corp also owns the bank the company who owns the helicopter makes payments to."

"Nakatomi?" Telma asked. "You didn't say anything about him being involved in this, Argent."

"I didn't know," Argent said. He laid down a blistering arc of fire that blunted another attempt by the attackers to regroup.

"I guess we're talking fragging bonus when we get out of here, huh?" Beedle said.

"We haven't made it out of here," Telma snapped.

"Details, details." Beedle gestured again. In response, a smoke cloud billowed up outside, swirling around the sec force. Many of the men collapsed, choking on the sulfuric fumes that made up the smoke.

Before Beedle could get back to cover, he spun around, blood flying from his shoulder. He cried out in pain, dropping to his knees.

At the same moment, three Asian Fuchi secmen fired through the windows at the tavern's side. A male and female elf went down under the bullets before they could defend themselves. Their ork companion rose up with a roar of rage and fired a cut-down shotgun at the secmen.

Argent didn't wait to see who was going to win. It was only a matter of how many the ork took with him. Reinforcements were coming up behind the sec force, revealed to the big warrior by the mini-cams linked to the Coronas. He crossed the floor, dropping the Ingram from his left hand and letting it hang from the Whipit sling around his shoulder. He closed his fist, trapping the material of Beedle's shirt.

Beedle looked at him, barely hanging onto his consciousness. The bullet had taken the young mage high on the upper chest, punching all the way through.

From the way his arm hung, Argent guessed the heavy round had broken the clavicle as well. He lifted Beedle to his feet and draped him across one shoulder. Before Argent could move, he felt a chill wind ghost across the back of his neck.

"Have you got him?" a voice asked behind him.

Argent spun, bringing the Ingram in his right hand up. He stared across the sights at Chandler.

The private investigator's clothing had been shot to hell. The turtleneck and mid-thigh khaki jacket hung in rags across his upper body. But there was no blood. He held a nickel-plated Ruger Thunderbolt pistol in his fist.

Seeing the man standing there, apparently unharmed, Argent knew then what had seemed so different about Chandler.

"Fragging vampire," Beedle groaned in a pained voice that was barely audible above the sustained bursts of gunfire filling the tavern.

Chandler grinned. "Not exactly my first career choice."

"Clear the area," Peg called over the commlink.

Argent caught the reason for her concern only a couple heartbeats after Peg did. He instantly recognized the vehicle pulling into the periphery of vision afforded through the mini-cams.

Then the sound of grinding tracks hammered into the tavern, rising above the din of wounded and gunfire. Staring through the broken plastiglass shards clinging to the window frames, he saw the dark green LAV-103 Striker Light Tank roll into position in the street.

The tank crew was obviously experienced, locking down quickly. The treads chewed into the street, ripping it up as the anchors resettled the weight.

"Oh bloody frag!" a woman screamed.

Argent kept the Ingram centered on the middle of Chandler's face. Even a vampire could die if its brain or spine were too severely damaged. At this range, both of them knew Argent wouldn't miss. "How did the tank get here?" he asked.

"Beats me," Chandler said. "But if I'd only come to set up you, I wouldn't be standing here now."

Argent ignored the man's words. As a vampire, Chandler didn't have to worry about injury as much as a human. He could regenerate any wounds he took, and turn to mist if things got too bad. Staying with them he could serve as a living gunsight.

"The tank was brought there on a truck transport," Peg answered. "I've got it on-screen."

Cycling through the images on the Corona, noting that he'd lost one of the mini-cams, Argent spotted the truck a few blocks down the street. Peg enhanced and magnified the image, showing the ramp sticking out the back.

"I've traced the license and the name of the company on the side of the truck," Peg said. "It's out of Los Angeles."

"You were followed," Argent stated, pulling the Ingram away from Chandler's face.

"No drek." Chandler looked uncomfortable. "Didn't figure on this little piece of biz getting slotted so drekking quick. And if they followed me, they must have been using some wiz tech. I'm no wannabe, and I've been to see the elephant."

Argent ignored the comment. He gathered Beedle's sagging weight, shoving the younger man toward the back door. "Telma."

She broke from her position at once, ramming a fresh clip home in the butt of her weapon. Two men near the back door on the other side of the bathrooms noticed the group moving toward the exit.

"You're the ones brought this down on us!" one of them snarled, lifting his pistol.

Without a word, Telma shot him through the shoulder, expertly hitting the nerve cluster that controlled the hand. The pistol tumbled from the joker's numbed fingers as he squalled in pain and fury. His partner dropped his weapon and stepped back.

Argent kept the Ingram moving, holding back the Lookers clientele. Beedle was nearly dead weight in his grip, his head lolling around on his shoulders. Watching the image of the Striker tank on the Coronas lens, Argent saw the turret turn, coming to bear on the front of the tavern.

Telma pushed through the door and into the dark, narrow corridor beyond. Glass doors beckoned at both ends of the corridor, letting out into the street in front and a parking area behind the building. "We can try for a vehicle," the bodyguard suggested.

"Not one of those," Argent said. "They'll have those covered." He gestured toward the stairs, knowing they'd be less vulnerable on them than in one of the elevators midway down the corridor. In the Corona lens, he saw

the Striker tank's turret turn more, coming to rest on the
corridor of the building. He didn't know how the sec force
had managed it, whether by infrared sights or by one of
the tank crewmen assensing them on the astral plane,
but the cannon was definitely pointed at them. "Move!
They've got a lock on us!"

21

Using the strength of his cyberarm and the leverage he'd
learned from years of having it, Argent hauled Beedle
over one shoulder and raced up the steps after Telma. His
breath came harshly from the exertion of the last handful
of minutes, but his body performed like a machine, flaw-
lessly and relentlessly, just the way he'd built it and
trained it to respond.

Telma ran ahead of him, graceful as an acrobat. She
held her pistol in both hands, twisting her shoulders as
she swept the shadows.

Beedle kept up a steady litany of curses. His words
and the breath jarred out of him as his abdomen slammed
into Argent's shoulder.

The cannon round from the Striker tank slammed into
the front doors of the corridor below. The plastiglass
doors didn't stand for a nanosecond against the projec-
tile, but the impact set off the shaped charge within the
sabot round. Designed as a tank killer, the sabot round
penetrated its target's exterior surface, then exploded a
secondary charge within that target's belly. In this case,
the target's belly was the corridor.

A sheet of coiling, racing flames speared out across
the corridor. The concussion and heat spilled over Argent,
knocking him flat as he reached the second floor, then

making the air too hot to breathe for a few seconds. If he hadn't had a damper in his cyberears to weed out sudden increases in sound, he would have gone deaf temporarily.

Dazed by the concussive force, he had to push himself back to his feet. Ceiling tile sections dropped from the grids above him, fragmenting against the floor, the railing around the second story balcony, his companions, and himself. White powder puffed up from the broken tiles, dispersing in clouds throughout the air.

A coughing fit racked Beedle, causing him to cry out in pain as well. The blood stain across his shoulder had spread, matting the material of his shirt to his flesh.

"They're getting set to fire again," Peg warned over the commlink.

"Do they still have a lock on us?" Argent asked. He glanced down at the swath of destruction that filled the corridor below.

Flames clung to the walls and floor, and licked greedily for anything they could claim as fuel. Debris scattered the floor, littered with gleaming diamond pinpoints of shattered plastiglass. Black shadows showed where holes had been knocked in the walls. A plastic rubber tree plant hung upside down from the ceiling, burning brightly.

"I don't know," Peg answered.

Chandler was the first to rise, whirling up out of the debris in mist form, then taking on flesh again. He picked his Thunderbolt up from the floor.

Telma shoved her way out from under tiles, covered in the white dust. She still held her weapon.

Kneeling, Argent reached inside his jacket and took out the small case of slap patches he carried. He opened it and took out a low-grade tranq patch and put it over Beedle's neck.

"No," Beedle protested.

Argent ignored the protest. The tranq patch would negate, or at least interfere, with Beedle's ability to work his magic. But Argent didn't want the man in pain because that could make him even harder to work with.

A second cannon round screamed into the interior of the building, impacting against the wall with a blinding display of pyrotechnics. The rush of heat took away the air again for a moment, and the vibration shook the balcony, stressing the supports enough to leave them bent and sagging. The balcony floor pulled away from the sides of the second floor, leaving gaps ten and more centimeters wide. The vibrations continued, accompanied by screeching as plastisteel rebar in the foundation gave way under the weight of the concrete.

Beedle's hand worried at the tranq patch on his neck, but his efforts grew rapidly weaker as the strong anesthetic surged through his system. His eyelids fluttered, slowly and finally closing.

The mini-cam locked onto the street view wavered, going gray, then flickering back into full-color mode alternately. The gray-toned projections started lasting longer and Argent knew he was losing the cam.

"Argent," Telma said.

"Up," Argent said.

The floor shifted violently, tilting toward the corridor below. Benches and artificial plants skidded toward the railing, then spilled over, falling into the flames.

Telma bolted up the stairs, having difficulty navigating them because they'd turned sideways when the bottom section had been blown loose. She paused at the top of the third-floor landing, sinking into cover provided by a pillar connecting the landing to the next floor.

To her left, an elevator opened, the floor level indicator light flashing on. The doors opened and a man stepped out, guiding two young girls.

Telma broke her stance. "Clear," she called back to Argent.

The big warrior never broke stride. Beedle hung limply over his shoulder, making negotiating the stairs harder.

Argent accessed the commlink. "Peg, what's on the top two floors of this building?"

"Primarily residences," she told him. "A few scattered individual businesses."

That agreed with what Argent remembered from the files Peg had sent him during the plane flight. He joined Telma on the landing, Chandler at his heels.

"We're about out of running room," Telma stated grimly.

"We've got company downstairs," Chandler said.

Argent peered over the railing's side. Nearly a dozen men fanned out below, taking up covering positions with overlapping fields of fire. The hard black armor reflected the flames. "We're not going to wait for them. Let's find the quickest way to the roof."

"I've got the building's schematic," Peg said. "At the top of the fourth-floor landing, turn left and go down twenty-five or thirty meters. There's a maintenance room there with a ladder that goes up to the rooftop."

Argent nodded at Telma, giving her the lead.

She took off in a sprint.

Argent followed her, feeling the steps jerk under the weight he was carrying. Groaning metal roared up from below as the bottom two levels of the stairs pulled free and fell. Bullets ripped through the air around them, tearing chunks out of the walls and ceiling.

The maintenance room door was locked when they arrived. Telma pulled on it in frustration. "I can pick it, but it's going to take time we don't have."

"I've got it," Argent said calmly. He released the Ingram and splayed his fingers out. Ramming his hand into the door facing around the handle, he closed his fist and yanked back. The maglock ripped free of the door. He tossed it onto the floor, then gripped the door and yanked it open.

Track lighting illuminated the room on the other side of the door. Shelves lined the walls, filled with cleaning supplies, spare bulbs, and carpenter's tools. Two washers and a dryer occupied a corner, their hoses wrapped up and thrust inside the compartments.

Argent scanned the room. "Where's the ladder?"

"Mounted inside the ceiling," Peg told him. "There's an access chute that runs to the roof."

"Here," Telma called out, moving into a corner at the back of the room. She leaped up and caught a dangling chain. The hatch mounted on the ceiling opened and a ladder extended down to the floor.

"Let's go," Argent said.

"You can't get Beedle through there on your back," Telma said.

Argent looked at the narrow chute and silently agreed. When he spotted the drive belts on the wall, he wasn't sure what they were intended for. But he knew how he could use them.

The belts were thin, hard plastic, with teeth cut into them to mesh with notches on pulley wheels. He took four of them, finding that number made a comfortable handgrip. A nearby box yielded an emergency flare that he pocketed. Turning back to Beedle, he looped them over the man's upper body and pulled his arms out.

"The sec force has taken the bar," Peg said. "Many of them are running into the corridor. I can't see them there."

Argent didn't have to guess to know that the sec force was dogging their footsteps. The secmen must have been thinking they had them cornered.

"Go," Argent said to Telma.

She stared up the ladder, going quickly hand over hand. "Running across the rooftops isn't a good idea. Most of them are too far away. Especially trying to carry Beedle."

"We're not going to run," Argent said. He motioned Chandler up next.

"You go," Chandler said. "I'll come up behind in case you need help with your friend."

Argent didn't argue despite the fact that he didn't like

to be contradicted in the field. What Chandler said made sense. He climbed the ladder one-handed, his move-by-wire reflexes allowing him to carry Beedle's weight perfectly balanced.

He was bathed in perspiration by the time he reached the top of the chute at the end of a five-meter climb. Judging from the distance, he guessed the building had storage space over the top floor. Breathing hard, he carried Beedle to a safe place near the roof's edge.

Blood continued to flow from the street mage's gunshot wound. Argent knew if it wasn't stopped, the young man was going to die. Just like Hawk and Toshi had.

Kneeling, Argent gently ripped the cloth from around the wound. He took the flare from his pocket and popped the self-starter. The flame sizzled to life, burning with a carmine and gold intensity.

"What are you doing?" Chandler asked.

"Trying to save his life," Telma answered. "Do it, Argent. There's no easy way."

Argent clamped down on his feelings the way Brynnmawr had taught him all those years ago, becoming as hard as the ferrous metals and ceramic that made up the cyberhand that held the flare. He shoved it against the bleeding wound.

When the pain hit his system, the young mage almost woke up, struggling against Argent's inexorable grip. Then he passed out again, a scream still-born on his lips.

Argent held the flare against the wound for a quick count of five, then pulled Beedle over and applied it again to the exit wound. Flesh sizzled and white smoke that smelled like frying meat twisted up into his nose. Raw, angry red blisters healed up at once.

But the bleeding stopped.

Argent hoped it would hold the wounds long enough to allow them to get Beedle to a medico who worked in the shadows and off the books. He closed his fist on the flare, crushing out the fire that still clung to it. When he tossed it to one side of the pebbled roof, a few sparks scattered, then the chemicals went inert.

"You did good," Telma said.

"I did what I had to," Argent replied. He stripped out of the jacket, laying it across Beedle. The street mage was already going into shock. Orienting himself, Argent approached the side of the roof above the front of the tavern four stories below.

The Commuter VTOL rested in mid-air, the props turned straight up, a little more than six meters below and nearly twice that distance away from the building. Rappelling ropes hung from the open cargo doors, and a man with an assault rifle stood guard there.

"Now what?" Telma asked, glancing over to the nearest rooftop.

"Wait," Argent said. He marked the plane's location in his mind, then jogged a few steps away. He turned and faced the rooftop, making sure the twin Ingrams were out of the way.

"Argent," Telma said softly, suddenly understanding what he was about to do.

Argent erupted into motion. Although his legs were flesh and blood, he'd had muscle augmentation done that made them incredibly powerful. Coupled with the move-by-wire system and the training he'd undergone, he was an Olympic-class athlete.

He drove his feet against the rooftop. At the rooftop's edge, he put his right foot on top of the edge and pushed himself out into the air. For a moment, there was no gravity, just him hung out over the street far below.

But the Commuter VTOL was there as well.

Gravity asserted itself and sucked Argent down toward the waiting prop at the end of the nearest wing.

22

The drone of the Commuter's flashing prop blades grew steadily louder in Argent's ears. He heard the cybernetic dampers cut in, lowering the incoming noise to something he could handle. The balance augmentor inside his ear kicked in, finding his balance point immediately.

Argent positioned himself as he fell, reaching out with both hands and activating the electromagnetic properties of both. He felt the suction of the madly whirling prop as it threatened to suck him into his deadly orbit.

He slammed his hands onto the wing when he landed on it, hoping the electromagnets would hold. His weight proved too much, drawing him to the edge. The wing dipped uncertainly beneath his weight, pulling toward the building Argent had leaped from.

The Commuter pilot compensated quickly, powering the craft up and regaining the lift.

Argent closed his hands on the wing's edge and held on. His shoulders ached with the strain, already fatigued from carrying Beedle.

"Argent!" Telma called over the commlink.

The Commuter dipped and rolled again, struggling with the unaccustomed weight at the end of the wing.

Argent held on, riding out the sudden shift. He craned his head toward the VTOL craft's cargo doors. The secman there was having the same problems he was, but the man had seen Argent.

Argent made his way toward the body of the plane hand-over-hand. He gripped the wing so tightly that his cyberhands left impressions in the metal. He'd nearly reached the cargo doors when the secman recovered his balance and raised his weapon.

The assault rifle kicked a line of bullet holes through the metal-covered wing with high-pitched pings.

Argent released one hand and hung from the other. Closing his free hand around the butt of the Ingram, he pulled it up, the smartlink connection painting cross hairs in his vision, and fired at the secman's face, emptying the man's skull.

Crossing hand-over-hand again, Argent reached the body of the plane. The cargo doors remained less than a meter out of reach. He let go of the wing and twisted forward to grab the lip of the cargo door. A quick pull and he was inside the Commuter. He filled his hands with the Ingrams and went forward to the pilot's section.

"They know you're aboard the plane," Peg said.

Argent wasn't surprised. The rigger flying the craft was in constant radio contact with the rest of the teams.

"They'll consider the plane expendable now," Telma said. Her words proved prophetic when bullets crashed into the Commuter from below.

Argent didn't worry much about pistol or rifle fire, and the Striker's cannon couldn't adjust to shoot into the air since the plane was well above the turret's elevation. However, with all of the ordnance already in evidence, he wasn't going to believe someone below couldn't pull an anti-aircraft gun out of their hoop.

The plane shifted, climbing. The flimsy door sectioning the cargo area off from the pilot's cabin didn't even properly slow Argent.

In the pilot's cabin, the rigger lay jacked into the Commuter and wearing it like a second skin. He was a thin man, human, who'd seen a lot of hard years.

"Hey," the rigger called out over the cabin's internal speaker system, "you don't need to flatline me. And if you do, who's gonna fly the plane?"

"I will." Argent yanked the rigger's trodes from the console. Being forcibly ejected from the deck system triggered dump shock that rendered the man unconscious. Argent slipped into the co-pilot's seat and pulled back on the yoke.

Sluggishly, the Commuter came under his control. Part of his training under Brynnmawr had included a familiarity with most known military aircraft. He was also well versed in boats, ships, subs, and wheeled and tracked vehicles.

Working the pedals, he turned the rudder and trimmed the flaps, then tilted the props to gain speed. He flew away from the building for a moment. When he had enough speed to gain altitude, he pulled back on the yoke, feeling the nose of the plane come up.

He accessed the commlink. "Telma."

"I'm still here, but we're not going to be alone much longer."

"Another minute," Argent promised, "you won't be there." The engines screamed as he brought the plane around, dropping the right wing and pulling back on the yoke hard enough that it seemed the Commuter was pirouetting on the wingtip. As he came around, he spotted green tracer fire arcing up at him from the ground.

Flying toward the target building again, he cut power to the props, then tilted them up. The plane settled into a descending glide path, then came to a dead stop over the building rooftop.

Telma started forward, carrying Beedle over her shoulder. Chandler followed close behind.

Watching the altimeter gauges on the instrument panel, Argent used the sonar scanner to put the Commuter's belly less than a meter above the rooftop. He locked the autopilot on to hold the plane in position, then reached for the unconscious rigger. Hooking his fingers in the back of the man's shirt, Argent dragged him to the cargo door and tossed him out as Telma reached the plane.

Argent took Beedle's weight, moving the man quick-ly but gently, not wanting to break open the cauterized wounds. "Belt him down," he told Telma.

She knelt to strap Beedle in. "They're on top of us."

"I know." Argent headed for the pilot's cabin.

"Company," Chandler called from beside the cargo doors. Bullets slammed into the plane's sides. Some of them were stopped by the reinforced plating in the cargo area, but others ripped through the tail section. Chandler fired his weapon.

Argent settled into the co-pilot's chair and took the autopilot off. "Hold on." He added more power to the tilt wings, pushing the craft toward the roof's edge.

Without warning, the escape route was suddenly cut off by a wall of fire that flamed up from the rooftop. The flames swarmed and grew taller, reaching a height of four meters or more as they twisted violently.

23

"That's no normal fire," Telma called from the cargo section.

Argent knew that. He also knew from experience that a normal fire might or might not explode any munitions that passed through it. But the firewall spell guaranteed detonations every time. If Beedle had been conscious, he might have been able to negate the spell or take out the mage that had used it. At the least, Beedle would have known who had performed the spell.

Glancing to his right, Argent halted the forward mo-mentum and brought the Commuter around in a tight cir-cle, taking full advantage of the tilt props. When the nose came around facing the group of secmen continuing to come up through the roof access door, he slid his thumbs over the heavy machine gun triggers mounted on the yoke.

The machine gun bullets ripped through the secmen, knocking some of them down and driving the others into startled lunges for cover. Return fire smashed against the plastiglass windows of the Commuter's nose, fracturing it till visibility was almost impossible.

The wall of fire disappeared.

Turning his attention back to escape, Argent powered the props again and tilted them forward. The Commuter streaked across the rooftop, through the smoky haze left where the fire had burned. Tracers lit up the air around them for a moment when they flew over the roof's edge and across the street below.

"Rocket!" Telma yelled in warning.

The plane's warning systems lit up, tracking the approaching anti-aircraft rocket from the Nakatomi ground crews in front of Lookers. Argent pushed the yoke down, losing altitude to gain speed, and dropped the left wing till the Commuter went vertical.

The rocket screamed by them, barely skimming past the plane's underbelly.

Argent fought the plane's inclination to continue losing altitude or flip out into one of the buildings they flew past. If the plane had been powered by jet engines, the outcome of the encounter would have been different. The anti-aircraft rockets were usually equipped with heat sensors that would have allowed them to lock on.

"Peg," he called over the commlink. "I need a place to drop the plane."

"Where do you have in mind?"

Argent mentally flicked through the terrain he knew existed around the L.A. area. "The Barrens. It's in Harbor Town."

"Got it," Peg said. "I'm sending you a map over your

headcom that will translate over the Coronas, but without a satlink, I can't vector you into the area."

"Just find it for me," Argent replied. "I'll get there." He aimed the Commuter south for the Harbor District. The Harbor District ran straight on to the Pacific Ocean.

The right lens of the Coronas pulsed, then filled with a map. Quickly, the map of Los Angeles grew more detailed, peeling away areas till it got down to the Harbor District. Streets and avenues around the area were clearly marked on the map, but the streets inside the Harbor District started and ended in a confusing maze. Security in the area was also reputed to be lax. The details came from the intel packet Peg had assembled on the areas around El Infierno during the night.

"You're taking a chance putting down there," Peg said.

"Yes," Argent agreed, "but it's the best one we have. Lone Star's activity there is minimal at best."

"That's because the local corps use the area as a dumping ground," Peg pointed out.

Argent knew that from the reports he'd read. There'd been numerous sightings of strange creatures lurking in the rubble left from the quake. He adjusted his approach, keeping his altitude low but not interfering with the surveillance systems protecting the corp buildings below. Still, he was high enough that he could see the lights of the plex below butt up against the darkness that evidently marked the Harbor District. The deeper black of the San Gabriel River lay beyond.

"You've got more to worry about than toxic chemicals," Peg said. "A thrill group called the Steppin' Wulfs has laid claim to that district."

Argent remembered that from the reports as well. The Steppin' Wulfs were reputed to be cybered crazies who zealously guarded their turf. Putting the Commuter down in the Harbor District was going to draw immediate attention. But they were all out of choices.

"Argent," Telma called from the back. "We've picked up a tail."

Glancing over at the cam console, Argent brought up the rearward-facing cam. Increasing the magnification, he spotted the wasp shape of the helicopter closing in on them. Green digital numbers marked the distance as 1206 meters and dropping steadily.

"We're going to need the safe house," Argent told Peg.

"On it," she said.

Coming into the area, Argent had known the run might turn dirty early, and he'd figured they might need a bolt-hole to run to. He concentrated on his piloting, watching the darkness that clung to the Harbor District swell till it filled the view behind him. Shoving the yoke forward, he began a sharp descent.

24

Tracerfire split the night around Argent, and a few rounds hit the Commuter. The altimeter dropped steadily as he continued the descent toward L.A.'s Harbor District.

Studying the controls, Argent found a switch that voided the fuel tanks. Normally it was used for flushing the tanks to expel bad fuel. He overrode the security controls.

At something less than sixty meters above the ground, Argent spotted a street two blocks into the Harbor District. According to the map Peg had sent over the Coronas, Hawaiian Street had initially been a nine-block-long two lane that had ran south down to the train tracks only a few blocks east of Interstate 110. Eight of those blocks still existed.

Argent hoped it would be enough to bring the Commuter

down safely. He dropped more altitude, looking for Los
Angeles Harbor College along Interstate 110 to get his
bearings.

He adjusted his approach, locking onto the street between the piles of rubble that filled the Harbor District.
The attack chopper was only 400 meters behind, and
the sec cam revealed that at least two more were coming
into the area. Heavy machine gun fire rocked the plane
steadily now.

Fighting the prop plane's inclination to go nose-up at
the landing, Argent guided it onto his chosen flight path.
He ignored the bullets shearing through his craft, ignored
the sparks that issued from the left tilt prop as machine
gun fire strafed the blades. Smoke belched from the rotor
housing as oil spilled out and burned across the heated
engine.

The altimeter dropped to 25 meters as the attack chopper zoomed in for the kill, closing to within 200 meters.

Argent waited, his finger poised above the fuel void
switch. He knew the pilot would be getting eager to hammer him to the ground. The smoke steaming from the
prop engine grew thicker and blacker.

The attack chopper's pilot opened up with the machine guns. Tracerfire filled the air.

Argent voided the fuel tanks in a liquid, gurgling rush
loud enough to be heard over the engines. He didn't see
the fuel in the rear cam until the tracer fire ignited it.

A large cloud of twisting, roiling flames lit up the night
and wrapped around the helicopter. It wasn't enough to
knock the helo from the sky, and wouldn't last long as a
diversion.

Argent powered the plane forward, listening to the
gut-wrenching noise made by the engines as they coughed
and died, reducing his control. He fought the yoke, forcing the plane onto the path he'd chosen. Barely ten meters above ground level, he sped between the huge piles

of rubble left by the quake. Chunks of brick, mortar, and concrete created hazards in the street.

He left the landing gear up, knowing they'd stand a better chance in the landing without risking a wheel that might collapse or get caught on an obstruction. Pulling the nose up, he gave the plane full flaps in an effort to slow their approach speed.

The Commuter's belly touched, and the grinding rush of the rubble and refuse underneath the craft filled the cockpit. Argent fought the rudder to keep the plane on an even keel. The flaps provided him a little control over the skid, but that was gone the instant the left wing contacted a pile of broken rock that towered seven meters in height.

The wing tore from the plane like tissue paper. The Commuter dipped forward, riding hard on her nose without the wing to help stabilize her weight. Sparks flared up and bounced against the bullet-shattered windshield.

The safety belts snugged tight against Argent, helping him maintain his position. They were on top of the railroad tracks before he knew it, cresting the small incline and going airborne again for an instant. When the Commuter came down, it slammed hard, the structure buckling.

The broken remains of a building filled the windshield. The impact ripped Argent's seat free of its moorings. He crossed his arms in front of him and blocked off most of the collision with the console.

The plane stopped dead in its tracks, shivering like a BTL junkie.

Argent ripped the safety harness free and went back to the cargo area. The plane was tilted, making it hard to walk. He switched on his low-light vision.

Chandler lay across Beedle's lower body while Telma sprawled over the mage's upper body. The vampire showed no signs of stress or damage, but Telma looked like hell.

"I think I broke my arm," she said, pulling back from Beedle's unconscious form.

Argent helped her to her feet and ripped free a cargo restraint. He fashioned a sling and cinched her arm into place against her stomach, immobilizing it.

"Can you handle it?" he asked.

She nodded, pain touching her dark eyes. "I've been hurt worse than this."

Argent knelt and picked Beedle up. The young mage was still under the effects of the tranq patch, and some of the bleeding had started up again, though it didn't appear life-threatening.

Chandler managed the cargo door, shoving it open with metallic squeals. The air outside was laden with noxious-smelling chemicals that burned Argent's nose. The olfactory booster receptors set into his nasal passages and at the back of his mouth damped down the effect immediately, and he kept the gas spectrometer in his main sinus chambers on-line so it would sift through all the unusual smells and identify any that might be biologically harmful to them. Of course, that warning would only activate if the spectrometer identified a chemical trace that was in its programs as harmful.

Argent settled Beedle over his shoulders in a fireman's carry that left both his hands free. Rotors droned overhead, letting him know the attack helos hadn't given up pursuit. A Lone Star helo had joined the collection of aircraft, circling along the outer perimeter and exchanging nervous fire with the corp helos.

Chandler scrambled to the top of the plane and wrenched the top off the in-flight fuel valve. "I know you voided the tanks," the vampire said, "but I also know you get more explosive effect from gaseous vapor than you do the liquid itself. I figure maybe this will confuse the issue a little more." He took a Zippo lighter from his pocket and ripped a shred of his torn turtleneck free. "You chummers get going. I won't be long."

Argent jogged through the piles of debris in the direction of Interstate 110. Telma stayed close behind, her pistol gleaming in her hand.

The bright flare of the material catching fire from the Zippo warned Argent of the impending explosion. Two of the helos descended from the dark sky at the same time, racing for the crash site.

Argent spotted Chandler on top of the plane, saw the vampire drop the flaming bit of cloth into the nearly empty tanks of the Commuter. The tilt-prop plane exploded, proving too much even for Argent's cybereyes. By the time they adjusted, only twisted and burning wreckage remained of the Commuter. There was no sign of Chandler.

"Did he—?" Telma asked.

"No," a strained voice answered.

Argent turned, watching as the vampire turned back into flesh and blood from mist form.

"But I admit that was closer than I thought it was going to be," Chandler said.

The helos swarmed the area. Argent knew they were going to split up into search patterns, looking for survivors, knowing that the plane could have been set off. But the fire would throw off all the infrared equipment in the immediate vicinity.

Argent moved out, taking the lead. His thoughts centered on Andi Sencio and the trouble she was now in. Getting to her wasn't going to be easy. Not if the combined forces of Nakatomi and Villiers couldn't reach her. Of course, the chip would give him more intel than either of those men had. But getting her out of her situation was going to put them all in harm's way.

25

"I'm sorry, Nakatomi-*san*, we lost them."

Clay Ironaxe stared at the vid-feed coming from Cal-Free over the telecom channel to which Nakatomi had linked him. The telecom also held calls on hold from Arthur Vogel and Shikei Nakatomi. The VaulTek CEO felt the pressure of the moment, but the adrenaline surging through him was an accustomed drug of choice, almost drowning out the anger that he felt.

The vid-feed from CalFree pulsed uncertainly across the telecom screen, showing the depth of the encryption process the Asian Fuchi deckers were using to keep the signal from the secteam inviolate. It displayed the battered remains of the Commuter plane. Flames still licked hungrily at the twisted fuselage. The incoming vid-feed had connected with the site in time for Ironaxe to witness the explosion.

The man speaking to Nakatomi was in charge of the ops unit that had attempted to take Argent. The number of dead hadn't been counted.

"I do not take failure lightly," Nakatomi was saying over the commlink connecting him to the ops unit. Ironaxe had been added to the aud transmission only after Argent's escape, and he knew the events coming now were designed solely to impress him.

"*Hai,* Nakatomi-*san,*" the unit commander said. He bowed stiffly, his face ashen. "This I understand."

"You know there is only one answer I will accept," Nakatomi said harshly.

"A finger or his life?" Bearstalker asked impassively. He stood slightly behind Ironaxe, gazing over his employer's shoulder. "I'm betting he's going to have the guy geek himself."

Ironaxe didn't comment. This part of Nakatomi's effort was pure sales job, showing how much control he had over his men. And the lengths to which he was willing to go.

"Know that I beg your forgiveness, Nakatomi-*san,*" the unit commander said.

"There is no forgiveness in this matter," Nakatomi said. "There is only weakness and failure."

The man bowed as a member of his team approached him, carrying a rectangular case. The commander opened the case and took out the short sword inside. The other man fell to his knees, reversing the sword and tearing the tail of his uniform blouse free. He wrapped the black material around the haft of the sword.

"One of the local trid stations has just arrived," Bearstalker said.

Ironaxe glanced at the large trid monitor built into the wall across from the desk. Nine smaller screens framed the one in the center, each a fifth the size of the central monitor. The central screen showed a CalFree channel tagline, and the scene was of the plane crash in the Harbor District. Lines of script ran across the bottom of the monitor because the unit was on mute. The footage was evidently being shot from an aerial unit—either a drone or a helicopter, Ironaxe wasn't sure which.

The snoop recording the story spoke with a lot of exclamation points in the script, but very few facts. There'd been a brawl in El Infierno and several people were dead. Then the vid locked onto Nakatomi's unit commander.

On two screens, getting two different perspectives, Ironaxe watched the man plunge the short sword into his own belly. The blade must have been equipped with a monofilament edge because the man sliced himself in halves. Both halves jerked as life left them.

The trid snoop kept filming, describing what his or her viewers were seeing in graphic detail. The vid tried to follow the other members of the secteam, but a hail of bullets smashed into the helicopter, causing it to break off course. The fact that the snoop was filming from a helicopter was confirmed when he dodged back and his cam recorded his own arm dripping with the pilot's brains. Even on mute, the hearing-impaired script prompter captured the snoop's last screams as the helicopter went down, translating them into written sounds as well as showing the decibel level on a graph that flickered into view.

The vid didn't end immediately even after the helicopter hit the ground, showing the way the snoop bounced. The cam came free and pointed to the downed helo on top of a pile of debris. The dead snoop's face was partially in the view, the single open eye only in fuzzy focus.

Almost immediately, a window opened up on the tridcast, framing a female anchor who went on air to continue fleshing out the story. But the window was strategically placed not to cover up the dead snoop's face or the broken helicopter. Background info on the dead snoop was spooned into the tridcast on the spot.

Ironaxe turned back to the vidlink recording the sec force unit commander's death. Only the body and the Commuter remained in view. He knew Nakatomi would wipe the dead man's records, making him appear SIN-less, another unidentified cipher in the plex.

"Whoever investigates this," Bearstalker said, "will probably think it was the yakuza fighting another border war with the Seoulpa Rings. They've been having turf battles with each other for years."

Ironaxe didn't know anything about that, but he knew Bearstalker did. Bearstalker hadn't always lived in the NAN, and he'd worked as a security specialist for smaller corps all along the West Coast. "So Nakatomi has deniability."

"Yeah. He's a smart fragger," Bearstalker admitted. "Having the commander geek himself like that is going to help the investigators leap to the quickest conclusion. Crime family violence with trid at 2300. Case closed."

"And by ordering the death of a man in front of me, he assumes he has deniability to me as well."

"Probably."

The vidlink ended, closing to an iris of black.

Walking back to his desk, Ironaxe considered all that he'd learned in the past few minutes. "This man, Argent, is a very capable warrior."

"From the way he busted out of that box Nakatomi's people had him in, I'd say so."

"But a man as valuable as that," Ironaxe said, "it doesn't make sense that Nakatomi would give him up. Not if Argent was in his employ."

"That depends on how twisted you think Nakatomi might play this. One man, even an operative as good as Argent, isn't worth more than what he hopes to gain by arranging a merger with you."

Ironaxe knew that was true. It wasn't just the Matrixware that was in development that Villiers and Nakatomi coveted; they wanted the leverage Ironaxe had with the Pueblo Corporate Council. An alignment like that would shore up either of the splintered Fuchis, and would be a hammer blow to the other unless they could find someone else with whom to work out an arrangement quickly.

Of the two, Richard Villiers's NovaTech was the stronger. At the moment. And that could change with the biz whizzing through Wall Street on any given day. One wrong move could possibly cost Villiers' his fledgling empire.

Villiers also had the inside track on the merger with Ironaxe because he had more to offer in North and South

American markets than Nakatomi. However, to complete the merger they were talking about, Villiers would have to give up some of the autonomy he'd maintained since the break-up of Fuchi. Ironaxe had to ask himself if the man would be willing to do that.

Nakatomi had never mentioned that Argent had worked for Fuchi in the past, yet Bearstalker had gotten the information readily enough. Of course, Aaron Bearstalker's sources among shadowrunners was quite remarkable. That was another of the reasons Ironaxe had hired him.

He looked at Bearstalker as he took his seat again behind the desk. "So which of them," he asked, "has betrayed me? Nakatomi or Villiers?"

"We'll find out," Bearstalker replied quietly. "Knowing you've been lied to is the most important part. When we find this Sencio, we'll find the truth."

26

"How do you want to handle this?" asked Miles Lanier.

Richard Villiers' impassive face gave nothing away. "Keep the coverage on Nakatomi and Argent going, but pull your team way back in CalFree. I don't want any repercussions from our involvement there."

Lanier phoned his unit commander and relayed the orders. He scanned the continuing trid coverage of the running gunbattle taking place in the Harbor District. The Lone Star helo had touched down within seconds.

Ground units had arrived on the scene where the Commuter VTOL plane had ripped her guts out, then exploded. Sec-clad Lone Star High-Threat Response Team personnel fanned out along the ground, sifting through the burning debris that could be approached for evidence.

"Argent will go to ground after this," Villiers said. "He'll investigate whatever Sencio's told him."

"I'd think so. After the telecom call I made to the private eye, Argent knows you're a player. Maybe he made some of Nakatomi's people while he was at it. And the information Sencio sent might name Ironaxe. Argent's too professional to miss an opportunity to learn more that might help him."

"Back when he worked for us in the Desert Wars," Villiers said, "he set up a communications system."

"Through the personal ads sections of the local screamsheets," Lanier said. "I remember."

"Since he knows we're involved, maybe he'll be ready to talk to us. Taking on Ironaxe or Asian Fuchi isn't something he's going to be ready to do. Possibly we can establish some kind of bargaining position."

Knowing Argent to be the kind of man he was, Lanier also knew that if Argent decided to try to make the save on Sencio and her people, he'd put their safety first. Even over the bad blood that had come from working with him and Villiers all those years ago. "You want to offer to help him?"

"Yes," Villiers said. "But only you and I are going to know about this. I want a position of deniability maintained on this whole operation. Whatever help he takes from us I want to lead straight back to Nakatomi. Pay him out of one of the bank accounts of Nakatomi's that we've penetrated if you have to. It'll expose some of the resources we've developed for keeping an eye on Nakatomi, but it'll be worth it."

"All right."

"And keep me apprised of anything that happens the instant it does." Villiers pushed up from his seat and walked across the room.

"There is the possibility," Lanier reminded, "that Argent may write Sencio off after this."

"No," Villiers replied. "We know Argent and this is exactly the kind of op he won't be able to walk away from. The man has a conscience. It's the only thing that ever kept him from being perfect."

27

[Chip file: Argent
Security access: ******—01:37:26/10-11-60]

BEGIN UPLOAD

Location: CalFree Safehouse

Before I'd gone down into California Free State, I'd made sure of two things. One was that we'd have a safe house if we needed it. And the second was that I had a street medico that would be ready and trustworthy if we needed him.

Either one of those was expensive. I'd paid no-return deposits on both, the balance due at the time the services were rendered.

Chandler helped me get Telma and Beedle to the medico, then vanished into the night. Beedle was in serious condition, requiring an immediate operation. If he hadn't been a mage, patching him up could have been made easier by artificially replacing some of the damaged bone instead of knitting it with vat-grown materials made from his own DNA. The medico guaranteed me that Beedle would make a full recovery.

Telma hadn't been as banged up. But after the medico got her back on her feet, she had a regular assignment to get back to. She'd arranged a bye on it to cover my back in CalFree, but she couldn't go any further.

I went to the safehouse alone. Except for Peg, who kept trying to draw me out into a conversation I didn't want to have. Or maybe didn't want to is too strong a declaration. I knew I needed to have that conversation with her, but I wasn't ready.

The safehouse was a flop based in Gardenia called Pierson Place where a shadowrunner could doss down into relative obscurity. The upper floors of the flop offered only conventional security. The basement levels, though, offered the max in secware and a shielded jack.

Nolly showed me to my room, taking me through one of the hidden passages to the lower levels. I'd never been able to verify how many rooms were in the basement. I took that as a good sign. If Peg and I hadn't been able to find the answer, I felt certain it would be difficult for anyone else to.

"Your fee pays for the room," Nolly said, "and guarantees anonymity while you're here." She was a thin wisp of an ork, wearing a peasant-style dress that fit the decor of the upper rooms. Her gray hair was pulled back in a bun that was counter-balanced by her thick jaw. "If you draw attention to yourself while you're here, or attempt to invade the privacy of anyone else in these rooms, you'll be evicted."

"I understand," I said, scanning the room. All I carried with me was the duffel containing my back-up gear.

She excused herself and left the room. I heard the door lock behind her. It wouldn't open again unless she opened it. I had the combination to another hidden door in the closet that led to a passage I could use to get outside the safehouse, but it was a one-time use.

The room was Spartan in furnishings. There was a small kitchen area and creatively stocked larder. An uncomfortable-looking bed pulled out of the wall.

I plugged in the encrypted telecom unit from the duffel

and plugged it into the shielded jack. Then I brought Peg on-line and she ran a diagnostics on the uplink.

"We're secure here," she announced.

"Good. Give me a few minutes more." Although the chip Sencio had sent by way of Chandler was locked away in the hidden compartment of my arm and weighed only a few grams at most, I remained sensitive to its presence. I finished searching for vid and aud transmitters but found none. Nolly's reputation was well deserved. I'd used the safehouse twice before, never the same lower basement room, and never the same way out.

Thankfully, Peg followed my lead and didn't talk much.

I finished setting up two of the minicams I had in the duffel. After placing them on the walls so they'd have overlapping fields of view, I tied them in through the encrypted telecom.

"The minicams are on-line," Peg told me.

Taking the motion-detector wands from the duffel, I set them up to cover the door I'd entered through, and the one inside the closet. Only then did I take the chip from my cyberarm and slot it in the telecom.

"Do you want me here for this?" Peg asked.

"Yes," I replied. But, in truth, I didn't know. I wasn't thrilled about having so much of my past life coming into her view. And Andi Sencio was a very confusing part of it. "I want you to upload the chip's contents to your deck," I said. "When I'm done here, I'm going to destroy this copy."

"All right."

I slotted the black chip into the telecom and punched UPLOAD.

"It's passcoded," Peg announced. "The copy's done."

I pulled the bed out and sat on its edge, willing myself to be calm. I turned out the lights, making the room dark except for the green glow of the telecom. One-handed, I tapped out the password Andi and I had agreed on the last time we saw each other.

Chrysalis. A time of change. The word had represented events that had been going on around us at the time, and the changes that had been taking place between us then as well.

The telecom screen flickered, then came on. The vid was sketchy at best, too dark and the chromatint jumped, causing tidal waves of explosive colors. At first I thought the vid had been shot inside a dark building, then I saw the rough stone around Andi and realized it had been shot while underground.

"Examine the files," I told Peg. "I want to know if they've been tampered with in any way."

Andi looked back at me from the telecom screen. She still wore her black hair hacked off street-short, a hold-over from our military days. Her skin was dark and burnished, tight over supple muscle. Every now and again the chromatint got her eye colors right: a turquoised hazel with a cyber sheen. She wore a black synthleather midriff shirt, black synthdenim jeans, and the go-ganger square-toed boots she favored.

She smiled, and maybe the casual observer wouldn't have noted the tightness behind that smile, but I did. Andi was nowhere near comfortable.

"Since you're getting this," Andi said wryly, "and you know how things were left between us, I assume you know that I'm probably in the worst drekpot of my life." She shrugged and paced, shoving her hands in the back pockets of her jeans. "And if I'm not, then I'm flatlined. Some choice, huh?"

UPLOAD TO CONTINUE

28

[Chip file: Argent
Security access: ******—01:55:10/10-11-60]

UPLOAD CONTINUED

Location: CalFree Safehouse

I watched Andi Sencio as she spoke, matching what I saw against what I knew I'd never forget. Andi knew a side of me that I didn't show. Her ability to reach that side of me hadn't ended just because the relationship had.

"You were never one to waste words," Andi said coolly, "and I don't have a lot of time here either. Even with the burst capability on the communications transmission we've cobbled together, we're pushing the clock." Despite her outward appearance, I picked up the tell-tale spike in her voice with my enhanced hearing that told how twitchy she was feeling.

As I watched Andi speak, I couldn't help thinking she might already be flat-lined. Even the com-burst getting off to Chandler only ensured that she'd lived that long, no longer.

"I'm still working for Richard Villiers," Andi said. "He assigned me to a covert run against one of the NAN-megas. We were on a major datasteal from a company in the Pueblo Corporate Council called VaulTek."

"I'm searching for VaulTek now," Peg told me.

"The CEO of VaulTek is a man named Clay Ironaxe,"

Andi said. "He's Amerind, always trying to learn more about his people and his culture. When Villiers put my team on the assignment, he had a good cover waiting for us as part of the research staff of LegacyTrax, an institution catering to the location of antiquities and information in the Awakened World."

LegacyTrax I knew about. They were a small operation that specialized in tracking down the reality of myths and legends that had been handed down before magic returned to the world. The big player in that field was the Atlantean Foundation. I'd done some close-cover work on some of Atlantean's fact-finding hunts over the years. But there were some who said Atlantean served its own purposes and not everything that was found was turned over to the contractors. LegacyTrax still enjoyed a good rep, as far as I knew.

"Some of my team were actual research assistants," Andi went on, "while the rest of us held sec positions. The assignment required that VaulTek open up many of their mainframes to us so our techs could confirm the mythologies being searched. Ironaxe had a number of security measures set up against what we accomplished, but they were easier to get around after we'd been given an invitation to be there."

The fact that Villiers had used Ironaxe's own curiosity against him wasn't surprising news. On the surface, Villiers had a reputation for acting quickly and ruthlessly. And there were some people in the plexes where he did the majority of his biz who considered him to be ready for sainthood. Every move was polished, though, and took into account any weaknesses Villiers could take advantage of.

"If you're wondering how Villiers worked our insertion into LegacyTrax," Andi said, "he did it by buying out the corp on a closed-market deal through other shell corps and dummy bank accounts. No one will be able to trace it back to him."

Without saying it, Andi knew I'd understand that she was the weak link in Villiers' covert datasnatch. Without Andi's testimony to tie NovaTech to LegacyTrax, Ironaxe might suspect, but he'd never prove, that Villiers had been behind the datasteal. And for one corp player to make a move against another corp player without gaining a bad rep, proof had to be involved at some point.

"While we had access to VaulTek's mainframes and cybernetic systems," Andi said, "we also managed to download information Villiers wanted us to retrieve. We used the open databases to patch and bridge our way into the R&D computers, then upload all the files to our decks."

I shifted on the bed and took a bottle of spring water from the stores Nolly had assigned me. I popped the tab unconsciously and drank off a third of its contents, focusing on Andi's words.

"You already know about all the in-fighting that's taking place between the three Fuchis," Andi said. "Any shadowrunner worth contracting has, and I'm guessing that you've been offered a lot of work in the past few months. Maybe you're too busy to handle the bit of action I'm trying to push your way. I hope not. If there was a way to get out without help, you know I'd never have contacted you. I gave you my promise back then, and you know I don't go back on those any more than you do."

I studied the way Andi was dressed, noting the scuff marks of gray-colored dust on the knees of the synth-denim jeans. Wherever she'd gone to tape the com-burst, there'd been some climbing involved.

"I uploaded most of the information we snatched to Villiers' cut-off team working the perimeter of our op," Andi said. "But they didn't get it all. Villiers also knows we're still alive. Some of us. And as long as we are, we're a liability. If he can't find a way clear to exfiltrate us from here without exposing himself and this op, I have

no doubt he'll have us chilled. I want to hire you to exfiltrate us."

Watching the way she moved, pacing as she spoke, I
knew her left leg had been injured. The movement wasn't
noticeable in a big way, but to someone who knew her as
intimately as I did, it was obvious. Andi had always carried a sinuous grace about her in anything physical: from
dancing to sex to assassination.

"You know the kind of money Villiers paid us when
you worked for him," she said, then gave me a wry smile.
"And you probably remember the way I liked to spend it.
Maybe you'd be surprised at how much of it I've put
back in recent years, though. I'll pay a fair price for your
time. Almost from the day you left me, I set up a joint account with the names of aliases you and I used to operate
under. The last report I saw showed a little more than
four hundred thousand nuyen in the account. It's with
Solar First in Washington, DC." She read off the account
number twice, speaking clearly both times.

I tapped the telecom and froze the chip play. "Run it,"
I told Peg. "But be careful. Things could get gnarly when
you access the information about that account."

"It's not like you to try to tell me how to do my biz,"
Peg said irritably.

I sipped my water and ignored the comment. When
she had Solar First's entry page on the telecom, I put my
thumb over the scanner built into the telecom and watched
the light bar flash across the print. It's expensive making
sure my thumbprints match after getting a cyberhand or
cyberlimb damaged, or losing one entirely, which has
happened as well. The cyberdoc I used worked at corp-
spec and was very expensive. But when my thumbprint was
laid into the bank's sec-systems, access to that account
was allowed immediately.

A short commercial played on the telecom display,
cramming as much info as the bank could manage about

their services into a ten-second burst. Then Peg went through the menu, fencing momentarily with the bank's sec-systems as they tried to track down my location. She sleazed through the defenses and fed them a false location. By the time they figured out their mistake, she was out of the system.

When the account opened, the balance was four hundred thirty-seven thousand, one hundred-thirteen nuyen and change. A quick scan of the account's activity log showed that monthly deposits had been made for the duration of the account, with no record of anything ever having been withdrawn.

I considered that maybe Andi had thought the longer we didn't speak, the more money it would take to bring me back around if she ever needed me. That realization made me feel uncomfortable, but I quickly pushed the feeling away. Operating out of an emotional frame of reference wasn't acceptable.

"She wasn't lying about the money," Peg said.

"No. I didn't think she was." I stared at the names on the account. Mr. and Mrs. Linda and Robert Raynes. They were two perfectly normal citizen names and carried none of the history that our real names or the names we wore now brought with them. Even the SINs would be spotless.

"Argent," Peg said in a quiet voice, "is Andi Sencio your wife?"

UPLOAD TO CONTINUE

29

[Chip file: Argent
Security access: ******—02:03:57/10-11-60]

UPLOAD CONTINUED

Location: CalFree Safehouse

I gazed at the still frame displayed on the telecom and considered how brainfragged answering that question had been even back then, without all the time and distance that separated us now. Even trying to wall myself off from the emotions that seeing Andi stirred up in me, I still wanted to touch her and smell her hair. More than that, I wanted to know she was all right.

"We were never married," I told Peg.

"Are you all right?" she asked almost immediately.

"I'm fine."

"I've never heard your voice like that before."

I only felt the tightness in my throat then. The cyberware I had installed was very sensitive. I cut out some of the feedback from my central nervous system, leaving only the mechanical application. Maybe I'd sound more like myself. "It must be the aud pick-up in this room."

"Maybe."

But I thought Peg was cutting me some slack. She wasn't ready to deal with that side of me any more than I was. I forced myself to go on because answering Peg's question was the only way I was going to get her to totally concentrate on what we were going to need to do. "We were close, Peg, as close as I've ever been to another person. There were days back then when it didn't even seem like we were two people."

"I see." The tone of Peg's voice told me she was uncertain about her answer. With her meat self getting kluged so early on, she hadn't never had the chance to experience a full physical relationship with another person. Toshi had told me that once, but I didn't know how he came to know it. There was sexually oriented simsense on the market, but from what I'd seen and heard, that medium allowed the human or meta participant too much control. A real relationship—at least to me, and maybe that was because of the upbringing and training I'd had—was a gestalt, something that was greater than the sum of its parts.

The relationship I'd had with Andi convinced me of that. She was the first to convince me that relationships weren't based purely on the physical, though that was a good springboard for them. And the friendship I'd had with Hawk and Toshi, the one I still had with Peg, remained proof to that belief. Over the years there'd only been a handful people I'd let close: Raven, Dirk Montgomery, and Rick Larson, a few others.

Maybe Peg had had some experiences in the Matrix that came close to what she considered meaningful relationships. I didn't know because she'd never mentioned them and I'd ask.

"What happened between you?" Peg asked.

"We both worked for Brynnmawr and the agency he represented," I said, wondering at how I was going to reduce all that history to just a few words. "She was on my team."

"But she was more than a team mate."

"Not at first. That came later. When things with Brynnmawr fell apart, we left together. It was safer for both of us. That way we each had someone who could guard our back."

"Was Sencio in agreement with leaving Brynnmawr?"

For someone who hadn't experienced much of life before she became a paraplegic, Peg was remarkably insightful. But that was one of the reasons she was so good at what she did. "No. Back then Brynnmawr was our only source of security. The things we were taught, the things we were encouraged to believe in—the ties were very strong."

"But you left," Peg said.

"I had no choice. I didn't believe any more. Not with them. Andi left because she wanted to stay with me." Even then I'd realized that Andi had come along not because she had problems with Brynnmawr's way of doing things, but to protect me. That realization had left me conflicted later, made it harder to do what I'd done.

"Then you went to work for Villiers?" Peg was pushing the limit and I was sure she knew it. However, she also knew she had a right to because her hoop was going to be on the line as well.

"Not immediately. For awhile, Andi and I freelanced in our . . . field. Our circumstances were very dangerous, and there was no security. Where we were, the situations we found ourselves in, we could be compatriots to our employers one day, then hunted outlaws the next. Villiers offered security. At least, he offered as much as we could expect in that part of the world at that time."

"There had to have been more. You're not an easy sell, Argent, and I can't believe there was a time you ever were."

Even back then, I hadn't been sold. But Andi had, and I'd gone along with what she wanted because I wanted her and because I was tired of running. And because she'd followed me when I'd chosen to split from Brynnmawr. I didn't mention that to Peg. "At that time, Villiers made a kind of sense. He was young, just putting together the deals that were going to make him big. He was cut-throat, but he wasn't like he can be now."

"That you knew of."

I nodded. "That made all the difference."

"Then when you found out he was like every other corp CEO out there, you quit."

"There was a certain amount of disillusionment on both sides. I didn't like the way he did some things, and Villiers didn't like it that I wasn't tractable."

"But Andi Sencio stayed?"

"Yes." The answer was simple now, but it hadn't been simple then.

"Why did she stay?"

"She wanted to."

"Why?"

"Because she wanted to." I stared at the screen where Andi stood frozen, knowing Peg was watching me. It made me feel uncomfortable. This was an area that I was supposed to be able to keep to myself.

"Did something happen between you?"

I hesitated.

"Argent," Peg said softly, "if you haven't talked to anyone about this, now might be the time." She paused, but I didn't reply. "And I need to know so I can watch— *things* better as we go into this. The situation she's in doesn't appear to be something you can handle by yourself. And you're not exactly in a neutral position on this."

"She made a choice." I kept my voice uninflected, surprised at how much of that old emotion was still alive inside me. "When I decided to leave Villiers, I asked her to come with me. She told me she couldn't. Our lives alone had been difficult. Brynnmawr's people still hunted us, and there were others by that time. You can't take sides without making enemies. And with the way things changed so rapidly back then, you couldn't count on your allies."

"Better to take the evil that you know than face more that you don't."

I nodded. It was a fair assessment.

"She let you go?" Peg asked.

"If I'd stayed, I wouldn't have been the same," I replied. "Andi knew that. Neither of us had a choice. About going or staying." And that was why, at the end, she'd let me go. If she'd tried harder to hold me, I honestly didn't know what would have happened.

"You haven't seen her since then?"

"No."

Peg waited a beat, then asked, "So what are you going to do now?"

I answered without pause. "It's a contract, Peg, pure and simple." I leaned forward and tapped the Play button again, sending the chip spinning to generate more of the message.

It was time to find out how hard the projected run could be.

UPLOAD TO CONTINUE

30

[Chip file: Argent
Security access: ******—02:08:12/10-11-60]

UPLOAD CONTINUED

Location: CalFree Safehouse

"It's more than just Villiers and Ironaxe," Andi said. "Shikei Nakatomi's involved as well. Villiers kept me away from Nakatomi while the Fuchis were one, so I don't think Asian Fuchi knows who I am. At least, they didn't. Nakatomi's corp espionage teams must really be earning their nuyen these days, because somebody tripped them to this run." She let out a deep breath and I could see the pain lines around her mouth. "Nakatomi smuggled a mole onto my team. A guy named Pendleton Frost. Villiers put the team together and I had the final say, but you know how that scans."

I knew exactly how that scanned. It was one of the chief reasons I was no longer a player in the corp scene. The corps looked at the bottom line, at what they wanted to accomplish rather than how feasible it was. Villiers was usually a joker who played his cards close to his vest, but he was also a risk-taker. Corp players had to be. Steady and conservative only netted modest profits. Someone willing to roll the dice on an all-or-nothing bid brought up the big payoff.

Villiers operated off the potential profit margins, using them as a benchmark to justify the risk. Money had never interested me as much as doing the right biz for the right reasons. Maybe it was all the early indoctrination Brynnmawr and his associates programmed into me while they were bringing me up. I liked to think I was that way because I chose to be. Walking away from Andi had been the hardest thing I'd ever done since leaving Brynnmawr, but both of those steps had been affirmation in my mind that I was my own man.

And being that was my bottom line, it was the only thing I could live with.

"By the time I found out about Pendleton Frost," Andi said, "it was too late. He'd compromised the run, too late to stop us, but early enough that four of my people died when we tried to get away." She smiled wryly. "*Almost* got away, I should say. The son-of-a-slitch sold DNA samples from my group to Nakatomi. While we were occupied dodging Ironaxe's corpcops, Nakatomi's people ambushed us. I lost two more people in a dustup with Asian Fuchi. The last report I got from my spotters surrounding the periphery of this site told me Ironaxe's people may be close to digging us out here."

I paused the chip-play again, keeping my emotions locked in. I had no way of knowing if Ironaxe had found Andi or not. "Peg, scan through the news trid and scream-sheet downloads coming out of the Pueblo Council lands."

"I've been doing that since Ironaxe's name first came up," Peg responded. "They've still got a lot of hot spots out there, and the number of acts of violence I've listed are in the dozens now. It's going to take some time ferreting out all of the information on them. I'm dividing them into two initial groups: ones where the victims are identified, and ones where they aren't."

"The corp could run Andi's corpse under a false name," I pointed out. "They could buy some time there."

"What would you suggest?"

"Break it down further," I said. "Assuming that the bodies have actually surfaced, and there's no guarantee of that, they'll be shipped to funeral homes."

"And any funeral homes owned by VaulTek or Nakatomi will be immediately suspect?"

"Yes." Not many people knew that most of the major corps own funeral-home chains throughout the plexes. Corp vengeance was quick as a striking deathrattle, but there was no getting around the habeas corpus writs the courts still handed down. However, if an ex-employee who'd been terminated was shipped to a corp-owned funeral home, that corp controlled the listing of the cause of death. Corp-owned on-site medical facilities could also generate a past medical record on the spot that would show the deceased's history of congenital heart failure and documented unwillingness to have a transplant or a cyber-organ installed. They had a menu of pre-existing conditions an employee could exhibit before flat-lining on the job.

"And if I find any," Peg asked, "what am I looking for then?"

"If any of Andi's people have been shipped to a funeral home that Ironaxe or VaulTek own, see if the family made arrangements with the funeral home for the body." Sometimes a corp made those arrangements, too. But Ironaxe and Nakatomi would have been working hurriedly. Maybe they'd made mistakes Peg could find. I released the Pause button on the telecom.

"We haven't made it out of the Pueblo Corporate Council lands," Andi said. "But you know me: never go into any place without someplace else to run to. I cut a deal with the Underground Awakened in Pueblo-Under to put us up for a few days. It helped that three of my surviving team are metas. With Nakatomi, Ironaxe, and Villiers all turning over rocks in the area, though, we're going to wear our welcome out slotting quick."

I knew only a little about the Underground Awakened. The Goblinization that helped remake the world when magic returned hadn't rested easily in the ranks of the Amerind cultures. Many of them ostracized children and adults that suddenly transformed into trolls and orks sometime around adolescence. In their own way they were as xenophobic as the Humanis Policlubs.

Mary Hawkmoon ran the Underground Awakened as tribal chief. Her father had been an influential subchief in Pueblo, but that hadn't kept her from being banned by the tribe when she'd morphed into a troll.

The little I did know about Mary Hawkmoon and her tribe of outcasts came from a report Brynnmawr had put together years back, and from sources in the shadows. At one point, Hawkmoon's assassination had been deemed necessary because the tribe was suspected of trafficking in BTL chips and Brynnmawr had been tentatively contracted to handle the wetwork.

Had it gone through, I would have been the point man on the op. Back then I wasn't asking as many questions, and

Hawkmoon would have gone down. But back then I didn't know how much of the BTL trade Brynnmawr's employers controlled—for financial as well as other reasons.

"If you choose to take this on," Andi said, "you need to know everything you're up against. I've got eight people in hiding, counting myself. Only four of them are physically able to move unaided. The other four are practically gurney cases that we'll need to med-evac to a shadow hospital ASAP. I'm not going to leave any of these people behind."

It was good to know that some of Andi's basics hadn't changed. Neither one of us had ever left a man behind.

"Besides ducking the combined forces searching for us, we'll also need to retrieve the DNA samples Asian Fuchi's mageslaves have," Andi said. "The nuyen's there in the account, so I guess it's up to you to decide if it's worth the risk." She gave me the location of the Underground Awakened safe house where she and her crew would be staying. When she finished, her hand filled the viewing area on the chip. Then it backed away and I saw the tears on her dust-covered cheeks.

Her emotion shook me, nearly toppling the control I stubbornly held onto. Even with all the death and hurt we'd experienced and dealt ourselves, I could count the number of times I'd seen Andi Sencio cry on one hand and have fingers left over.

"I hate to ask this, Argent," she said in a soft, ragged voice, "because I know you won't walk away from this. At least, the man I remember wouldn't. But I don't want to be stuck here thinking I got you geeked."

Her hand came down and broke the connection, ending the recorded segment. The telecom monitor turned black as death.

UPLOAD TO CONTINUE

31

[Chip file: Argent
Security access: ******—02:21:43/10-11-60]

UPLOAD CONTINUED

Location: CalFree Safehouse

I played the chip three more times, but nothing new came to my attention. When I was finished, I stored it back in the hidden compartment in my arm.

"The safest thing to do would be to walk away from this," Peg told me.

"Yes."

She hesitated, putting it into words since I wouldn't. "But you're not going to, are you?"

"Not till after I've looked into it," I answered. I at least had to do that.

"Then give me a game plan," Peg said. "Something I can work with."

"Run the names you've gotten tonight," I told her. "Get all the data you can. Dig into Nakatomi's and Villiers' current operations. The shadow boards will be filled with truth, lies, and speculations. See if there's anything there that applies to the current problem."

"What are you going to do?"

"Make a few calls," I said. "If you call back soon, I'll be out for a little while."

Peg's silence told me she didn't like the idea. I knew

she was worried about me, and she had every right to be. We'd worked together so long that we'd left traces on each other. There was a good chance that if I went down in a nasty piece of biz, anyone looking too close might be able to tie her with me.

I shut the telecom down. I wanted the solitude the doss offered. Forcing myself up from the bed, I went to the fresher and showered. When I emerged a few minutes later I wasn't feeling at my tiptop form, but I felt better than I had.

I took a pair of creased slacks and a loose printed shirt from my duffel, then got dressed. Leaving the tails of the shirt out gave me enough cover to tuck the Savalette Guardian at the back of my waist. I dropped spare magazines into the deep pockets of the slacks, fitting them into the specially tailored bands inside the pockets to hold them in place. I added a couple of CarbEnergy Bars rather than risk boosting some stuffers. I eat healthy when I can.

Then I buzzed Nolly, asked her to open the door, and left.

I walked fourteen blocks south, then another eight to the east till I reached a Stuffer Shack that had a working public telecom.

The first number I entered was to a cut-out I kept in a warehouse in Raleigh, North Carolina, in which I had an investment under another name. The warehouse barely broke even, but having the cut-out available was worth it. I'd designed the system myself. There were things I had in place that even Peg, Toshi, and Hawk hadn't known about. The system was antiquated next to anything Peg could put together, but it had a lock-down that flushed automatically if anyone tried a trace-back.

Once I had the North Carolina number up, I worked through its system and punched in an LTG I knew from memory. I didn't worry about the time; Rottstein was always up.

"Yeah," a phlegmatic voice answered.

I told him who I was.

"Just a minute." Rottstein turned away from the telecom—I could tell because the sound of hacking and coughing receded somewhat. After much spitting and wheezing, he came back on the line. "Time for a new set of fragging lungs, omae."

He wasn't kidding about the lungs. He's had four transplants in the time that I'd known him. Rottstein had been one of the groundpounders I'd worked with in the Desert Wars, but he'd been in the nastiest part of the firefights toward the end. His entire unit had been hosed with a bacterial bug that concentrated in the respiratory system. Even the transplants didn't remove the bac-agent; it had started on his lungs again immediately, deteriorating them day by day.

"Sencio's between a rock and a hard place," I said. "She asked me to dig her out."

"You want my advice, omae? She made her bed, let her lie in it."

Rottstein had known both of us from the old days. "Can't."

His sigh of disgust broke into a painful fit of coughing. "I know. I was just hoping you'd listen. I don't have that many friends as it is. Can't afford to lose one. What do you need from me?"

"I'm running too hot down here to try to set up anything in the shadows. Peg's up against the wall, too. I need to recruit for the op."

Rottstein was a fixer, a joker who could get whatever someone needed—for a price. He networked between Mr. Johnsons and shadowrunners, arranged buyers for boosted data and physical swag. And he could get in touch with the people I wanted to work with.

"Who?" he asked.

I gave him the list I'd worked up in my mind on the way over to the Stuffer Shack.

"Give me till noon tomorrow."

I didn't like the time frame, but I didn't tell him. Gathering the runners was going to take time, too.

"I'll shave time off where I can," Rottstein promised, "but you're talking about an up-scale crew here. What kind of contract price should I mention?"

"Fifty thousand nuyen," I said. "It'll be paid up front. You can mention that there's a chance we'll turn another profit along the way if we can grab some of the data involved."

That surprised Rottstein. "Not like you to handle a datasteal."

That was how I'd built my rep. I wasn't a conventional shadowrunner. A lot of them were thieves who broke through corp security and boosted data from personnel or research and development branches. Industrial espionage wasn't honorable, and I'd never done it. However, if a Mr. Johnson could convince me he was entitled to a piece of data, I'd retrieved it.

"It won't be a datasteal," I replied. "But there're a number of angles to play on this op. We may be in a position to blackmail our way out of it. If we do, the price goes up."

"I'll tell them," Rottstein said. "Fifty thousand is a lot of nuyen for some of these people, but it's a drop in the bucket to others."

"Make the offer," I suggested. "We'll go from there."

"Sure, omae." Rottstein paused. "I don't want to come across sounding selfish, but where's my fifteen percent coming from? If we cut into that fifty grand apiece, we're knocking it down another seven-five."

"I'll pay the freight on this," I replied. "You'll have the nuyen slotted to one of the accounts I have access to by morning."

"That's a big handle to carry over," Rottstein said. "Unless you're taking a large cut."

"Mine's the same as theirs," I said.

"You're going in the hole ten thousand nuyen on this op?"

"I'm paying the handle," I said.

"Slot me for a sympathetic brainwipe," Rottstein sighed. "I'm not going to see you go in the hole. I'll get it connected for fifty thousand."

"You don't have to."

"I know. Maybe I don't like everything there is about Andi Sencio, but she was one of us. Capish?"

"Yeah."

"Call me tomorrow."

I broke the connection, listening to a fresh burst of gagged coughing from Rottstein. I stood in the shadows of the pay telecom shell and considered my options. Nakatomi and Ironaxe were going to be dangerous players, but I thought I knew how to leverage Villiers. Turning back to the telecom, I slotted my credstick and brought up the on-line screamsheets.

I found the note from Neon Rose in the personals of six screamsheets. The message was the same.

CASSIDAY,
    WOULD LOVE TO HEAR FROM YOU TO TALK OVER OLD TIMES. IT'S POSSIBLE WE STILL HAVE SO MUCH IN COMMON. IF YOU THINK SO TOO, PLEASE CONTACT ME SOONEST.
                                    —NEON ROSE

I slotted the credstick and placed the call to NovaTech. It was time to start putting the pressure back on the players.

END UPLOAD

32

Miles Lanier punched the telecom to Connect on the first warble for attention, recognizing Argent's broad features even before the pixels repainted the image properly.

"Hello, Mr. Lanier," Argent said in that calm voice he had. "Is Mr. Villiers there?"

The professional stance Argent displayed at all times was also one of his trademarks. "I'll get him patched in," Lanier promised.

"Stop the trace-back as well," Argent warned. "If your people get too close, they're going to get hit with some black IC that could damage some of their systems. I'll also be gone before you talk to me. And you want to talk to me."

Without hesitation, Lanier opened an audlink to the dataslaves. "Break off the trace."

"What is it, Miles?" Villiers asked as the view to his telecom sliced the screen in half.

"I have Argent on the line." Lanier tapped the circuits, opening a three-way on the telecom.

"You seem to have stumbled onto a piece of my biz," Villiers accused.

"I was invited in," Argent said. "And since I plan on taking a hand, I wanted to establish some ground rules."

"You're hardly in a position to be giving—"

"I'm in exactly the position to be giving orders to you," Argent interrupted. "I've got a chip recording with a confession detailing how you attempted to breach the security at VaulTek. I also know you're trying to put a deal together with Clay Ironaxe to shore up some of NovaTech's holdings in North America. Earning the enmity of the Pueblo Corporate Council wouldn't do you any good at all."

"If you'll let me," Villiers said smoothly, "I could be of help to you. I've got men and equipment in that area. I could—"

"No." Argent's reply was cold and hard, leaving no room for argument. "You've got a different agenda than I do."

Villiers' eyes darkened with anger. "Your involvement represents a serious threat to my efforts in this arena."

"Mr. Villiers," Argent said, "that was the path you chose when you assigned Andi Sencio to this shadowrun. If I'm successful, Ironaxe will never know you crashed his computer systems. If you don't do as I say, I'm going to see to it personally that Ironaxe gets a copy of that chip file."

"What about the rest of the data Sencio was supposed to send out of there?"

"We'll see," Argent replied. "But I don't want your people cluttering up the field. Pull them now." He broke the connection.

Lanier watched as the half-screen faded to black. A tick more and Villiers' face filled the screen again. Villiers smiled and placed the fingertips of both hands against each other. "This isn't exactly how I'd intended it," he said, "but this is going to work out nicely."

"He could trade the information he has to Ironaxe," Lanier pointed out.

"Then he'd lose the leverage he has over me. I'd have Sencio geeked for it, and he knows that as well." Villiers shook his head. "No, he's as trapped by these circumstances as we are. And that's how we're going to keep him."

33

The telecom in the safehouse buzzed for attention the next morning. Argent woke quickly, his body responding to the move-by-wire system. Sitting up on the edge of the bed, he tabbed the telecom, knowing it could only be one person.

"Are you awake?" Peg asked.

"I am now."

"Get dressed," Peg said. "There's someone I want you to meet."

"Who?"

"If you intend to go after Sencio, you're going to need a decker because I can't physically go with you. I can cover you from outside, but if you run into systems and can't patch a commlink into them that I can work through, you're going to need someone who can handle the scutwork."

Argent considered that. He'd worked with Peg so long that he hadn't thought about that possibility. But every contract he'd taken before had allowed him work an angle that allowed Peg to piggyback into the systems they went up against. "You've got someone?"

"I recruited the best I know. We're just drekking lucky she was available. Get moving."

"Sure." Argent tabbed the telecom off and headed for the fresher.

The decker was elven. For her to have come to El Infierno in the heartland of gangers, yakuza, Seoulpa Rings, and the dregs of metahumanity was a big statement of how much nerve she had.

Seated at a back table of the Chinese restaurant, she stood out like a flower in a snowfield. Her complexion was a milky white without flaw that Argent could see even with his enhanced vision. Wraparound Whitelaw sunglasses covered her eyes as she turned to look at him. Her platinum blond hair was pulled back from her heart-shaped face in a style that was attractive and served to keep it from being loose enough to be grabbed by a prospective attacker. Metal glimmered at her right temple, advertising the datajack there. She wore a mid-thigh-length jade green jacket over a lighter green blouse and matching skirt that ended well above the knee. An Armanté briefcase occupied the seat beside her.

Argent stopped at the counter and ordered two waters that matched the brand on the table in front of the elven decker. Before he could finish slotting his credstick, one of the trio of roller-blade gangers near the front door wheeled over to her table.

The ganger was young and Hispanic, his hair buzzed and the color of watermelon taffy. Gold necklaces dangled around his neck. "Hey, hermana," the ganger said, "my amigos and I were wondering."

Argent stayed by the counter, watching the exchange. He adjusted his hearing to pick up the conversation.

The elf said nothing, regarding the ganger from behind her sunglasses.

Her lack of response seemed to throw the ganger off. He shrugged, getting himself back on track. "We were wondering what a beautiful woman like you is doing down here?"

She remained silent, but one of her hands dropped down to her lap.

"Mis amigos," the ganger said, "they tell me you must be some kind of corp exec come down to El Infierno to check out some of the corp housing. But me, I say you're a joygirl here to do some biz."

If she was offended at being mistaken for a prostitute, the elf didn't show it. "What's your name?" she asked in a soft voice.

The ganger rolled on his blades till he was snug up against the table, within arm's reach of the elf. He smiled, flashing gold-capped teeth. "I am called Luís."

"Well, Luís, why don't you roll back over to your muchachos and tell them you were wrong," the elf said.

Still smiling, Luís leaned forward on the table, placing both hands on the tabletop. "How do I know that I am wrong?"

"Do you like my legs?" the elf asked. "I saw you and your friends looking at them earlier."

"*Sí,*" Luís responded.

"Do you know why you can see my legs?" the elf asked.

"Because you like showing them off. You have good legs."

"Thank you, but no, that's not the reason I wore a skirt today. Come a little closer, Luís."

The ganger leaned down further.

She whispered and Argent's cyberears picked up her words. "Guess what I'm wearing under the skirt, Luís."

An even bigger smile split the ganger's face. "Must be nothing, hermana, for you to tease me like this."

"Wrong." The cool look never left the elf's face. "I'm wearing an Ares Light Fire 70 in a thigh holster. Actually, I guess I'm only wearing the holster now, because I'm holding the pistol."

The ganger's eyes dropped from her face to the arm concealed beneath the table. "You're lying."

"Want to find out?" the elf asked. "I've got sixteen rounds in the clip before I have to reload. I plan on putting four of them through your cojones, then another four through that cute little belly button of yours showing beneath that half-shirt. Then I'll find out how far your amigos want to press their curiosity."

Argent placed the bottles of chilled water on the counter, waiting to see how the biz played out.

34

"*Puta* daisy eater!" the ganger snapped, not moving.

"Now I'm offended," the elf said with no change in her voice at all. "I'm going to give you to the count of three to clear my table before I start squeezing this trigger. And move slowly or I might misinterpret your actions."

The ganger pushed back angrily, moving slowly.

"Hands over your head," the elf instructed.

Anger suffusing his face, the ganger obeyed. The other people in the restaurant glanced in his direction but seemed unaffected by his behavior. El Infierno, Argent decided as he picked up the bottled water again, had become jaded to violence. As long as bullets didn't start flying, everything was normal.

The elf left her hand in her lap as she gazed at Argent.

"May I sit?" Argent asked. "I believe we have a mutual chummer."

"Give me a name," the elf said.

"Peg."

"All right, Mr. Johnson."

Argent took a chair opposite the elf. He placed the bottled water in front of her, then adjusted the empty plastiglass napkin dispenser on the table so he could see the reflection of the gangers behind him. He wore the Savalette Guardian under his shirt at the back of his pants. "You can call me Argent."

"Fine."

"Peg didn't give me your name," Argent said. That had surprised him, but then he supposed they each had their secrets.

"There's no point in it," the elven decker said, "until I accept the contract."

"Peg didn't fill you in?"

"I told her I'd rather hear it from you," she said. "I'm better at convincing myself than having other people convince me."

Argent was impressed. Most shadowrunners only looked at the bottom line: how much up front, and how much on the back end.

"I was told there would be some risks."

"There are," Argent agreed, then he began spinning it out for her, leaving out the particulars and the names of the main players. Even if she bought into it, there were some things he was determined to keep only on a need-to-know basis. He was surprised when he got through the whole set-up and she hadn't buzzed turbo.

"I can handle this," she said. "You can call me Archangel. Let's take a walk. I'm sure you have some questions you want to ask me, and the atmosphere in this place has definitely lost its appeal."

"Two sloppies," Argent told the street vendor outside the laundry two blocks down. He took the time to make sure they weren't being followed. He'd contacted Peg over the commlink, but the decker had refused to talk to him until he'd finished his conversation with Archangel.

The vendor doled out the sloppies, covering them with relish, chili, onions, and cheese.

Argent slotted his credstick to pay for them, then gathered the food in one huge hand. He picked up extra napkins. Returning to Archangel, he gave her one and kept the other for himself. He'd pointed out that they could have eaten in the restaurant or gone to another one. Archangel had responded that she liked to think while she was on her feet.

"Peg tells me you're a drek-hot decker," Argent said.

"And you're wondering what a drek-hot decker is doing operating solo," Archangel said.

"Yes."

"You're direct," she told him. "I like that. Cuts through a lot of unnecessary bulldrek."

"You haven't answered my question." Argent matched her long stride easily as they walked past the six stories of plascrete rectangle that was the Eli Whitney Tower, a corp-sponsored housing project. The corps funded several of the housing projects in the area, primarily so they could have a hostage test group for products they developed.

Archangel bit into the sloppie with clean, white teeth. She chewed, swallowed, then answered. "I choose to work solo, contract by contract."

"There's not much security in that."

"You make do without a team."

"There's Peg."

"Most of my work has been solo," she said. "If you know who to check with and the places to ask, you'll find I've been a busy girl. I was with a team for awhile."

"What happened?"

"I'm a professional. I got too close to one of the team."

"Caring about the people you work with isn't a bad thing."

"The way I was starting to care," Archangel commented softly, "was definitely a bad thing. I need distance in my biz to be good. If I start concentrating on one thing, on one person, wondering what'll happen to him when the drek comes down on a run, how the frag am I supposed to keep everybody else out of the drek?"

"Does he know?" The story touched Argent; he could hear the pain and confusion still in her voice despite her attempt to cover it up.

"I told him."

"What did he say?"

"I left a note."

"That's one way to avoid things."

She turned her black-lensed gaze on him. "There was nothing to avoid, Argent. What I did was a career choice. You should appreciate how professional I can be. I've made it my biz to know limits. Especially my own."

"You're right." Argent also knew how exacting that professionalism could be. The only time he'd truly felt alive since leaving Brynnmawr and Sencio had been when he was with the Wrecking Crew. Part of him had died again when Toshi and Hawk had flatlined. "How long ago was that?"

"Three years." Archangel looked away and started walking again.

"Three years is a lot of time," Argent stated.

"Meaning?"

"You could have hooked up with another team."

"I haven't found one I'd want to stay with."

"Why?"

"They weren't good enough. Their agendas didn't fit mine. They had manners I didn't appreciate. Why? Are you trying to put a permanent team together?"

"No." The thought twisted Argent's stomach slightly, surprising him. Getting close to someone again and losing them wasn't something he wanted to go through again. Having Andi Sencio in her present predicament was reminder of that.

"Why not?" she pressed. "You've got a good rep in this biz. You wouldn't have a problem enlisting a team."

"I'm more comfortable organizing specialty teams for specific runs. If you put a team together, you become responsible to it."

"Only if you let yourself."

"You have to take care of the team if you expect it to take care of you," Argent said, and it was one of the most

basic lessons he'd learned even when he'd just been starting out with Brynnmawr.

"I don't need to be taken care of," Archangel said. "I
take care of myself. I like it that way."

"Three years and you haven't gone back?"

"No."

"Keep in touch?"

"I've got a friend who keeps me updated."

"But you ask?" Argent asked.

"Yes."

"You haven't gotten past those feelings."

She regarded him. "You're pushing."

"I'm learning," Argent disagreed. "If you still have
feelings for this joker it means you're capable of deep
commitment. That you haven't gone back because you
can't make it right in your own mind tells me that you're
capable of deep convictions—no matter how much they
hurt."

"Did you interview the other people on this run as
closely?" she demanded.

"I know them," Argent stated flatly. "I know what I
can expect of them, and what I can't."

"You could trust Peg."

"I do. That's why I'm talking to you now."

Archangel gave him a cold smile filled with the promise of bitter winter. "You can be a son of a slitch, Argent."

"Do you still want the contract?"

"Then I meet with your approval?"

"Yes."

She turned from him. "I'd already accepted the contract. From Peg. That's why I was here."

"Peg isn't managing this run."

"Whether you use me on the run or not," Archangel
said, "I made the deal with Peg. I don't put myself through
this kind of drek. I handle myself, and the people I work
with are glad to get me."

Argent believed her.

* * *

Argent made the call to Rottstein from a pay telecom outside of a barber shop that he was sure fronted for a bookie operation. Commlinks in the El Infierno neighborhood were at a premium so the gambling operation still worked off shoe leather. A dozen small kids of different colors and metahumanity sat on the curb beside the street.

He placed the call through the protected North Carolina exchange and got the fixer on-line almost at once. "It's me," Argent said.

"Yeah, yeah. Gimme a minute."

Argent listened to the racking coughs that followed, only partially muted by Rottstein turning away. He glanced at Archangel across the street. She was looking in the window of a second-hand store that specialized in children's clothes. Her attention seemed captured by a little girl's sky-blue dress.

"Got some bad news," Rottstein said when he came back to the telecom. "Cholonga got whacked in Philadelphia last week. You're looking for a back-up long gun on this op, you're drek outta luck."

35

"What happened to Cholonga?" Argent asked.

"Skinny I get is that he went on the corp-dole as a black-ops specialist and got geeked running what was supposed to be a buy-back from another corp. At least, that's the scan they're giving out."

"But you got it another way?" Argent said.

"Yeah. The street buzz is that Cholonga was a sacrificial offering. He blew up somebody at a corp where his boss corp was making nice-nice again. In order to do biz, the other corp wanted Cholonga's brainbox on a stick."

"You've got addresses for the others?" Argent asked. Cholonga would be missed on this op; he was a true professional.

"Yeah. You ready?"

Argent took a blank chip from his forearm and slotted it into the telecom. "Push it through."

"Coming."

The telecom whirred for a couple heartbeats. Argent scanned the encrypted information feeding into the chip.

"You got times and places on there," Rottstein said. "An LTG if your timetable gets fragged along the way."

Argent took the chip out of the telecom and housed it inside his arm again. "Thanks."

"Null sweat," Rottstein said. "Just keep your head low, omae. You're one of the few who I can still do biz with and not end up with herniated bowels 'cause I'm trying not to drek myself."

Argent punched the Disconnect and crossed the street to Archangel. She had her sunglasses off as she studied the children's dresses. Her eyes were bronze with startling gold flecks in them. He couldn't quite identify the emotion in her eyes, but part of it was sadness.

"Like to buy something?" he asked.

Smoothly, the sunglasses slid back into place. Her expression was neutral when she turned to face him. "No."

"You can have it sent."

"No. Cut to the chase."

"Sure." Argent led the way down the sidewalk, searching for an El Infierno cab. Most of them were armored up like tanks, and very few of them existed at all. "Do you speak French?"

"I speak eleven languages," Archangel replied. "French is one of them."

"Good, because speaking English in Quebec City isn't a good idea."

"We're headed to Quebec?"

"As soon as we can catch a plane," Argent replied. "We're going to be traveling a lot over the next few days."

The jet touched down in Quebec City at 21:43:11, local time. Secmen and sec-systems filled the airport. Argent's cyberware sent the silent alarms into a panic frenzy as soon as he stepped off the plane.

A half-dozen men, rendered faceless by the riot helmets they wore and covered in kevlar, pointed their weapons at him. "Down on the floor!" ordered a man with sergeant's chevrons marked on his shoulder. He spoke in French, then repeated himself in English. "Hands on your head!"

Argent complied, moving lithely into position and staring full into the sergeant's facemask. "I've got papers," he said in French. The remainder of the plane's passengers cowered in the tunnel leading to the jet. The people in the airport itself stared in frozen curiosity.

The sec sergeant nodded to one of his men. The secman came forward cautiously, remaining small in the field of fire.

"I'm a bounty hunter," Argent said. "I've got a work visa."

Peg had supplied the cover, including the visa. Quebec didn't recognize the sentience of paranormal creatures, and even wanted to put trolls on the bounty lists the government paid off on. The problem was, even though those sentient creatures weren't recognized as intelligent, they often turned the tables on the people who hunted them. Bounty hunters regularly crossed the borders seeking gainful employment.

The bounty hunter cover explained much of the cyberware Argent had.

The secman pulled the Quebec-stamped document from Argent's blouse pocket. He scanned through it quickly. "It's a certified license, sir," he reported. "His name is Kortmunder."

"Run it," the sergeant ordered. Neither he nor his men lowered their weapons.

Argent waited on his knees, watching as the secman crossed the boarding cubicle to the telecom on the greeting desk. He spoke briefly, then scanned the visa in. Argent felt his stomach tighten involuntarily, wondering how well Peg had been able to sleaze her way through Quebec City's bureaucratic systems. They should have been easier than any corp's in the plex.

"It's valid," the secman said.

The sergeant nodded, waving his troops into parade rest. They holstered their weapons. "Enjoy your stay in Quebec City, Mr. Kortmunder," the sergeant said.

"It's got to be better than this," Argent said, standing up and grabbing his duffel. He made his way through the packed airport and to the baggage claim area. After he had his gear, he went to the rental car area. Finished with the paperwork and scanning the Kortmunder thumbprint he was wearing into the contract, he found the Americar he'd been given and drove to the upper levels of the airport.

Archangel stood in front of the main entrance.

Argent pulled to the curb and reached across to open her door.

"Now that was exciting," she said as she placed her briefcase in the back seat.

Argent said nothing, pressing on the accelerator as he roared away from the curb and slid into the shadowy maw of Quebec City. He headed for the newest section of the plex. Locals called them the Enterprise Zones because the corps had built there with exactly that in mind.

When the work had begun, thousands of plex natives had been displaced as room was made for the Enterprise Zones. There'd been five in the beginning, representing MCT, Aztechnology, Fuchi, Yokogawa-Honeywell, and

Yamaha. Three more opened in 2054, bringing the total up to eight.

"That has the distinct look of a demilitarized zone," Archangel commented.

"It's more dangerous than that," Argent said quietly. "The Enterprise Zones are treated as extraterritorial and beyond the laws of Quebec. The corps can kill whomever they like over there, and Quebec City won't do a thing about it as long as they don't advertise the fact."

"We aren't going there, I hope."

"No." Argent leveled a forefinger and pointed through the mosquito-smeared windshield. "There." The Hilton International Quebec stood twenty-five stories tall in the distance. Lime-green neon advertising raced up its sides, blending it into the rest of the plex's lighted Upper Town area.

36

"Do you want to tell me who we're here to meet?" Archangel asked as they stepped off the elevator on the eighteenth floor of the Hilton International Quebec.

Argent scanned the hallway as he stepped out. He'd taken the Savalette Guardian from his bags in the parking lot. The hotel security systems weren't designed to keep out people with weapons, but a sec-force was in evidence in the foyer. The elevators were also bugged with audlinks and vidlinks. Except for a few watercolor prints on the walls, the hallway seemed clear.

"Her name is Laveau," Argent said. "She's a street shaman. I've worked with her a few times before. She's in eighteen-fourteen." He counted doors down, closing on his objective.

"What's she doing here?"

"Her latest gig," Argent answered. "She's set herself up as a card reader for the corps, telling fortunes, creating good luck totems, and the occasional love potion. With all the corp action here, she's doing quite well, from what I hear." Rottstein had filled him in on the specifics. "Here we are." He pressed the button beside the door and stood in view of the button-cam at the top of the door so Laveau could see his image on the scanner inside.

Argent counted the ticks, waiting for the door to open.

"You're early," Laveau complained as she swung the door wide. "I'm still with a client." She was a black ork, her hair cut and styled in curls, the canines jutting up from her lower jaw gleaming and white. She stood almost as tall as Argent and wore a flowing white dress covered with silver embroidery in the shape of skulls, grinning, leering, angry, and sad.

"We can wait," Argent offered.

"Madame Fontaine," a man's voice called from inside, "don't hesitate to invite your next client in. I'm quite satisfied that we've done all we can with this visit."

"As you wish, Tajira-*san*." Laveau stepped back into the well-furnished apartment, waving Argent and Archangel in behind her.

Stepping into the room, Argent automatically dimmed his olfactory sensors because of all the accumulated incense smoke. The decor reflected Laveau's shamanistic roots in Jamaican voodoo. Lit candles occupied nearly every flat space in the living room, glinting from ceramic and plastimetal surfaces.

A hand-woven tapestry representing Damballah Wedo, Laveau's chosen patron loa, hung above the synth-fireplace against the opposite wall. Rendered in psychedelic colors, Damballah Wedo was a gleaming serpent winding through a tall forest to reach for the moon-kissed clouds above.

"I'm sorry to interrupt your time," Argent said, turning to face the man in the room.

"Arne Gemmell," Laveau said, introducing Argent as the alias he traveled under, "this is Hideo Tajira."

Argent kept his hands at his sides and performed a perfect bow. "Tajira-*san,* I'm honored to make your acquaintance."

"And I to make yours," Tajira answered.

Argent read the man as a corp exec at once. He was a half head shorter than Argent and moved with a smoothness that suggested a long familiarity with marital arts combined with boosted reflexes.

Tajira wore a black Armanté and went smooth-shaven. His long hair, exceeding the specs of most corps, was pulled back in a ponytail. His green eyes glimmered for just an instant, registering more fully on Argent's face than was proper in the Japanese culture. "Madame Fontaine, you'll find your account credited properly. I thank you for your time." Tajira pulled on thin black gloves. "The evening has been most *enlightening.*"

Laveau took his arm and moved him toward the door. "Shall I schedule you for the same time next week?"

"Of course. I'll look forward to it."

Argent took in the ashtrays containing the burning incense unleashing coiling smoke trails against the ceiling. His mind sped up, recognizing the danger they were suddenly in.

Tajira paused in the doorway, turning to take a final look inside the room. He locked eyes with Argent for just a moment.

Laveau closed the door, then turned to face Argent. When she spoke, her English took on the slurred tones of her native New Orleans. She didn't speak French to let the big shadowrunner know how upset she was with him. "Ever hear of a leetle thing called de telecom, *cher*? It takes all de inconvenience from dese messy meetings."

"It's about to get more inconvenient," Argent said,

freeing the Savalette Guardian from his waistband and activating the smartlink. His vision blurred for the instant it took for the cross hairs to form. "Your client is with Asian Fuchi, right?"

"Yes, cher. But how you know that? You got bad juju between you?"

"I've never seen him before," Argent answered. "But he recognized me."

37

"They know we're coming."

Belted into the opulent comfort of the Agusta-Cierva Rotorcraft, Clay Ironaxe peered down into the purple twilight staining the city of Pueblo as night swept in over the desert. The plex had once been prosperous, not the darkened and dying husk it was now. The warehouse district lining the Arkansas River below was desolate.

"It doesn't matter," Ironaxe told Bearstalker. "They won't be able to run." He looked through the window and up, spotting the other two helos that accompanied the one he occupied.

Their espionage teams had born fruit. Only hours into his assignment, they'd turned up the fact that Nakatomi had a sec-force housed in one of the empty warehouses below through one of the spies he regularly employed. The Asian Fuchi CEO hadn't bothered to mention the presence of the team.

Even as the helos descended like hunting hawks, ground units poured in through the main entrance and swept toward the targeted warehouse. The Agusta-Cierva touched the pockmarked tarmac below with an audible thump. Its spotting lights centered on the warehouse doors as a large team of black-outfitted men circled them.

Fisting his Seco LD-120 pistol, Ironaxe stepped out of the helo. He put on the kevlar helmet Bearstalker offered as he strode toward the thriller graffiti covered warehouse doors. His sec forces moved to the walls of the warehouse. Chainsaws ripped through the thin sheet plastimetal skin into the rooms beyond. In seconds, Ares tear gas canisters were shoved through the holes, making the place look like it had been hit by a fumigator. Ironaxe breathed easily inside the kevlared helmet because it had a filter and a miniature air supply.

The small force inside put up only token resistance. They knew they were heavily outnumbered, and the tear gas took away the last of their resolve. The interior of the warehouse had been superficially changed to house the men inside. The electronic equipment was only rudimentary. Hammocks and sleeping bags littered the floor. The fifteen men and women lay scattered across the floor as well, all writhing painfully in the throes of the tear gas.

Ironaxe bent down and caught a young Japanese woman by the back of her blouse. She groaned in pain, her hands clawing at her eyes. He propped her against the wall near a work bench, then squatted down so she could see his eyes through the visor of the kevlared helmet. "You're working for Nakatomi, aren't you?"

The woman started to deny the accusation, but Ironaxe raised a big hand and scared her out of it. "*Hai.* I work for Nakatomi."

"Doing what?"

"He put us into place here to find the slotters that jacked your decks. We're trying to do you a fragging favor."

Ironaxe ignored the anger. "How were you going to help me?"

"We had DNA samples of the shadowrunners," the woman replied.

"How did he get the DNA samples?"

"I don't know. I think he managed to turn one of the runners against the others."

"Did you find them?"

She shook her head and wiped at her mouth again. "Not yet, but we know they have to be in this area somewhere. They've just dug in deep."

"How do you know that?"

"Because this is the last place we traced them to."

The medic arrived and Ironaxe left the woman to him. Then he joined Bearstalker in searching through the personal effects the Asian Fuchi team had. Bearstalker had already found the DNA samples. Ironaxe had a mage sent over. The female mage came over and sketched out the things the mage team had discovered.

"They were using ritual sorcery," the mage stated. "Very expensive and very time consuming. Evidently they weren't successful."

"Can we use the DNA samples?" Ironaxe asked.

"No." She shook her head. "Only the mages who began work on these can use them. Ritual sorcery is much more proprietary."

Ironaxe dismissed her, scowling.

"Having the DNA samples here could mean a number of things," Bearstalker said.

"I know." Ironaxe's mind was already leaping to the more obvious of solutions. "That Nakatomi really is trying to pin the blame rightfully on Villiers. That Nakatomi was running the operation from here and kept the DNA samples on hand so he wouldn't lose the group he'd put into LegacyTrax himself. That the DNA samples are fakes and the shadowrunners we're searching for have already buzzed turbo, taken out by Nakatomi." He glanced at the DNA samples spread across the corpmage's knees. "Or those DNA samples are fake and we were supposed to find them, then waste time looking for matches that don't exist."

One of the sec people came running up with a portable telecom. "Your office, sir," the man said. "They said it was important." He extended the handset. A cord connected it to the encrypted backpack commlink across his shoulders. The signal was relayed to the lead helo managing the satlink.

Ironaxe said his name into the handset, listening to the echo of the voices and the helos trapped on the open line.

"I do apologize for the deception," Shikei Nakatomi said without hesitation. "I'd truly planned in being in possession of those shadowrunners before now."

"You should have told me you had the DNA samples," Ironaxe said.

"If I had informed you," Nakatomi pointed out, "we couldn't have been sure that Sencio and Villiers wouldn't have found out we had the DNA samples."

Ironaxe watched as his sec guards gathered the scouting team from the floor and marched them out into a waiting Roadmaster converted into a containment vehicle. "For all I know, these people are a support group for the runners who infiltrated LegacyTrax."

"If you believe that, you'll be making a mistake," Nakatomi assured him smoothly. "Also, I didn't just call you because you'd raided the team I had in place there. I just received word from an employee in Quebec City that Argent is there now. I have a team en route to his position. He'll be in our hands in minutes."

"You'll call me?"

"Immediately."

"I'll be waiting." Ironaxe punched the Disconnect and handed the phone back to the comm officer. His brain whirled, figuring all the angles. That Nakatomi hadn't told him about the team for the reasons he gave made sense, but he knew none of those were the real reason. If the team had pinpointed Sencio's group first, Nakatomi would have recovered all the data she'd stolen before

killing her and turning her over to Ironaxe, *regretful* that
he hadn't been able to bring her in alive.

Or Nakatomi might have had her killed because she
could have fingered him for contracting her.

It was hard to know, or even guess, which was the truth.

38

Showing the professionalism that had marked everything
she'd ever done, Laveau scrambled through the doss and
grabbed only the things that were essential to her continued survival. It didn't prevent her, though, from hurling
curses in Argent's direction and bemoaning the fact that
she was leaving behind very expensive things.

Argent stood at the door to the doss, the Guardian tight
in his fist.

"You never mentioned Asian Fuchi as being a problem, cher," Laveau said. "Else me, I would have had dat
boy long gone from here, yes."

Archangel remained calm, sizing up the rest of the
rooms in the doss. She was the first to think of removing
the telecom and dialing out to a pay service so it couldn't
be tapped into and used as a spy device inside the room.

Argent appreciated Archangel's thoroughness and calm.
"The people you worked with must have been good,"
he said.

"The guy who ran the team was clever," she admitted.
"There isn't much in the way of a run that gets by him."

"Was he the one?"

Archangel fixed Argent with a chill stare of her bronze
and gold flecked eyes. "That question is out of place."

"Yes." But Argent knew they were both aware that
she'd answered it all the same. Still, her own plight mir-

rored his to an extent and it made him more curious about her than he normally would have allowed himself to be. She had bailed on the guy she'd fallen for because she couldn't handle the emotions and still be as professional as she wanted to be. And Argent was being pulled into Sencio's problems because he hadn't been able to walk completely away from his own feelings. Nor would he have chosen to. Admitting those feelings existed would have been detrimental. The last person he needed to lie to was himself.

"Let's go, cher," Laveau said. She'd slung everything she could carry into a backpack, Argent noted with approval. The ork street shaman was as efficient as always. As a girl in New Orleans, she'd grown up in the streets, making her way as a thief before turning to magic. As a result, her lifestyle had never taken on more than the semblance of permanence. She carried a Colt Manhunter at her side. "I'm correct thinking dese men be wanting to flatline you dey catch you, cher?"

"Yes," Argent replied.

"Den we get out drekking quick and make no hesitation."

Argent took the lead, stepping out into the hallway while using the doorway as a shield. "The fire escape," he said. "They could already be tapped into the audlinks and vidlinks in the elevators."

"They'll have them in the fire escapes as well," Archangel said.

"We'll have more room to move," Argent said. "Does Tajira come alone to these meetings?"

"He's a corpexec," Laveau said. "Ever know one of dem to come alone to anything? No way. He keeps men stationed in de bar downstairs."

Movement caught in his peripheral vision, sending him into motion. A hail of bullets slammed through the airspace where he'd just stood. The Guardian came up in his fist, spitting and snapping.

The bullets crunched through the face of the man standing at the corner at the other end of the hallway. Before the body fell, Argent fired again as another man moved around the corpse. His second burst only succeeded in smashing against the second gunner's kevlar jacket, driving him back.

"Move!" Argent ordered.

Archangel and Laveau fired as well, keeping the gunner back while Argent reloaded.

The big shadowrunner streaked for the fire escape. His move-by-wire system kept everything flowing smoothly, taking in information in nanoseconds and making corrections. As always, even moving at full tilt his body felt like a greased bearing rolling through its tracks.

His infrared vision lit up the shadow through the window on the fire escape door. He brought the Guardian up in his fist, not breaking stride as he squeezed off two rounds in quick succession.

The bullets ripped through the plastiglass a heartbeat ahead of Argent. The big shadowrunner thought that both rounds had scored on their target, but he didn't take any chances. He spread a big hand out and caught the door against his palm.

With the enhanced weight the cyberware added to his body and the strength possible in his cyberlimbs, the reinforced door shrieked out of its moorings and exploded backward in a warped rush. The door smacked into the man and shoved him down the steps, over the top of two more men charging up after him.

Argent activated the electromagnet in his palm and slapped it against the wall beside the steps. The effect helped anchor him and brought him just short of making the same fall. The smartlink brought his gunhand up and fired the Guardian dry at the two men, targeting the exposed faces rather than the areas protected by bulletproof armor.

Archangel was at his heels, cradling her pistol in both hands. She didn't fire because it wasn't necessary. All three men were geeked.

Without warning the *whumpf* of a set explosive shivered through the building and filled the halls with noise. Immediately afterward, klaxons screamed stridently.

Argent looked back at Laveau and spotted the remote control device in her hand.

"Just a precaution, cher," the ork shaman said. "You know I don't never figure on staying in any one place too long, me. Ol' Laveau, she knows she gonna be a traveler most of dis life." She smiled and dropped the detonator. "Firebomb in de apartment, dat explosion gonna give dem something to think about, yes?"

"Yes."

"Those fire alarms are also going to put everyone in the hotel out into the fire escapes," Archangel said. "That's putting a lot of innocents in harm's way."

Argent was thinking the same thing. He'd worked with Laveau before and found her to be competent at her craft, but it was generally her neck she thought of first. He moved his estimation of Archangel up. He missed having Peg inside his head, but they'd agreed to keep the commlink silent unless necessary to cut down on the chances of them being picked up.

"Very few staying in dis place got any claim to innocence, dem," Laveau said.

Argent moved through the dead men, keeping a pace that he figured would keep the women stressed to match. Archangel seemed to flow along behind him, but Laveau was breathing hard after six stories. At least it was downhill all the way.

"Nakatomi's people should know they don't have to watch the elevators," Archangel said. "By now the fire alarms will have made them all return to the lobby floor."

"And they won't have found us on them," Argent said.

Dozens of people filled the fire escape now, all of them in varying degrees of panic and demanding to know what had happened. "So the elevator shafts should be the safest place for us."

"Yes."

Argent had already thought of that but he didn't mention it. That Archangel was thinking as quickly and clearly as she was only impressed him more. Who had she been working with before that she thought so quickly on her feet?

He led the way down to the ninth floor, then apologized as he forced his way through the packed throng barring the way back into the hotel corridor. He jogged halfway down the hallway till he reached an elevator. The way he had it figured, the elevator would put them over the lobby and the underground garage below. It was on the right side of the underground garage that he'd left the rental car.

Slipping his fingers between the locked elevator doors, he leveraged them open. The interior of the shaft only held red warning lights advertising the absence of the elevator cage.

Operated by the maglev systems, the egg-shaped cage sat at the bottom of the shaft. There were no connecting cables, no infrastructure offering extra support. Only smooth sides of plastisteel for the next eight stories.

"Laveau," Argent said.

"Yes, cher." The ork shaman crowded close and peered down into the inky depths.

"Can you clear the way to the underground garage?"

"Through de floor?"

"Yes."

She shook her head. "You ask a lot, cher, but I think dese old bones up to de job." Chanting to herself, her voice rising, she gestured at the cage below.

With his infravision on, Argent thought he saw the

waves of disruption spike from Laveau's fingertips. When they made contact with the elevator cage, the cage crumpled at once.

Continuing with her chanting, her voice hoarse with effort now, Laveau gestured again. This time the crumpled mass of the elevator cage exploded through the floor below, opening a hole almost two meters across.

"That'll do," Argent said.

"Good, cher, because dere was no much else dese old bones had to give, I tell you dat." Laveau's color had faded and perspiration covered her face. "Been living easy maybe too long, I have."

"That's eight stories," Archangel said.

"Trust me," Argent said. He powered up the electromagnet in his palm again and flexed it at her. "The current generated won't be enough to stop us from falling, but it should slow us."

The look on Archangel's face told him she didn't like having to depend on him. But she didn't argue. She slipped her belt off and ran it through his, making a loop she could hang onto.

Argent stood at the edge of the shaft and let Archangel stretch out, hanging over the abyss as he took her weight. Grimly, he stepped over the edge, clapping his hand against the plastisteel wall. At the mercy of gravity, they fell.

The trip lasted only seconds, faster than Argent would have wanted. He was aware of Laveau levitating herself after them, her dress furling around her legs. Then they hit bottom. Argent's move-by-wire system and strength kept him on his feet, but Archangel went rolling away with a groan of pain.

"Archangel," Argent called, disengaging his magnetic hand.

"I'm fine." She forced herself to her feet shakily, her pistol still gripped in her hand. "You're wasting time."

Argent dropped through the hole and into the underground garage, landing almost five meters below with some effort because the debris of the floor and the elevator cage lay scattered across the garage floor. He started to reach back for Archangel, but she had already lowered herself from the lip of the hole, then dropped carefully to the floor.

Laveau floated through with no problems at all.

A few of the hotel's guests were moving among the parked cars now, talking anxiously. Argent didn't see anyone who looked like they worked for Asian Fuchi. The big shadowrunner led the way to the parked rental.

In minutes they were outside the building, on their way back to the airport. Argent breathed a sigh of relief when they were in the air, but his thoughts were already turning to Atlanta, Georgia.

39

Miles Lanier paced behind his desk, trying to exercise away some of the tension he was feeling. In his experience, it would have been better to be in front of a group and have to mask those feelings. Being on-stage was where he excelled at duplicity. Being alone with the tension was much worse.

And having Argent out there roaming while the shadow op team sat like a ticking nuke in Pueblo was increasingly nerve-wracking.

"What is it, Miles?" Richard Villiers asked over the telecom.

"Argent was just spotted in Quebec City less than an hour ago," the security chief reported. "One of the moles we've got in with Yamaha informed me that Nakatomi's people tried to close in on Argent. He killed four of their people and escaped."

Villiers leaned back in his chair behind the desk. "What was Argent doing in Quebec City?"

"Seeing a fortune teller named Antoinette Fontaine according to my source. She had an expensive SIN, but once we started investigating, we found out it was pure sim."

"Argent's recruiting," Villiers announced.

"Yeah, and at the same time there's been a new problem added in Pueblo," Lanier went on. "Ironaxe just hit Nakatomi's scouting party in the warehouse district. Our spotters in the area confirmed that Ironaxe is now in possession of the DNA samples Pendleton Frost got to Nakatomi."

"I know," Villiers said. "Ironaxe was tipped off by his espionage teams."

"And who tipped them?" Lanier asked, not liking it that their control over the op seemed to lessen with each passing minute.

A half-smile flirted with Villiers lips. "Why I did, Miles."

"Why?"

"To get the DNA samples out of Nakatomi's hands. Argent had to know they existed because that would have been one of the first things Sencio would have told him. Getting the DNA samples from Nakatomi's group would have been hard because he'd have had to find them first. Finding Ironaxe once Argent knows the man has them, will be easier."

"We could have taken the DNA samples off the board and left the way clear for the exfiltration."

"Not without showing ourselves," Villiers pointed out. "Also as a result of doing things this way and exposing the Asian Fuchi team covertly in Pueblo, Nakatomi's position has gotten soft. He's put on a front of being honest with Ironaxe. Now he's had to admit that he was hiding things as well. Ironaxe will have no choice but to realize believing in Nakatomi could be very dangerous."

Lanier considered the implications. "If Ironaxe has the DNA samples, he's going to figure that Sencio and her crew are hiding out in Pueblo-Under. You've just cut the safety margin on her."

"Drastically, I hope," Villiers stated.

40

Argent abandoned his initial plans for getting a nearly straight flight to Atlanta. Having to dump the cover ID after Laveau had mentioned it to the Asian Fuchi corp-exec meant having to activate a backup ID. That wasn't hard because he and Peg kept a number of them active for him. He'd also had another set up for Laveau. But outfitting Archangel for another proved time-consuming.

He'd paid for tickets at Quebec City only minutes before the flight out to Cleveland, Ohio, but they'd left the plane at Buffalo, New York, dumping the SINs they'd been traveling under before they cleared the airport.

They also gained back an hour in crossing the time zone. Just after midnight, they were dossed down in a motel near the hub of the plex under other names. Argent paid for a suite of rooms, then spent twenty minutes talking at the table in the center room. He filmed the conversation, having already primed Laveau and Archangel for the subject matter. Their cover was investments and they'd studied financial screamsheets on the plane, learning a number of the current markets and the pro/con index on them.

He found two button cams in the room with an overlapping field of view of the table. Using two mini-cams from his duffel, he wired them into the hotel cams, mirroring the fields of view. He keyed the RECORD function on both mini-cams to shoot him as he approached the table where Archangel and Laveau were. He cued the mini-cams again after he sat.

Then they talked investments for twenty minutes, all of them professional enough to put their fears at rest while they finished the performance. Argent figured the only glitch in the plan was if the sec-team monitoring the room actually listened to more than twenty minutes of conversation coming from the room.

But he didn't know anyone who'd want to listen to talk about over-the-counter trading stock.

When he finished the twenty minutes, he used the remote control again to cut his mini-cams into the hotel's system. When the sec unit checked their monitors, all they'd see was the conversation continuing at the table. It didn't offer the security of a safe house, but it was the best he could do under the circumstances.

"Okay," Argent said as he pushed up from the table, "as long as we don't move from this room or into view of the main hallway we should be fine."

The two women stretched and got up from the table as well.

"You realize dat de bathroom, it be down dat hallway as well," Laveau complained.

"You had your chance," Argent said. He glanced around the suite. The rooms offered nothing extravagant in the way of decor, just the typical couch, desk, table and chairs. A wet bar was in the corner of the room, but the shelves were barren except for no-name brewkaf. He started a pot, then dragged out three disposable cups with the hotel's logo on them.

Activating the commlink inside his head, he placed a call to the number Peg had set up to run this part of the op. It was answered on the second ring, and a recorded uni-sex voice informed him that Glatenstatt's was closed for the evening, he should call again at ten in the morning. He disconnected, then heard the telecom line jangle again immediately when the call-back feature Peg had programmed into it kicked in.

The original call went through the Albany LTGs, lighting up the hotel on their mainframes. But when the call came back from the Glatenstatt number, the call was piggy-backed through the LTGs so it was almost impossible to trace. Even if someone decided to check it out. The call was also encrypted.

"Argent," Peg said, "I heard about the biz in Quebec City. Are you all right?"

"Yes," Argent replied. "We all are." He brought her up to date quickly. "How much of the news is already out?" He tuned the hotel's telecom, bringing one of the 24-hour news stations on-line, setting it for closed caption. He scanned the news as he talked.

"Nothing in the regular media," Peg told him, "but your name has been bounced around some in the shadow-boards."

"Who's doing the bouncing?"

"Asian Fuchi. I tracked back two of the entries and found they originated in Quebec City and in Tokyo."

"Nakatomi's staying involved."

"Yes, but they don't seem to have anything definite. Other than one of their corpexecs IDing you."

"Getting our travel plans back together is going to set our schedule back a half day or so," Argent said. "Call the others and let them know when we finish this call."

"I will. I'm still working on getting the Pueblo maps," the decker said. "Some of those are locked up tighter than I'd expected. There were clandestine military ops in that area before the NAN took over."

"How many of the terrain maps do you have?" Argent asked.

"Above ground I've got all of them. Old maps as well

as new ones that have been shot from the air and ground. I've got a cache Archangel can retrieve for you."

Glancing across the room, Argent saw that the elven decker had already jacked out of her meat body and into the Matrix. She sat on the floor with her back to the wall, her deck across her knees. A cable inserted into the datajack on her temple connected her to her deck.

"The underground maps are the ones I need most," Argent said.

"I know. I'm trying. I've got a friend who knows a source who has a number of pre-Awakened World documents, but you know how hard some of those can be to come by."

Argent did know. When magic had returned, followed by the killer computer virus that caused the Crash of 2029 and succeeded in toppling world governments, a lot of knowledge had vanished with those political bodies. Part of it was wiped out when the computer systems went down, but the physical records were destroyed in the fever of independence that swept around the world. Some runners, though, had discovered several small fortunes in documents they'd been able to find. By then, most of them were hard to find.

"Pueblo's records should be easier to locate than most," Peg said, "though Mary Hawkmoon and Pueblo's Underground-Awakened have gone to considerable trouble to eliminate those records. Luckily, Pueblo didn't have much industry go into it even before the NAN took over."

"I need them, Peg," Argent said, "if I'm going to make this work."

"I'll have them for you," the decker promised. "I've got Archangel's new SIN ready. At least, it will be by morning."

"Thanks. I'll call you then." Argent broke the telecom connection inside his head and walked to the nearby window looking out over the front of the hotel. The streets of the plex were still alive with movement.

"Cher."

Argent turned around to face Laveau. He knew it was bad from the look on her dark face.

She licked her canines hesitantly. "Man I know, he does biz with Asian Fuchi. Leetle things dat require a deft hand, you know what I'm talking, but his loyalty, it can be bought. Well he, dat man be doing some checking as a favor to me. Said dat scuttlebutt he hears along de way is dat VaulTek discovered an Asian Fuchi covert op in Pueblo."

Argent felt his stomach tighten, thinking maybe he was too late to help Sencio after all.

"Not dat woman you be after, cher," Laveau went on hurriedly, "no, not dat one at all. Dis be another group, one holding de broom, you know what I mean."

"They were the ones who had the DNA samples," Argent stated, getting the feel for the op. The Asian Fuchi group had been a sweeper team, designed to tidy up potentially embarrassing situations by whatever means possible. "Nakatomi had them in the area trying to run Sencio and her group down."

"Dis man I talk to, he don't know what dey be doing dere, but I dink you're right. We both right, cher. Nakatomi, he get ambitious, dink maybe he can get some leverage over Ironaxe, maybe de man figure he owe Nakatomi a big favor. Instead Nakatomi, he gets caught fisting his own wanker, you know."

"How?"

Laveau shook her head. "Dis man I talk to, he don't know. He lucky to know what he know."

Argent silently agreed, but part of him thought maybe the knowledge getting out to the shadowboards that Laveau had access to was deliberate. Nakatomi wouldn't have sold out his own team—unless there was a profit in it.

That line of thinking only left Villiers to be at the root

of it. The NovaTech CEO wasn't going to quietly sit on the sidelines. Argent hadn't expected it anyway.

"Dis thing going to be a nasty bit of biz, ain't it?" Laveau asked.

"Having second thoughts?" Argent asked.

"Fifty dousand nuyen still fifty dousand nuyen, cher. And you talking to a woman, she ain't got no home no more." The ork shaman looked up at Argent. " 'Course, dat's a foolish thought. People like us, we ain't never going to have no home because we be thinking somebody done come along and snatch it from us."

Quietly, in the still part of his soul that still remembered Andi Sencio and what life could be like at times, Argent fervently hoped that wasn't so.

41

Argent left the rental car in the huge parking lot in front of Rebel Hell. The parking area covered acres of black-topped countryside, and he'd been forced to park near the outer perimeter. They'd flown into Hartsfield International Airport from Albany after a brief layover in Memphis and driven straight out to the bar in the plex's Southtown district.

Calling the establishment a bar was a major understatement, the big shadowrunner knew. It was a lot like calling Southtown a bad place to be. On a good weekend night, Rebel Hell could provide sex, drugs, and southern rock and roll to forty-five thousand citizens of Atlanta's over six million inhabitants. And on the weekends, Southtown only saw an increase in the crimes that were committed there on a regular basis. The Yakuza ran most of the black market biz in Southtown out of warehouses.

Neon lights flashed across the front of the bar, alternately displaying an original Confederate States of America flag flying in the breeze and a cyberware cowboy mounted on a heavily cybered bull bucking for all it was worth. Strident music hammered the still, humid night around Argent as he made his way to one of the half-dozen entrances guarded by yabos and mages.

Laveau and Archangel both wore street dress, taking their lead from Argent, who wore slacks and a loose print shirt, pulling it all together with a synthleather covered Kevlar jacket. The women were overdressed for the event, but Argent hadn't bothered to tell them. They weren't staying.

Most of Rebel Hell's clientele appeared young and daring. Argent saw hairstyles he was certain he'd never seen before, as well as colors he hadn't thought possible. And it would have been easier to describe what the clothing covered rather than what it didn't. He also noticed that the clothing had a habit of not always covering what it started out covering.

The doormen were hulking bruisers who looked like they'd been bottle-fed on steroids and hadn't lost the taste as they'd grown. All of them were also heavily cybered. Standing at the door, Argent felt the music hammer into him, literally setting up vibrations inside his flesh.

He slotted his credstick when he got to the door, indicating he was paying for himself as well as the two women. "Can I get a message to Travers?" he asked.

The doorman regarded him with heavy lids. "Which one?"

"Doesn't matter," Argent said. "I'm looking for them both."

The doorman smiled without mirth. "Biz or pleasure?"

"We're chummers."

The doorman didn't appear convinced. "Guess we'll see about that. Jesse and Jason, they're already having themselves a time tonight. Go to the main bar. I'll get a message out. Want to leave a name?"

"Bobby Lee."

The doorman smirked. "After the Civil War Confederate general? Think you're a flip joker, huh?"

Argent dropped folded nuyen into the doorman's hand and passed through the door.

Tables and chairs formed a loose ring around three different dance floors that he could see. Smoke wreathed the air, and the smell of alcohol burned his nostrils. He drew several hostile stares as he made his way through the crowd to the main bar.

More than a dozen bartenders worked behind the polished synth-pecan bar. The music made conversation almost impossible, and the unseen DJ kept spinning the tunes together so tightly there was almost no break at all.

He placed drink orders, Tir na nÓg berry water for himself and Archangel, and a Virgin Mary for Laveau.

"Who are we here to meet, cher?" the ork shaman asked.

"The Travers twins," Argent replied.

"I don't know dem boys."

Argent glanced at the crowd moving across the bar's open spaces, ebbing and flowing like a human tide to the crescendo of music. Rebel yells punctuated the noise. "Jesse and Jason are street sams," he told her. "Some of the best I've ever worked with. And they have a tendency to stick no matter how bad the drekstorm is when it comes down."

"I've heard of them," Archangel told Laveau. "They're supposed to be good."

"They are," Argent confirmed. He waited patiently at the bar, conscious of the stares he received and of the time passing. The news that Ironaxe had pinned down Sencio's location in Pueblo had preyed on his mind during the few hours of sleep he'd gotten.

Thankfully he'd been able to keep focused while putting the plan together using the information Peg had turned up on the terrain. Detailed notes were already stored in his personal noteputer where he kept his journals.

Two trolls shoved their way through the crowd around Argent, vectoring on the big shadowrunner with deliberation. They were both over three meters tall and nearly half of that across. Scarred black go-ganger synthleather covered them.

"Dese be dem boys?" Laveau asked hopefully.

Argent knew the ork shaman had scanned the malicious glint in the trolls' cybered eyes. "No." He pushed away from the bar and turned to face the trolls. They weren't the Travers twins, and they definitely looked like trouble.

42

"You don't look like a local," one of the trolls told Argent as they spread out in front of the shadowrunner in Rebel Hell. The shadows around the bar intensified as the trolls blocked off the light.

Argent didn't respond to the taunt. He knew from experience that anything he could have said would have only been used against him.

"Me and Dweedle don't like people sniffing around our bar that we don't know," the troll went on. He triggered the synapse link that popped the heavy forearm snapblades he wore. The points gleamed in the low light, matching the silver caps on the canines of his lower jaw that jutted almost to his eyes.

The immediate crowd hugging the bar began pulling back, creating a widening circle.

"You and Dweedle keep on sticking your nose in other people's biz, Khelp," a light-hearted voice behind the trolls said, "you may end up sniffing your own hoop during a dirtnap. If you've got a nose left to sniff with."

Khelp turned slightly, looking confused by the interruption. "This ain't any of your biz, Travers."

"Long as I'm working this floor to keep browncones from flatlining each other or anyone else it's my biz." Travers stopped well out of range of the snapblades and without interfering with Argent's maneuvering room.

Travers was at least eight centimeters taller even than Argent, and broader across, not yet out of his early twenties. He looked like a young giant. Dressed in a flimsy Confederate gray tank top and maroon synthdemin pants, Travers' muscular build was intimidating. His hands looked as big as pie plates and hung easily at his sides. Curly dark brown hair fell to his shoulders. His eyes shown cerulean blue, a hint of a flash that revealed they'd been cybered. The jawline was firm and hard, but the grin on his lips was irreverent, almost juvenile.

"You may think you're big," Khelp said, "but you ain't troll-sized yet. Me and you have never had any problems."

"Meaning I should wonder if I can take you?" Travers shook his head and laughed derisively. "Couple of things you don't get, scrod-head. One: when I walk this floor, I think I can take any son-of-a-slitch out here, and maybe any two or three, or I'd head back to the doss and drek myself every night. Two: I don't let any mother's son tell me what I can think or not think. And three: Letting you take that man on might get you flatlined for sure when I'd only slap a knot on your head. It's not him I'm worried about."

As Travers spoke, other troll go-gangers gathered around them, adding encouragement to Khelp. Argent noted the alcoholic flames burning in the go-ganger's eyes, but the quick, jerky motions he moved in spoke of other types of chem fragging his system as well. Common sense wasn't on the agenda anymore.

"Frag you, Travers," Khelp said. "For all I know, this

guy's a Lone Star groundhound you let onto the premises to snare me and my buds to keep your own hoop out of the slammer." He spun without warning, flicking the snapblades out.

Guided by the move-by-wire system and his own training, Argent reached out for the snapblades. He caught them one-handed, a heartbeat before the blades could have turned into cleavers that might have shorn through even his cybernetic limb. He closed his fingers on the blades, breaking them off. They dropped to the floor, seemingly soundless with the music crashing throughout the room. Before Khelp could draw his hand back, Argent seized that as well, controlling the man with crushing force.

The troll go-ganger's eyes rounded even more when Argent placed the biz end of the Guardian at the center of his forehead.

"Breeze or bleed," Argent offered, his face impassive. "Your choice. I don't care which you choose. Either way, I don't want to see you again."

"You won't," the troll said, trying not to show the pain he was in. But he meant the answer to come across as intimidating.

Another troll suddenly flew backward, propelled by a barstool that flew across the air with the force of a battering ram. He landed in the midst of a group of dancers who protested loudly.

"Don't be so unwise, *vous enfants miserable,* to dink dat only one man stands before you." Laveau's voice was cold and hard. She held out a hand, palm up. The smoke in the area twisted into a miniature hurricane that spun in her palm. "And do not dink we are without resources."

The show stopped any thoughts of retribution on the part of the go-gangers. Argent released the troll's hand and stared the man down. Trying to hang onto the shreds of his dignity, Khelp turned and shoved his way through the trolls around him, cursing at them and slapping the ones who didn't move away quickly enough.

"Hoi, Argent," Travers said, approaching with a hand out.

Argent took the young man's hand and shook it. The brief grip Travers showed only hinted at the strength that even exceeded the massive build he showed from steroids and weight training. Argent knew both of the twins well enough to know that they'd had massive amounts of muscle augmentation in addition to the other cyberwork they'd had done to make themselves bigger and taller.

"Hello, Jesse," Argent said.

The young giant smiled. "You always know, don't you?"

"I have so far," Argent replied.

"Even a lot of our family still can't tell us apart all the time," another voice said.

Argent turned slightly and saw Jason Travers approach from beside the bar. The other twin samurai carried an Ares AZ-150 Super Stun Baton in his left hand. "Hello, Jase."

"You knowing how to do that is kind of disconcerting," Jason said. "In our biz, we sometimes depend on people losing track of who's who."

Jesse grinned. "Makes it easier for them to think we've got them surrounded."

"You're late getting here," Jase said.

"Made us start to worry," his brother put in.

"We kind of counted on this piece of biz com," Jase said.

Jesse leaned against the bar and scanned Archangel from head to toe. "Didn't count on the lush scenery being thrown in, though."

"Always love the fringe benefits when we work with you, Argent," Jase said.

"Zero out," Archangel said in a frosty voice. "If you get the wrong ideas in those tiny little brainboxes of yours, taking on a bar full of troll go-gangers is going to look wiz by comparison."

"Spunk," Jesse said, smiling and nodding in approval.

"We always like spunk," Jase stated.

"But," Jesse took up the slack, "Argent doesn't allow any poser behavior while we're working."

"And you're working now," Argent told the twins. He'd worked with them six times before. Despite the irreverent attitudes and macho complexes they exuded, the Travers always came through when the heat turned hottest. And for sheer mayhem, pound for pound, Argent had never seen anything like the twins.

Jesse came away from Archangel still smiling. "Good to know we're working."

"This past year," Jase said, "we've been saving back a little out of each contract."

"Investing." Jesse raised an eyebrow salaciously.

"Thinking of the future," Jase said.

"*Our* future, of course," Jesse said.

"We wanted something we understood."

"And something close to home."

"So we've been putting our extra nuyen into the bar," Jase said.

"We share in the quarterly profits," Jesse said.

"Feels kinda strange being legit," Jase confided.

Jesse nodded. "That's why we were glad you showed up with the offer."

"We'll be back in a couple ticks," Jase promised.

"We've got to get our stuff."

Argent watched them go, neither of them breaking stride but managing to talk to several of the bar attendees along the way just the same, calling out to them by name, although the bar patrons seemed confused as to which brother was which.

"Are they that hyper all the time?" Archangel asked quietly.

"No," Argent said truthfully. "Sometimes they're worse. But when they're working, they don't get any better."

"Where to next, cher?" Laveau asked, swirling her drink in a long-nailed hand.

"Fort Worth, Texas," Argent said. "There's a guy I've got in mind to replace the long gun on the team, but I know what he'll probably say."

43

"Go with you to Pueblo just to get my fragging hoop shot off?"

"All I could do was ask," Argent said. He was seated in a booth at the Satin Doll, a night club rendered in an opulent Japanese decor, the next morning. Only members and their guests were allowed entry. Argent finished his glass of water and started to rise. "Stay healthy, Harrison."

"Spirits." Harrison Dane reached out and caught Argent's thick wrist in his hand. He was elven, long and lean, sporting fiery red hair that framed his angular face in an expensive cut that made him look like a trid version of a Mafia don. The expensive Armante suit carried out the appearance. He cursed fluently in Sperethiel. "You're going to walk out of here just like that?" He glanced around quickly, as if to see if anyone else had noticed his guest leaving so quickly.

Argent resumed his seat. "I've got things to do. I'm pushing the time frame on this one. You said no."

"And I meant no, fraggit," Dane growled. "Do you realize what you're asking me to do?"

"That's why I'm here."

"Well, you can't just ask that anymore."

"So ka," Argent said. "Then I've got to go." He started to rise again.

"Sit down," Dane pleaded. "Please. I've got an image to maintain here. The trid show is hanging in at one of the top ten consistently, and has for the last two seasons. Do you know what the chances of that are?"

"No," Argent replied. Trid was not one of his interests, but he knew the show Dane was talking about.

Kase for the Defense was one of the hottest action/adventure trid shows on the air. And Harrison Dane was a mega-star. Dane starred as Konrad Kase, an ex-Texas Ranger turned defense attorney who defended sympathetic shadowrunners and individual companies from the evil clutches of mega-corporate bad guys. During the course of an action-filled hour of trid, Kase could be counted on for shoot-outs, car chases, explosions, and babes.

Argent had gotten the information from a local scream-sheet he'd read on the flight into Dallas/Fort Worth International Airport from Atlanta. He hadn't talked to Dane in over two years. At that point, *Kase for the Defense* had been in its premiere year.

"Let me tell you," Dane said. "These days any kind of success on trid is a rare and wonderous thing. Most trid series die within their first six outings." He quieted as three young women came up and asked for his autograph. He smiled generously and signed their books, then waved good-bye to them. "Fans, spirits love 'em."

Argent waited, letting Dane catch him in the act of checking the time.

"You're busting my stones here," Dane said.

"I took no as your answer," Argent said.

"But you didn't argue. You didn't mention how much I owe you." Dane looked uncomfortable bringing the matter up.

"You don't owe me," Argent said. "I never thought you did."

"Then why are you here?"

"To ask you if you could cover the action on this. You said no. There's no problem." Argent meant it. Back in the days when he'd worked with Brynnmawr, he'd learned all about manipulation and he'd promised himself never to use it. The confusion over the answer lay within Dane, not him.

"And you're not even going to mention the fact that all this success I'm enjoying now is due to you?" Dane asked.

"I didn't train you to be an actor," Argent pointed out.

"No, but if you and Peg hadn't helped me build this new SIN and identity a few years back, I'd still be a wanted assassin with a price on my head."

"I'm glad it's worked out for you."

"But?" Dane prompted.

"No buts," Argent said.

"I couldn't have done it without you."

"You couldn't have done it without someone who could have manufactured the new ID."

Dane still didn't look happy. "So you're just going to let me off the hook?"

"There never was a hook," Argent said.

"Everybody in the shadow biz is out for some kind of payback," Dane said. "They call your marker because you owe them, or they want to frag your hoop because you slotted them over."

"You don't want any part of this," Argent said. "I can respect that."

Dane sighed and looked pained. "What about Cholonga?"

"He got flat-lined in Philly," Argent said. "Tried to go corp-issue and they offered his head up as penance for a piece of biz that got slotted."

Dane massaged his jaw, thinking. "Cholonga was the only guy I knew who might have been as good as I am." Then he paused and looked directly at Argent. The elf's almond-shaped chartreuse eyes glittered as they narrowed to slits. "You called Cholonga first? Before me?"

"You've been out of the biz a few years," Argent pointed out. "Maybe you've lost your touch."

"Bulldrek!" the elf said. "If you thought that, you wouldn't be here now."

"I figured I could ask."

"I haven't lost my touch. I still shoot with the stunt guys working the set on *Kase*. I don't show them everything I've got, but I show them enough to take their nuyen when they're pushing it around."

"A chummer can lose his edge and not know it," Argent pointed out.

"I haven't lost my touch," Dane repeated. "I get off to myself, I can still peg a shot at two kilometers."

"Glad to hear it." In his day, Dane had been the finest sharpshooter Argent had ever worked with. Even better than people who'd been chipped and hardwired. The elf seemed to have a sixth sense for his targets, knowing if, when, and where they'd move after he fired his shot, allowing him to place the bullet exactly.

"Look," Dane said in a gentler voice, "you have to understand why I can't do this. The show, chummer, it's going through the roof in a biz that normally eats talent like troll kibble. That's not happening with me. I'm a fragging star."

"So I've been told."

"We're doing a thing with the show," Dane went on. "Do you know what an arc is?"

"Probably not when it comes to trid," Argent admitted.

"It's a series of stories," the elf replied, "that kind of make up one really big story. This arc is going to cover nine weeks. We're only halfway through that now. We've had two- and three-story arcs before in the series, and I thought the sponsors were going to drek themselves then. Nobody watches a fragging story arc anymore. Tune in for instant gratification, chummers, that's the only road to go. But our fans made those story arcs some of the biggest events to air on trid. Frag, they were picked up as straight-to-chip releases, putting both or all three episodes together and packaging them to sell. And they did. Now they're talking about a premiere release on the big screens. This nine-show arc is important. I just wanted you to know."

"I understand," Argent said.

Dane twirled the tail of one of the shrimp hanging on the cocktail in front of him. "I don't like the way you understand."

Argent nodded, conscious of the time going by. If Dane wasn't going to buy in, there were other arrangements he needed to make.

"So who are you going to get to cover your back?" Dane asked.

"I was told Mellion was free," Argent said.

"Pathetic. Who else?"

"Kristos."

"Little more than a poser wannabe. Who else?"

"Chalmers, Garrett, or Torkelette."

"Chalmers won't stick if things get tight. Garrett's a maybe on really long distances at best. And Torkelette's working with a BTL-chip monkey on his back these days. You use any of those people, you're going to end up slotted."

"I need the long gun," Argent stated. "The joker we're 'fronting will have armored cav in the area."

"I've been wondering about that too," Dane admitted. "How do you plan on getting around the ground and air forces he can put in there?"

"I've got an idea."

Dane looked at him steadily for a moment, then broke out into a big grin. "Love to hear it, chummer. You're facing rugged terrain, an incredibly large army, and limited resources."

"The terrain is going to work for me," Argent said. "I've just got to make an exfiltration. Nothing fancy like a prolonged insertion."

" 'Nothing fancy,' " Dane repeated. He leaned back in his seat and shook his head. "Still hard for you to admit the impossible, isn't it?"

Argent thought back over Toshi and Hawk dying. At the time, that had seemed impossible. "It's easier these days."

"But you think you have a shot at this?"

"If I didn't, I wouldn't go."

"Who have you got working on it with you?"

Argent shook his head. Unless someone was confirmed for a run, no one got any information. And then, if it was truly sensitive, only when they needed to know.

"You knew I'd be curious," Dane complained.

"Maybe I'll tell you about it sometime." The waitress approached, wearing a cocktail dress split up high on the sides. Argent waved her off. "I've got to go."

"For curiosity's sake," Dane said, "how much was this gig going to pay?"

"Fifty thousand."

"Fifty thousand!" the elf spluttered indignantly. "Do you know how much I get for an episode of *Kase*?"

"No. I only know how much this was going to pay."

"Well, it's a lot more than that, I'll tell you," Dane said. "And I get paid that while some stunt double gets paid a whole lot less to go in and risk getting his hoop slotted."

"I'm glad everything's going so well for you." Argent stood. "Be seeing you around."

"Yeah." Dane didn't look comfortable saying good-bye.

Argent left the elf sitting there and headed for the door. Before he reached the main foyer, though, Dane was at his side.

"Can't let you go, chummer," the elf said. "I owe you too much."

"You don't owe me anything," Argent said.

"Then I owe me something," Dane said.

"What about the show?"

Dane grinned. "Frag, I'm a star. *The* star. They'll work around me. I've just got to make a few calls, clear up a few problems. Drek, truth to tell, just sitting there thinking about doing something like this again was making me quiver all over. I can always count on you to get my adrenaline up, chummer. Hasn't ever been a time I've worked with you that the odds weren't against us."

44

Argent arrived in Denver at Lowry Airport with the team that evening. The SINs and IDs Peg and Archangel had managed to cobble together for them over the past two days held up under the scrutiny of the flesh and blood and cybernetic security in place to protect CAS interests. Hard-eyed secguards covered the airport, weapons in sight. The security tech was also top of the line. Laveau registered the magework done to keep the integrity of the airport secure.

Denver was also known as the Front Range Free Zone. Independent and dependent all at the same time, the mile-high city was divided between six political sectors that included the UCAS, CAS, Sioux Nation, Aztlan, Ute Nation, and Pueblo Corporate Council.

With the way the relationships between the six countries remained within the plex, no trade or currency could legally travel between the sectors. If it hadn't been for the runners plying the shadows between the sectors, commerce of any kind would have died in the area, or would have been bitterly fought over on six armed fronts.

Argent was counting on the Wild West nature of the area to help with the exfiltration efforts he had planned. Once they'd dropped into the CAS, getting permits for weapons hadn't been a problem. The CAS had a permanent soft spot for allowing personal defense weapons to its citizens and guests, and that courtesy continued to be respected in the CAS sector of Denver. The SINs Peg and Archangel had put together covered the weapons the group carried.

The only thing that wouldn't have made it through security had been Archangel's deck. Knight Errant provided the security for the sector regarding decks, and even those that were properly licensed by the CAS sector of Denver had ID-trace chipsets installed so Knight Errant could monitor activity going through the Matrix.

Then again, with the black market running rampant through Denver, Argent knew they could replace the deck within an hour after they started looking.

The only potential hose-up had been when a group of fans had recognized Harrison Dane from the trid show. He'd split off from Argent at once and started signing autographs. It also provided him the opportunity to check along their back trail.

Outside the airport, Argent flagged down a cab. He and Archangel took the first cab while the Travers twins and Laveau went on to the hotel the big Shadowrunner had set up in Chinatown. With all the animosity running through the areas regarding Chinatown, Argent had figured it would be the safest place to be. Luckily, they were trying to stay hidden, not find anyone. Digging someone out of the sectors was much harder than disappearing.

Argent and Archangel made the rendezvous Rottstein had fixed up with the CAS Yakuza at half-past 2200. After slotting the credstick he had for the transaction with the black market dealers the fixer had recommended, Argent and Archangel walked away with a top-of-the-line NovaTech Slimcase 10 cyberdeck.

Inside a cab Argent flagged down a few blocks from where the transaction had taken place, Archangel ran her hands across the NovaTech cyberdeck. "Expensive," the elven decker said quietly.

"You can work with this?" Argent asked. Peg had set up the specs while Archangel had been deep into the Matrix.

"Easily. What I'm talking about is the cost of the deck. Even without the black market prices, this unit is over two million nuyen."

Argent was aware of the price. Being selective about the work he did in the shadows didn't always push him toward the big money. Even with the impressive brag sheet on the shadownet, there had been lean times, or runs that had doled out a high cost. Leveraging the two million nuyen to buy the deck had left him tapped out, especially after the shadow tariffs Peg'd had to pay to jockey the money around. And if he had to cover the whole cost of the unit if it was damaged or destroyed, he'd be broke for a long time to come.

"We can't keep it," the big shadowrunner told the elven decker. "That investment has tied up all of my liquid capital and then some."

"I can understand."

"In case you were thinking out upping your end of the contract price," Argent said, "I'm broke."

She looked at him thoughtfully, studying his face, his eyes.

For a moment, Argent got the impression that she was looking straight into whatever was left of his soul.

"I wasn't scamming toward that at all," she said softly. "I'm not that way. I've got standards, and I stick to them."

Argent nodded.

"Why?" she asked.

"Why what?" Argent didn't understand the question.

"Why risk everything for a woman you haven't seen in years?"

45

Argent didn't say anything for a time and sat draped in the shadows filling the back seat of the CAS Denver cab.

"If I've stepped over the boundaries, I apologize," Archangel said quickly.

"No," the big man replied. "I was just thinking how best to answer your question. I think you asked it wrong."

She glanced at him.

In her eyes, Argent again saw some of the pain and confusion that she worked so hard to mask. "It would be easier to ask me how could I *not* risk what I'm risking."

"Okay."

"The answer is that I couldn't *not* risk it."

"Why?"

"Part of it has to do with the way I see myself," Argent answered. "When chummers need me, I'm there. When I hire on with a Mr. Johnson, if I'm not lied to, or if I understand why I was lied to at the time, I stick. How many absolutes do you see in the world we live in?"

"I don't know that I've ever bought into the metaphysical," the elven decker said.

"I've seen the Matrix," Argent said. "Being involved with that world involves buying into a lot of concepts. Not everything is as it looks in the Matrix."

"But there is something there," Archangel said. "And if you ignore it, it will slot you fragging quick."

"My behavior is my own, but only to a degree. I was raised with absolutes. The . . . training . . . I experienced allowed only absolutes. I walked away from much of that. But I couldn't walk away from it all. If I had, there would have been nothing left." Argent paused, looking at the elven decker. "Do you understand?"

"Maybe," she answered. "When you run the Matrix and encounter IC that you've never seen before, you can't depend on what you think you know about all the IC you've seen before. You have to depend on what you know about yourself, about what you can handle. It gives you a certain perception."

"Close enough." Argent rubbed his face, feeling the stubble there and knowing he'd need to shave soon. His appearance was one of those absolutes he kept for himself. "Most of your world stems from your encounters in the Matrix."

"And yours is based on what you can accomplish while working with people and the situations they've involved themselves in."

"Yes."

"But what made you develop this . . ." Archangel seemed at a loss for words.

"Code of behavior?" Argent supplied.

"That'll do."

"Because there was nothing else," Argent told her honestly. "Everything I was trained to believe in was taken from me. All I am is the way I conduct myself. I was all I had left."

"And Sencio."

"Yes."

"Only her code of behavior ultimately proved different than your own," the elven decker said.

"Yes."

"That left you and how you saw the world."

Argent nodded. "It's a strength and a weakness, Archangel. My view makes me strong because I believe in it."

"Even to the point of putting your life on the line for it."

"There's no other way to truly believe in it."

"Then how does it make you weak?" the elven decker asked.

"Because I could be wrong."

"Wrong to believe?" She seemed confused again.

"No. Believing is never wrong. But belief isn't fostered only out of passion. There has to be logic behind it as well. I can't just believe because I want to. I have to believe because I *know* I can believe, not because I have to."

"Even if it's something you've never done before?"

"Do you always know you can defeat IC in the Matrix?"

"Of course not. I've found some that I haven't been able to sleaze my way through."

"But any time you set yourself to take it on, you believe you can sleaze your way through it?"

"Yes. Otherwise, why try?"

"Exactly."

Archangel shook her head and turned away, staring out at the passing street in the downtown CAS sector of Denver. "I don't see how what I feel about the Matrix applies to relationships."

"You're the one who's drawn the lines," Argent told her.

"What do you mean?"

"You feel the way you do about your skills inside the Matrix because you want to."

"I have to feel that way in order to get my job done."

"Then you have a reason to feel that way," Argent granted. "But you've chosen to have that confidence. Just as you choose not to have that confidence in relationships."

She was quiet for a time and the hum of the cab's tires rolling across the street filled the compartment. "You make it sound easy."

"It shouldn't," Argent said. "Because it's not. Belief is a very strong thing, but it's also the most demanding emotion you'll ever know."

"How do you get it?"

"You don't," Argent said. "It gets you for the most part.

When there's nothing else to turn to, when you're at the most alone you've ever felt in your life, that's when belief will come to you."

"Just like slotting a datachip?" Archangel snorted derisively.

Argent ignored the emotion. What he was dealing with, what she was feeling at the moment, was a very powerful thing. It wasn't just an epiphany for her or him; it was a shared thing that came out of both their needs to know. "No. It's always a very small thing at first, and if you don't recognize it for what it is, don't nurture it, it'll die."

"And if it does?"

"It's only because you discovered you weren't as alone as you thought. People turn to other things during those crises. Some to chem, some to BTL chips, some to other people or religious trappings. Most people can probably get by without believing. There are too many other things to lean on."

"But you can't?"

"No."

"That's such fragging bulldrek." Tears sparkled on Archangel's cheeks, but she quickly wiped them away and no more reappeared.

"You weren't asking those questions about yourself, were you?" Argent asked.

"No."

"They were about someone else? The guy you started to get involved with from your old team?"

"In some ways, you remind me of him," Archangel said.

"How?"

"He has to believe too," she replied. "He has to know what he's doing is right. But I don't think he's as aware of the process as much as you are. He's always tried to keep his life simple, with no attachments to anyone. Because he doesn't trust himself to be what he needs to be for other people. But he can't walk away from things, either. His life just continued to get more complicated."

"Because of you?"

"Jack—" She stopped herself. "He didn't even know I was starting to care too much about him."

"He didn't see it?"

"There were other problems at the time. Other commitments."

"You didn't tell him how you felt?"

"No. He had enough to worry about. I felt it was unfair to pull him in so many directions. And I knew for fragging sure I wasn't going to get involved with something like this. It was a dead-end street. Not going to happen no matter what."

"Why?"

"Because I *choose* not to let it," Archangel responded. "I am going to be in charge of my life, in charge of the decisions I make without having them influenced by other clutter in my life. I'm good at what I do because I'm a pro."

Argent considered her words, then chose his next tact, feeling there was no convincing her. The elven decker didn't want to be convinced; she was trying to understand because the run had touched her own feelings more deeply than she'd thought it would. "You don't think we can pull this run off?" he asked.

"I do," Archangel said. "Otherwise I wouldn't be here no matter how much Peg wanted me to be."

"Then what?"

"You're doing it for the wrong reasons."

"How do you figure?"

"I'm getting fifty thousand nuyen for my part in this," Archangel said. "You aren't getting that. In fact, even after reselling this deck when we're finished with it, you're going to end up in the hole."

"You can look at it that way," Argent admitted. "But the way I look at it, if I didn't attempt to rescue Andi Sencio and her team, I'd end up a lot further in the hole than a few nuyen."

"Only because of the expectations you place on yourself."

"Yes. But without those expectations, I wouldn't be who I am. Saving my life only to lose my self doesn't sound like a good trade-off."

"That isn't what would happen."

"I think it is," Argent said. "Let's turn things around for a moment. Suppose this *friend* of yours got into trouble? The worst trouble you could imagine, and he asked you for help. What would you do?"

"If I could help, I would."

"Even if it meant risking your own freedom, your life, your financial well-being?"

"Yes."

"And you think he'd do the same?"

"At the time," Archangel said, "I didn't have a doubt about it. But things have changed."

"Because you left?"

"Yes."

"How long has it been since you've seen him?"

"Three years."

Argent got the feeling she could have let him know the time to the hour and minute. "Then why haven't your feelings about it changed?"

"I don't know."

"Maybe you should see him," Argent said softly.

"I think that would be a mistake," the elven decker replied.

"You don't know till you try."

She faced him, sliding her sunglasses into place and tripping the night-vision function. "Look, we got a lot deeper into this than I wanted to. I was just looking for a perspective point, not a lecture."

"Sure," Argent said. "Lecture's over." He leaned back in the cab's back seat and turned his vision outward. Despite the elven decker's discomfort with the conversation, he'd found that it strengthened his own resolve to see it through. He was right about what he was doing.

All that remained to be seen was if he was skilled enough to see it through. Or lucky enough.

46

"Where are we going?"

Argent slotted his credstick in the cabby's reader, adding a generous tip. Most sec forces in the sectors knew better than to ask the cab drivers for information about people they ferried around. In Denver, it paid to make sure memories remained dim, unless someone had a big enough hammer or could offer proof.

"We've got one more meeting," Argent said. "We'll need transport out of Pueblo when we manage the exfiltration."

The section of town the cab had let them off in looked even more run-down than the warehouse area where they'd cut the deal with the Yaks for the cyberdeck.

Argent watched with approval as Archangel took her small pistol from its shoulder holster and tucked it into her jacket pocket where it was immediately accessible.

Three blocks down Means Street, he turned left into an alley and followed it down. Chem-guzzlers on the skids lounged in the shadows, asking for money with practiced pitches. A clutch of thrillers stood outside the single door of a bar at the end of the alley. A listing neon sign hung over the single, weather-beaten door that had shed its synthwood veneer years ago.

Before Argent could step inside, a heavily cybered troll stepped out of the shadows beside the door. Green neon spitting from the failing light above the door gave the troll a sickly cast, but there was no mistaking the augmentation.

"You got biz inside, omae?" the troll asked. "Because it's off-limits to anybody ain't a member."

"I'm here to see Wakiza Summertrees," Argent said.

"You got a name?" the troll asked.

"Fullburn," the big shadowrunner said.

The troll popped the top of the wristphone and spoke briefly. "So ka," he said, closing the device. "You can go on in." He opened the door with a large hand.

Argent stepped through the door and turned his low-light vision up higher. The interior of the bar was dark, filled with smoke-tainted shadows that seemed to writhe restlessly to the heavy clangor of troll rock stemming from the system buried in the walls.

The Ridgerunner was a T-bird bar and made no bones about it. The walls held scale models of LAVs. The low-altitude vehicles were definitely the hardware of choice favored by the bar's owners. Most of the featured models were GMC Banshees that looked like stripped down whales arcing through the air sans flukes. The majority of them also featured cannon on their forward firmpoints.

T-birds and their crews were the life's blood of Denver. Without the runners and the jammers taking on the border guards to move product around, the shadow commerce would have died in the area. And the T-birds didn't just handle the locals. They made runs across the North American continent, including Quebec and Aztlan.

Several of the people in the bar reacted to Argent, reading him as someone who didn't belong in the bar. He drew hostile glares the way cyber took to electricity.

"Hoi, Argent, my friend," a deep voice called from the group of tables around a simsense competition table. In the holo presented by the competition table, two ancient biplanes battled to the death amid a blue sky full of white clouds. Machine guns ripped sparks between them.

"Hello, Wakiza." Argent stuck out a hand.

The Amerind took the shadowrunner's hand briefly, his eyes flicking over Argent's face. Wakiza Summertrees was young and reed slender, only coming to Argent's shoulder. He wore a red synthleather flightsuit with a blue-black dreamcatcher woven over his left breast. His dark hair hung in a long braid down his back. High cheekbones made him look thinner and almost buried his almond-shaped too-blue eyes in slits. The datajack gleamed behind his left ear, lending him an even more alien appearance.

"In a hurry?" Summertrees asked. "Or can you take a trip?"

"I've got time," Argent said. "I want to see the hardware."

Summertrees smiled. "It's one sweet machine. I've upgraded since I saw you last." He started toward the back of the bar. "Come on through. I've got a car at the other end of the alley."

47

On the outskirts of the Denver plex where the CAS sector nearly bumped up against the UCAS to the south in a thin strip that barely marked territory before the Pueblo Corporate Council's claims began again, Argent studied the T-bird that he had hired with the last of his liquid assets. With all the planning he'd done, trying to take advantage of the few weaknesses he'd found in Ironaxe's control over the area, he'd known from the beginning that getting Sencio's team evac-ed without a LAV was drekking impossible.

The warehouse was only one of several structures honey-combed into the side of the red clay foothills. Enough corp and black market influence was in the area to make sure that no surprise raids by law enforcement personnel from other Denver sectors or nations would be successful. Or be accomplished without immediate retaliation. The black market biz was a protected investment of the whole Front Range Free Zone.

Argent walked around the massive vehicle as it sat in the garage on its three fold-out wheel struts. The Banshee held a Victory Rotary Assault Cannon on its forward firmpoint, backed by two belt-fed SMGs that covered the back and both sides.

Black European Arm Works modular ablative armor covered the exterior of the LAV. All of it appeared in pristine condition. With the reactive explosions trapped inside the armor, when it took a hit, the armor defused the attack by blowing up back and throwing the used ablative section off. Like the ablative armor, the LAV's hull was black and radar-absorbent.

"When do you plan to make the run?" Summertrees asked.

"Tomorrow night," Argent answered. He'd worked with the Amerind rigger before, on other ops that weren't quite so close to home for Summertrees. The rigger was one of the most capable T-bird jammers he'd ever seen, guiding his vehicles only centimeters above the ground at times and pushing everything to the edge of control.

"Still Pueblo?" Summertrees asked.

"Dead center," Argent told him.

Summertrees' facial expression didn't change much but Argent knew the man well enough to know he wasn't completely happy. "Things have heated up down there. Joker named Ironaxe is turning over rocks all through Pueblo looking for some runners."

"The runners are the cargo," Argent told him. "And I knew about Ironaxe."

"He's got a big crew down there."

"We're not going to take his crew on," Argent said. "We're just going to get away from them."

"When I first checked into this op," Summertrees said, "there wasn't that much activity down there."

"Events are getting closer to the bone." Argent surveyed the black-out windows in two of the warehouse's walls. "I'm going to have to know if you're in or out."

"You never have said who's picking up the bottom line on this run," Summertrees said.

"I am," Argent replied. "This one's for a friend. Where's the second unit?"

"Further back in the warehouse," Summertrees answered, taking the lead and heading back into the darkness.

Argent adjusted his low-light vision automatically and picked out the crates stacked neatly on pallets and the work benches built into the sides of the walls. The LAV-98 Armored Personnel Carrier sat in the middle of the floor. Code-named Devil Rat, the LAV-98 was a piece of equipment Argent was extremely familiar with from the Desert Wars. It was painted a flat, non-reflecting black as well, and covered with the ablative armor.

The Devil Rat was a work horse of military hardware. Capable of going off-road and amphibious, it was the choice of armies in the CAS and CalFree for combat and combat-support missions. A heavy machine gun was mounted on the top turret.

"Have you arranged transport for the LAV-98?" Argent asked.

"Yeah. Got another rigger friend of mine who thinks this has got to be the most bimble-brained thing he's ever heard of, but he's agreed to provide the air transport because the chance to do it would be so wiz. And there's the nuyen involved. You realize, of course, that even after I drive this monster out of the cargo plane and start the drop, there's a better than even chance it's going to get lit up by hostile fire long before it hits the ground."

"Ironaxe's teams are going to be having problems before we drop the LAV-98," Argent said. "By then, there should be a major amount of confusion going on."

"And if there's not?" Summertrees asked.

"Then you don't make the drop," Argent said. "Simple as that."

"You realize that we're going to lose the LAV-98 if we make the exfiltration?" Summertrees asked.

"It's an acceptable loss," Argent replied. "And it's actually a loss from the minute it comes out of that cargo plane and starts the descent."

Summertrees shook his head. "Chummer, even getting the deal I got on it, you're talking about shucking a hundred and seventy thousand nuyen in flames. And then there's the costs on the upgrades to the ECM hardware."

Argent knew. The electronic countermeasure hardware remained a constant expense, based on improvements and changes in the field. "I know. Are you in or out?"

Summertrees extended a hand and flashed a crooked grin. "I'm in, chummer. This is the kind of run legends are made of. Drek, it might even make a good epitaph."

48

The hotel room in Denver's CAS sector's Chinatown was small and cramped, filled with the smells of the Cantonese restaurant occupying the lower story of the building. Archangel encrypted the telecom transmissions at that end, allowing Peg to be present during Argent's briefing as well as the rest of the team. To prevent eavesdroppers and electronic surveillance, Argent set up white noise generators in a perimeter that cut off the outside world, blanketing all four walls, the floor, and the ceiling. As a further precaution, Laveau kept a watcher spirit in the astral around the room.

"We only get one take on this op." Argent stood in the center of the room, his hand resting on the holo projector control he'd set up and programmed for the brief. "If it gets fragged at any time, drop it in the drekker and pull out however you can. For most of you, we've already established SINs that will allow you to leave Denver. Those of you who end up in-country have no choice but to try to get free on your own."

"Nice of you to set it up so we have such a cheery beginning." Harrison Dane lounged in a chair and sipped a whiskey sour. He wore street clothing and looked like he'd just put in a hard eight at a nearby loading dock. Wherever the elf went, from gutter to social club, Argent had always known him to blend in.

Argent swept the team with his gaze. "This is the last night you have that you may draw an easy breath for awhile. I want you to know what you're risking."

"Dey know, cher," Laveau said, lights glinting on the many silver rings she wore. "Else dey not be here, no?"

"The upside," Argent went on, "is that I think we can do this." He flicked the holo projector on.

A bright bubble of color filled the air above his head. In heartbeats, it sorted itself out into a trid image. Darkened plexscape showed lights from businesses and dwellings, advertising as well as defensive perimeters.

"This is downtown Pueblo," Argent said. "Our target is in the Underground-Awakened."

"The local rally point—" Jesse Travers said, leaning against one side of the room's door back to the main hallway.

"—for metahumanity," Jason Travers continued, standing on the other side of the door. "Primarily for the victims of goblinization—"

"—who got kicked out of their own tribes," Jesse said.

"We read the downloads you had on the noteputers you outfitted us with," Jason finished.

"Sencio and her team are with the Underground-Awakened," Argent said, "under the warehouse district." The holo tightened up its focus, sweeping to the warehouse area.

"That's also where Ironaxe and his sec teams have started to concentrate their search," Peg commented over the telecom. A map of bright red stars suddenly shot through the holo. "Each one of these stars signifies a vehicular unit Ironaxe has put into the area. As you can see, there are dozens."

"And you plan on evading all those units." Wakiza Summertrees sat cross-legged on the floor.

"Are you sweating this, flyboy?" Jesse Travers asked.

"You're the last man to be committed to this free-for-all," Jason said.

"Evading them is the only chance we have," Archangel spoke up from her corner of the room. "But we're going to manage that in stages."

"As you know," Argent said, "we've got to consider more than the physical transportation of the team trapped in the Underground-Awakened. Ironaxe has a comm-base set up inside his search perimeter."

"And you've found it?" Harrison Dane asked.

"Peg did," Argent answered. A yellow triangle lit up on the screen. "Ironaxe set up ops in one of the warehouses, complete with sat-link and troop-link capability."

"So we blow it up and we no longer have to worry about a sat-link scanning the area. I can punch holes in most of that for you with a Barrett Model 121 from nearly two thousand meters out, using thermographic sights. Next thing the guys know inside the comm-base, they're geeked."

"That's part of it," Argent agreed. "However, Ironaxe has been establishing negotiations with Asian Fuchi and NovaTech. It's a safe bet that both of those entities have satellite recon in the area."

"Dey be waiting to jump in and help ol' Ironaxe, him find himself in a fix," Laveau said.

Argent nodded. "So what we have to do is take an alternate comm-relay point, patch into their deck feeds, and prevent Ironaxe from falling back on either Asian Fuchi or NovaTech."

"Do you think he'd use one of them if he's as suspicious of them as you think he is?" Summertrees asked.

"In a heartbeat," Argent answered. "First, he's pretty sure whoever set the shadowrunners loose in his biz hasn't completely gotten everything they wanted on the datasteal. And second, if either of the two corps try to turn him down when he requests assistance, he may have his guilty party."

"He may not go for them," Summertrees said. "An APC, even an accomplished rig like the LAV-98, isn't going to be able to fade the heat in a combat situation like the one you're going to be addressing down in Pueblo."

"What's this about an APC?" Dane demanded. "Nobody mentioned using a fragging Devil Rat on this op. Spirits, tooling around in that, we're going to be sitting ducks on a hot zone evac."

"That's where everything gets interesting," Argent said.

49

Argent hadn't revealed everything to the crew yet, and Harrison Dane's reaction in the briefing room only underscored that. Before anything went down with the op, he had to sell them on it. He could almost feel Toshi and Hawk in the background around him, almost hear their approval for the daring route he was going to take with the exfiltration. "We'll leave that for the moment. Before this run gets that far, other things have to be taken care of."

"One of those things being that a patch has to be made into Ironaxe's cybernetic systems," Archangel said. "That's where I come in. After I get into position, Dane will take down Ironaxe's sat-link. Peg has found a probable point of entry."

"Here," Peg announced. A purple light joined the others on the holo representation of the Pueblo warehouse district. "While I was sleazing my way around Ironaxe's on-site systems after tracking them through his corporate systems, I found the back-up system linking him directly into the local telephone grid."

"So when the sat-link gets slotted by Dane—" Jesse said.

"—then Ironaxe will try to go on-line through the LTG," Jason stated. "Only Archangel will be there—"

"—and she'll feed in the data we want the other corps to have—"

"—fragging their systems."

"If everything works right," Argent said, "that's exactly how it will go down."

"And if it doesn't?" Summertrees asked.

"Then everybody buzzes turbo and clears the hot zone," the big shadowrunner said. "Everybody scan?"

Nods circled the room.

"Step One is to shut down Ironaxe's sat-link and re-establish a patch with NovaTech and Asian Fuchi that will allow us to sideline them as well. Hopefully that will create even more of a diversion because Ironaxe will have to put some people on that end of his ops to find out if he's been betrayed and if any more is coming. Once we control the comm-links, we move directly into Step Two. And that's to create confusion at the physical location in Pueblo." Argent glanced up at the Travers twins, forcing himself to concentrate on the logistics of the plan and not all the things that could go wrong during the implementation of it. "Dane, we're still going to be needing the long gun at this point."

"Have you got a position marked for me?" the elf asked. The trid star demeanor had dropped away, replaced by the canny gaze of the trained assassin Argent was most familiar with.

"Peg," Argent prompted.

"Here," Peg replied. Obediently, a green light winked on in the holo, topping one of the taller buildings in the warehouse district. "This location will give you an overview of Ironaxe's whole Pueblo operation. The longest shot you'll have to make will be somewhat less than twelve hundred meters."

"Cake," Dane stated. "Simhard at best."

"Ironaxe's ground troops are going to be around—" Jesse Travers said.

"—and they're going to try to light you up if they find you," Jason added.

"The Barrett I got for you is also going to be equipped with APDS rounds. They'll punch through the armor."

"Should be enough to slot somebody's day," Dane commented. "That fragging Barrett is a big drekking weapon, though. I assume I'm going inside Pueblo earlier than the rest of you?"

"You're out of here in the morning," Argent said. "You're going in with Summertrees when he stashes the T-bird. If you get caught before tomorrow night, the run is off."

"How will we know?" Laveau asked.

"If he's in place, he'll call," Argent said.

"What about comm-links?" Jesse Travers asked.

"By twenty-three hundred tomorrow," Argent said, "we'll have a sat-link up and running. Peg made a time-buy from one of the T-bird comm-links in the area to back our action. The time was expensive, and they're giving us only eleven minutes to make our play. Then we lose everything they give us."

"But during that time we'll all be linked?" Jason asked.

Argent nodded. "From what I remember, everyone in this room is checked out on the BattleTac Integration System." When no one disagreed with him, he went on. "I've also got my hands on some Esprit light military armor for the on-site teams. You won't be invulnerable, but it should help out."

"While Dane's flat-lining everything he can put cross hairs over," Jesse asked, "what are we going to be doing?"

"Creating havoc along the warehouse district," Argent said. "We're not stinting any on heavy bang-bang for this run. After we take out the sat-link, after Dane opens fire on the vehicles that could offer pursuit, you'll drop from the cargo plane with Summertrees and hit the ground running. You'll have a backpack filled with mines and incendiaries. Put them to use."

"And me?" Laveau asked. "Where will I be during dis time?"

"With Summertrees," Argent said. "Since we can't get word in to the Underground-Awakened or Sencio, I want to make sure we don't get blasted for our trouble by the people we're trying to rescue."

"Also to let dem know dat you have one of deir kind among you," Laveau said.

Argent returned her gaze full measure. "Yes." There was no other answer. "Also, Sencio has people who aren't going to be able to move under their own power. You can help out with that and get first aid going. And when that Devil Rat hits the ground, rest assured that you're going to draw more than your share of attention. You and Summertrees will have to hold them till Archangel and I can double back to your position."

"What's this about a Devil Rat?" Dane asked suspiciously. "I thought we were going to use the T-bird to get out of there."

"We are," Argent said. "*After* we get out of Pueblo. That was the interesting part I told you we'd get to." He told them the rest of it, beginning with the way the APC was going to be air-dropped into the hot zone. He watched as conviction gave way to surprise, then to disbelief. Finally, he reeled them back in to his way of thinking, convincing them how it was going to work, convincing himself one more time.

Interest, Argent had always found, was in a direct ratio to how close a chummer cut it to getting geeked. And interest on this run was off the charts.

50

Argent braced himself in the back of the Hawker-Siddley HS-895 Skytruck and gazed down into the black night seen through the open cargo door at his feet. The twin rear-facing pusher propellers set up an unusual vibration he hadn't quite gotten used to in the short flight from the CAS sector in Denver.

Wakiza Summertrees and Laveau stood behind him, to the right of the LAV-98 strapped down to the bottom of the Skytruck. Archangel stood at his side, clutching a handrail mounted on the side of the plane's immense cargo hold.

All of them were dressed in the black Espirit light military armor Argent had purchased on the black market. He missed having Peg inside his head as he got ready to make the drop a little over twenty klicks outside the Pueblo plex. He wore the Ingram machine pistols in double shoulder slings and the Savalette Guardian on his thigh. The BattleTac wrapped securely around his left wrist. Pouches and slings on his armor held reloads for his weapons and incendiaries.

He took a deep breath to clear his lungs of carbon dioxide, then checked his retina chron. He and Archangel had a little over an hour to make the rendezvous with Ironaxe's back-up comm-link in Pueblo before 2300.

He glanced at the elven decker and used the short-wave radio built into the suit's helmet to communicate with her. "Are you ready?"

Archangel ran her hands over her gear. The cyberdeck hung in a special bulletproof and impact resistant case across her lower back under her parachute. "Yes."

"See you on the ground, Wakiza," Argent told the rigger.

"We'll be there, omae, but I sure hope this comes off the way you say it will."

"Have a little faith," the big shadowrunner said. "If there's one thing that can be counted on in this world, it's corporate greed. Too many interested parties have too much at stake on this play. It's not just about Sencio and her people any more."

"Take care down dere, cher," Laveau said. "Dese old bones feel good about dis, but dey say you watch your hoop all de same. And you know dat Hawk, he be watching over you from de other side tonight. I feel him with you, cher."

"I hope so," Argent said. Without another word, he kicked the pack at the side of the cargo door out into the slipstream following the plane. Then he leaped out and followed it.

The big pack Argent kicked out had a static line pull cord. A hundred meters back of the Skytruck, the black parachute belled out and filled with air.

Argent popped his own parachute and followed the cargo chute down, glancing up only briefly to make sure

Archangel had cleared the Skytruck safely. The elven decker's synthsilk opened above him, a black oval that blotted out the stars above.

Long minutes ticked by. If it hadn't been for the cargo chute, Argent would have popped synthsilk much closer to the ground. Losing it was possible because the Battle-Tac system wouldn't be on-line till the sat-link they'd arranged to cover the op came to life. There was no way to replace the equipment the pack carried if something went wrong. Safer was slower but surer.

The pack touched ground first, almost disappearing against the shadow-wrapped crest of a hill. The terrain in all directions was broken and uneven.

Argent unstrapped the chute and gave it to Archangel. The elven decker took his chute and hers, then covered them with loose rocks she found. There was nothing on the chutes to tie the team to them, nothing even a mage could dig up because no personal contact had been made with them that hadn't been with gloved hands.

Using the tool kit that came in the pack, Argent assembled the two Artemis Industries Night Gliders in something under twelve minutes. They sat on the ground when he finished, two hang gliders with wedge shaped sails. Luckily, Archangel had used an electric-driven turbofan powered Night Glider before, though she hadn't informed Argent as to when or what the circumstances had entailed.

Switching the batteries on, Argent took a running start with the lightweight Night Glider and leaped into the air. Rather than use the vertical lift that was possible from the unit because it was such a drain on the batteries, he opted for the gradual lift as they flew away from the hillside. The southwesterly wind filled with the chill that came over the area at night provided a crosscurrent and made Argent grateful for the heavy armor he wore.

They switched off the helmet comm-links, preferring

to give off no electronic signature. The turbofan engines were whisper quiet and couldn't be heard from more than a few meters away. The glider's mesh skin was radar absorbent so Argent wasn't worried about tripping any of the electronic security Ironaxe had surrounding the warehouse district in the Pueblo plex.

He glided, barely aware of the turbofan humming in his ears as he watched the lights of the plex grow stronger and closer. His heart hammered in his chest and he tried in vain to sort out all the emotions that filled him.

The retina clock whirred by, and time chased Argent all the way into Pueblo.

51

Argent and Archangel dumped the Night Gliders two klicks out of the plex and jogged into Pueblo without incident. Ironaxe's team were gearing toward not letting people out of the area instead of guarding against people coming in. The entrance to the Underground-Awakened Sencio had given Argent was through an abandoned warehouse on Creel Street, on the outer perimeter of the loading docks fronting the Arkansas River.

Leading the way through the tangle of broken and empty streets, Argent spotted the helicopters hovering over the central area of the warehouse district. Ironaxe hadn't spared the expense in his search, which gave the big shadowrunner hope. Sencio and her team were still free.

Perspiration covered him under the light military armor. He gazed out at the black water of the river, smelling the pollution that had tainted it from the mining operations that had created a rat's warren under Pueblo. The steel industry had been demanding, and the plex had fed on itself before the world had Awakened. Mounds of tailings from all the mining efforts stood in tall near-mountains beyond the plex's rim and on the other side of the river.

A third helicopter dragged the river in front of the warehouse district, working a route that kept it above the dark water. There was no doubt that the crew aboard the helo swept the river as well as the banks with their surveillance equipment. The river would be the most likely route of escape.

On Creel Street, Argent paused in the shadows and glanced across the broken thoroughfare to the two-story building that had once housed a machine shop that had supplied the various mining companies and smelting factories in the area.

He crossed the street at a jog, his hands filled with the Ingrams. Boards covered the door and the broken windows of the building. He scanned the door carefully and found the miniaturized silent lock-squealer that would signal if the door was opened. Evidently Ironaxe's teams had already searched the building.

Holstering the Ingrams, he knelt and fished a screwdriver and wirecutters from his armored vest pockets. A lock-squealer wasn't hard to work around; the trick lay in spotting them before it was too late. Using some of the electrical wire he carried in the vest, he wired around the contacts, then opened the door.

His low-light vision amplified the light streaming in through the dusty panes of the board-covered windows. The room beyond was empty, the concrete floor littered with debris that squatters had used to make their stay in the building more comfortable. The smell of fresh ashes lingered in the air.

There was no sign of any squatters, though. Either

they'd taken the hint when Ironaxe's troops had invaded the area, or they'd been routed when the door-to-door search had begun.

Closing the door behind him, Argent made his way deeper into the building. He knew the way from the floor plans Sencio had sent. Archangel stayed at his heels. Machine pistols in his hands, he found the door leading down to the basement and followed the switchback metal stairs down.

Six rooms lined the basement, three to a side. All of them showed signs of having been used by squatters before. In the third room on the right, Argent crossed to the line of rusty metal lockers covering the wall. All of them had bent and warped doors, totally empty of contents that would be helpful in any way.

He counted six down, just the way Sencio had called it, then bent down and caught the bottom of the locker. His fingers just made it under the clearance provided by the locker's stubby legs. He found the catch hidden there and released it. Then he lifted the locker, having to use the greater strength provided in his cyberlimb.

At first, the locker resisted. Then the resistance gave way and the locker moved smoothly upward, taking two on either side of it. The lockers shoved upward nearly a meter, not quite half their length, stopping just short of the ceiling. There were no tracks or scrapes on the wall behind it to reveal that the lockers could be raised.

Adjusting his low-light vision, Argent peered into the waiting darkness. Nothing moved. But a tunnel, hewn from the rocky strata, drifted down into the ground, opening into a chamber beyond.

"Well?" he said to Archangel.

"If it's according to the gameplan," the elven decker said, "we go. We're losing time sitting here wondering."

Argent silently agreed. He sniffed the air, using his cyberware to gather the trace scents of minerals, the river, and human and meta perspiration. All of it seemed old, like it belonged there.

He slid through the opening under the lockers and waited till Archangel joined him. The tunnel beyond left enough room for him to stand if he hunkered over slightly. He reached up and pulled the locker down, closing the hidden entrance.

Resuming the lead, he made his way toward the chamber, recognizing it as one of the mine shafts that had been driven deep beneath the city. Before the world had Awakened, Pueblo had continued to grow as a plex, soon stretching out over old mines that had been abandoned and closed up. When metahumanity had filled the ranks of the Amerinds, they'd found living quarters already established for them beneath Pueblo.

Shadows suddenly filled the chamber, and the harsh clacks of weapon safeties being released filled the air.

"Drek," Archangel said quietly behind Argent.

"Put your weapons down!" a male voice commanded from the shadows.

Argent stared through the shadows, seeing the trolls and orks dominating the ranks of the Amerind metahumanity lining the opposite side of the underground chamber. He released the Ingrams, letting them fall to the length of their Whipit slings. "Do what he said," he told Archangel.

His retina clock showed the time as 22:42:12. He had less than eighteen minutes to get into place to make the call to Harrison Dane. Otherwise, the team buzzed turbo and they were all trapped.

52

[Chip file: Argent
Security access: ******—22:43:21/10-14-60]

BEGIN UPLOAD

Location: Seattle Safehouse (recorded at a later date)

"Argent."

I recognized Andi's voice at once, and I felt the pull of it despite all the years and distance that had been between us.

I stood in the darkness with my hands raised over my head, the weight of the Ingrams pressing against the sides of my chest only an eyeblink away if I chose to go for them. And if Andi hadn't been among the group of two dozen there in front of me, maybe I'd have taken my chances.

They couldn't see it, but I'd palmed an AFR-7 flash grenade from my weapons rigging. The pull-ring looped over my thumb. One flick and I'd yank it free. A heartbeat after that and the chamber would have been filled with blinding light that my cybereyes could adjust for. In the instant after that, there'd have been a lot of flat-liners filling the chamber.

Andi limped from the shadows, favoring her left leg more than she had in the vid-file she'd sent me by way of Chandler. Her face showed efforts of cleaning, but her complexion was off, waxy with pain. "I was starting to think you weren't coming," she said.

I took my hands out of the air as her temporary allies lowered their weapons. They didn't fully trust me, but they were sociable enough not to be obvious about it. I spoke for the others to hear, not wanting them to make any mistakes. "I've got a noteputer in my chest pouch." I reached in and took it out, using sleight of hand to return the flash grenade to my weapon webbing.

"I didn't doubt you," Andi said, "but I didn't know if the message got through." She didn't stop coming till she reached me.

I took her into my arms to help support her.

Andi touched my face with her hand, drawing it slowly down the line of my jaw. "You look like you haven't changed at all."

I felt her body briefly against mine, but as familiar as it seemed, there'd been changes too. Holding onto the past was never a good thing. It had a tendency to make you question things you had no business questioning, and made you slow to react to things you didn't have time to question.

She must have felt it, too, because she drew away. And in that instant, so cold and hard and crystal-clear between us, we both knew that the ties that bound us were no longer the ones we thought had been there. But neither were they completely gone. And I think both of us knew they never quite would be.

I took a comm-link headset from my chest pouch. It was encrypted and set to the frequency the team was using. "You'll need this."

She took it without a word, standing apart from me now.

I also handed her the noteputer, switching it on. The pale green screen filled the darkness of the chamber. "This is a map of the mine tunnels under Pueblo. There's a destination marked on it that's less than a klick from the present position here. Can you get your people there," I consulted my retina clock, "in fourteen minutes?"

"I can try." Andi glanced at the noteputer. "You got maps of the mines."

"A friend of mine did," I said, referring to Peg. "We got maps of most of the mining areas, but we weren't sure about all the changes the Underground-Awakened have made."

"Not many," a strong, clear voice advised.

I looked up, spotting the tall troll as she stepped from behind two yabos sporting assault rifles. I recognized her from the file Peg had uploaded me regarding the Underground-Awakened: Mary Hawkmoon, the meta tribe's chosen chieftain.

There'd been two pictures in the file I'd scanned. One showed her as she was now, a brutish looking troll with canines that reached up to the bottom of her eyes. The other picture was of her before she'd goblinized: a petite girl of about twelve or thirteen, raven's-wing dark hair, and a smile full of joy.

The goblinization had eradicated all the appearance of the young girl, leaving what her family and tribe had considered to be a monster in its wake. Gray filled her hair, making her look ancient.

"If we made too many changes in these tunnels," Mary Hawkmoon said, "our movements would be too easily found out."

I nodded. "There's also a path marked from that point," I said. "If you can get word to your people that we'll be traveling that way, it'll help keep them clear of the firezone."

"You're going to bring Ironaxe and his people down here?" Hawkmoon seized the noteputer from Andi and gazed at it.

"Can't be helped," I said. "Escape overland isn't an option."

"How dare you do so," an ork told me, his dark eyes flashing as he stepped threateningly toward me. He carried an assault rifle and let the barrel drift in my direction.

UPLOAD TO CONTINUE

53

[Chip file: Argent
Security access: ******—22:49:03/10-14-60]

UPLOAD CONTINUED

Location: Seattle Safehouse (recorded at a later time)

"Look," I told Hawkmoon, shifting slightly to give myself some maneuvering room against the assault rifle the ork held on me in the underground chamber, "you knew the risks you were taking when you offered sanctuary to these people. And Ironaxe is already closing in."

"He's right," Hawkmoon said. "We've lost six of our people to Ironaxe's sec forces."

The ork backed down, but he obviously didn't like it.

"Clear your people out of those tunnels," I said. "Ironaxe is going to know we're moving in"—I checked the time—"eight minutes. When we do, he's going to follow us. Then we'll either get away from him, or he'll geek us where he catches up to us. However it goes down, he should leave the rest of the Underground Awakened alone."

Hawkmoon called out names, sending her warriors on their way. "The Spirits look over you, warrior, and I wish you well with your war." She turned and headed out of the chamber.

I shifted my attention to Andi. "See you on the other side."

Andi looked like she wanted to say something more, but there was no time. And more than likely, she didn't know what to say.

My heart beat like a leaden gong as I watched her. I guess I'd fantasized somewhere in the back of that lizard brain that pushes us all through life, figuring how she'd react when I rode in to save her. Brynnmawr programmed me to be a hero, or maybe he only helped shape that innate need within myself to push myself to the limit to be more than I ever could be. Being a hero was only a manifestation of that.

How I conducted myself, how I saw the world and my place in it, that only mattered to me. And looking into Andi's eyes, I finally saw the true distance that really separated us.

I'd always believed in what I was doing because I felt the actions I'd taken were to make the world a better place. It sounded altruistic to admit it to myself, but that was when I knew. Brynnmawr had groomed me, made me what I was, because *he* had recognized what was within me.

And in that moment, I also realized that maybe I'd never truly understood what it was that was within Brynnmawr. We were more alike than I'd ever imagined. Only somewhere in there, he'd broken, lost the faith that I needed so desperately to survive.

An image of Brynnmawr living in the Matrix in that empty, grave-filled world of his blurred in front of me, and I realized my time with him hadn't been finished after all.

But I did see Andi clearly, saw her as she was and not as I'd wanted her to be. She was a true professional at what she did. And she did what she did to benefit herself.

I couldn't fault her for it. Most people lived their lives that way.

"I'll be there," she said finally. Then she stepped through the mouth of the chamber into another tunnel and was gone.

I went back to the hidden entrance and opened it, surging through. The retina clock was clicking off the seconds, adding up to minutes. There were only three of them before Archangel and I had to be in position.

"How do you feel about the situation now?" Archangel asked as we ran up the shaking metal stairs.

"With Sencio?" I asked.

"Yes. There wasn't all that chemistry and sparks I'd expected between you two."

"Disappointed?" I asked, trying not to let my own confusion sound in my voice.

"Maybe a little. You've got all this advice on how I should look at my own situation, and you've been pretty fragging free with it."

"My advice," I said, "is to get a good look at your situation, then decide what to do with it. Don't just run away from it."

"I didn't ask for your advice."

I ran to the door leading out into the street. Two minutes and twenty-eight seconds remained for us to get to the secondary comm-link, and to give the signal to Harrison Dane. "The only reason I offered it is because you're tearing yourself apart with it," I said.

Maybe she wanted to argue, but I never found out. In the next minute we were buzzing turbo down the street, staying in the shadows. At something less than a minute remaining on the chron, I knew there was no time for finesse when we reached the targeted warehouse.

Three members of Ironaxe's sec forces stood at the doorway to the warehouse, all wearing the dark blue light military armor his troops favored on the op. Still at a dead run, coming out of the shadows and drawing their attention now, I extended the Ingrams and gave myself over to the smartlink capabilities and move-by-wire systems.

There could be no hesitation now, no false moves. And if I couldn't fight for Andi in quite the way I thought I'd be able to, I could still fight for the way I saw myself.

My fingers caressed the triggers of the Ingrams as Ironaxe's sec guards brought their weapons up.

UPLOAD TO CONTINUE

54

[Chip file: Argent
Security access: ******—22:59:57/10-14-60]

UPLOAD CONTINUED

Location: Seattle Safehouse (recorded at a later date)

Hardwired into the move-by-wire and smartlink systems, time slowed and I became a gunsight. The initial bursts from the Ingrams slammed into the three men guarding the door to the warehouse and dropped them meters from where they'd been standing.

I raced by the falling sec guards, aware that they hadn't even gotten a shot off. But I also didn't doubt that they'd been in contact with their commanding officers, announcing the attack.

"Back," I yelled to Archangel as I slapped a Kleen-tac coated chunk of Compound 12 boomjelly to the locked doors. I set the two-second timer with a flick of my forefinger, then turned away.

The shaped charge took out the doors, blowing them inward.

Wheeling, I darted in after the smoke, the Ingrams in my hands again. The warehouse had a wide open pit area at the center of it. Memory of the schematic dropped into my head as I vaulted over the torn and buckled sheet plastimetal of the door.

Bullets cut a swath around me, ricocheting from the floor and walls. Tracer-fire gleamed at the periphery of my vision.

I leaped, going into an immediate tuck and roll, firing the whole time because the cybersystems I had allowed me to do so. Most of my rounds found their targets, knocking down men wherever they touched them, punching small holes in the walls when they didn't.

I came up on my feet, finishing the clip in the left Ingram by taking out two men entering the room from a door on the ground level. I emptied the clip in the right Ingram by taking out the track lighting overhead, plunging the room into darkness. I had my cybereyes and I knew as an elf, Archangel would be able to see well in the darkness even if she hadn't been cybered. But Ironaxe's men were dependent on the night-lenses most of them weren't wearing.

Dropping the Ingrams to hang from their Whipit slings, I drew the Savalette Guardian and flicked the safety off. The sounds of the gunshots, muted though they were because of the selectivity permitted from my cyber-ears, seemed to echo forever in the cavern of the empty warehouse.

A man appeared at the railing on the stairway above me. He raised a hand and started to gesture.

Magic takes time to use, and that's where a street sam has the edge on a mage. I lifted the Guardian, feeling the pistol's smartlink programming rushing through my palm and up my arm, replacing the Ingrams' programming. By the time I had the Guardian extended, it was as much a part of me as one of my cyberarms.

I shot the mage through his hand, interrupting whatever spell he was about to cast, then I placed two rounds through his head. I was moving as he fell and broke through the frail railing.

Hitting the bottom step of the stairway, I legged it up the stairs, pushing off on every third or fourth one. I knew it was twenty-three hundred hours and the sat-link Peg had set up was suddenly working because her voice filled my head.

"Argent!" she called out.

"Here, Peg," I said. And there was more pure emotion, rich and deep, in having her back than there was in seeing Andi again.

"Are you all right?"

I pulled up short against the edge of the doorway and tucked the Guardian in close. I listened, adjusting the perception of my cyberears, and ferreted out the sound of a man's frightened breathing inside the room. I tightened my grip and waited just a little longer, realizing the breathing was actually coming from two men. "I'm fine," I told Peg.

Then I turned, dropping and bringing the Guardian up. The smartlink lit up both targets, painting one of them red to mark him as primary, and ghosting the other in orange to mark him as secondary.

Bullets slammed into the door frame and cut the air beside my head. The second man had an external smartlink. I put a pair of rounds through the first man's chest, blowing him through the boarded over window behind him. He flailed weakly as he fell, letting me know the kill hadn't been instant.

I shot the second man through his smartlink goggles. There was no doubt about when he flat-lined. He was DOA before his shattered face hit the floor.

The room had been an office at one time. The comm-link gear occupied a scarred plastimetal desk that was covered with rust spots. Empty filing cabinets, their function going back decades, were over-turned in one corner. Bookshelves filled with spiderwebs covered one wall.

"I've got it," Archangel said from behind me. She came into the room with her pistol naked in her fist and carrying the cyberdeck in her other arm.

"Count it down," I rapped into the comm-link. "Team leader is One."

"Two," Peg called.

"Three," Archangel said as she placed the cyberdeck on the desk next to Ironaxe's back-up comm-link systems. Her hands moved fast and sure, feeling the coaxial cables between the two decks.

"Four," Harrison Dane called, "and I'm in position, ready to jam my primary target."

"Five," Jesse Travers said.

"Six," Jason Travers said almost immediately.

"Seven," Laveau continued.

I watched as Archangel slid the deck cable into the datajack in her skull. An instant later, her whole body relaxed as she entered the Matrix.

"Eight," Summertrees finished.

Crossing to the broken window one of my targets had dropped through, I glanced out across the warehouse district. Ironaxe's people were in motion, getting their response together. In seconds they'd be breathing down the secondary comm-link station. Turning to the east, I pinpointed Dante's position. "Dane."

"Yo," he answered laconically.

This was the elven master assassin I remembered. Cool and competent, not full of himself. Even Toshi had acknowledged Dane as being better with the long gun. I reloaded my weapons, knowing we were all about to be in the fight for our lives. "Light up your first target."

UPLOAD TO CONTINUE

55

Harrison Dane lay prone across the rooftop of the building twelve hundred eighteen meters from his primary target. He breathed smoothly and easily, and focused on his target through the thermographic sights of the Barrett Model 121.

The thermographic sniperscope reduced the three men inside the sat-link command center to garish red, yellow, and orange simulacrums of human beings. Dane didn't see them that way. To the elf assassin, the three men were objectives and dangers. But they were dangers only if they were allowed to live. For the moment, they were objectives.

Dane took his finger from the trigger guard and placed it carefully over the trigger. He breathed easily, smoothly, focusing on the man seated at the desk next to the sat-link deck. Then he pulled the trigger through.

The Barrett jerked slightly against the shooting pad he'd Kleen-tacked to his right shoulder. The bullpup design of the sniper rifle, putting the ejector behind the trigger, also aided in recoil reduction. Still, the round was massive. Since he was using caseless ammo, all the ejector expelled was non-traceable smoke as the next bullet jacked into place.

The APDS round streaked through the plasticrete side of the building without a problem, then struck the decker in the back of the head. He had the second round in the air before the first one hit, and had locked onto the third man just as the first round struck home. The third man didn't even have time to move as he watched the other two men flatline in front of him. Then he was dead as well.

Dane put two rounds into the deck, making sure it was taken out of commission, then locked onto the sat-dish bolted onto the side of the building. His sixth shot sheared the plastimetal support strut and the power cord in two, dropping the sat-dish to the ground.

"Argent, your primary targets are down," he said quietly. Spirits, he thought, tracking onto the first of the vehicles open to his field of fire, the trid show's success notwithstanding, there was *nothing* like being on this end of a rifle.

"Message received," Argent replied. "Move onto your secondary targets."

"Locking on." Dane put the thermographic cross hairs over the driver's side of the Landrover streaking toward Argent's position. He squeezed off another round, putting a bullet into the man's chest.

The Landrover went out of control immediately, smashing into the side of a building. Before the men riding inside it could clear, Dane put a follow-up round through the gas tank, turning it into a burning pyre that killed at least four men.

Swiveling his attention to a Leyland-Rover Transport van, he put two rounds through the front seat area, then targeted the gas tank there as well.

Movement in the dark sky above drew his attention. Gazing over the top of the thermographic sniperscope, he spotted the Hughes WK-2 Stallion helicopter coming toward him. The Vanquisher heavy machine guns opened up, scattering scarlet fire from their barrels. The bullets ripped into the rooftop to Dane's left, closing in and letting him know the pilot must have been chipped to the max for weapons proficiencies.

Coolly, Dane ignored the line of fire tearing across the gravel and tar surface. He put the cross hairs over his target. Shooting straight wasn't a problem as long as a chummer had the right equipment. And making a great shot was usually a matter of standing ground and taking that shot.

He squeezed the trigger when the Vanquisher was laying down a spray of bullets less than a meter from him. The bullet hit the plastiglass nosepiece of the helo and cored through, striking the pilot in the head and doing its best to blow the man's head through the helmet in all directions.

The Hughes went down in a skewed path, crashing into a warehouse and erupting into a red and orange explosion that lit up the battlefield.

Dane didn't watch it burn; he was already moving on to other targets.

56

Miles Lanier watched the vid feed coming in from the sat-link over Pueblo in disbelief. Explosions rocked the warehouse district where he knew Andi Sencio was holed up. At first, he'd thought Sencio had finally gotten desperate enough to attempt to break free on her own.

Lanier wouldn't have blamed her. Ironaxe and his people were practically breathing down her neck.

Even though they had the vid, there'd been no way to get aud from any of Ironaxe's sec teams. He pressed one digit on his desktop telecom to connect him to Villiers.

"I see it, Miles," Villiers replied calmly. "I'm watching it now."

Lanier watched as one of the helicopters suddenly slid sideways and smashed into a fireball against a warehouse. "At first, I thought this might be Sencio's doing, that maybe the Underground Awakened had gotten cornered by Ironaxe's people and struck back. But as I look at it now, I see it's too deliberate." He glanced at Villiers on the telecom screen.

"If it's Argent, he's running a higher profile on this than I'm comfortable with," Villiers admitted.

"We still have the teams in Pueblo," Lanier reminded. "They could be there in five minutes, probably take Sencio and her team five minutes after that. But at the moment, I'd prefer to keep them there. As long as we know what's going on, let's keep our distance. Nakatomi has teams in the area as well, and that could still work to our advantage."

Villiers's eyes cut away from the telecom screen. "Hold on a minute. I've got a call coming in on my other line."

Lanier continued watching the destruction on the screen, amazed at how surgical it appeared. As a military specialist himself, he appreciated the action. Two men, possibly three, armed with armor-piercing rounds, he guessed. But he didn't think there were many in the Underground Awakened who had that kind of skill. And Sencio's people, the ones she had left, weren't capable of that kind of long-distance killing.

That meant that the efforts he was watching had to be a result of Argent. But what was the shadowrunner trying to do? Any attempt he made to get Sencio out of the area would be a covert one at best.

"Miles," Villiers called from the telecom.

Lanier regarded his employer and friend, mentally prying around the dangerous edges of what he saw transpiring, trying to guess at the depths of the biz Argent must have put into action. "Yes?"

"Clay Ironaxe is on another line," Villiers said. "He wants to use whatever satellite access we have over Pueblo. Somebody took his sat-link off-line. He's wanting to patch through our vid-feeds to coordinate his defense."

"What are you going to do?"

"I'm going to let him. Under the present circumstances, I can't see how I can refuse him."

"If you turn him down, tell him you don't have a sat-link over the area—"

"He's going to know I'm lying," Villiers said. "If I tell him no, he's going to take that as a breach of faith."

"And adding him to the sat-link feeds is going to jeopardize the integrity you have over that area," Lanier finished.

Villiers nodded. "He's going on-line in forty-seven seconds."

"Make sure those vid-feeds from that sat-link are separated from everything else we've got running through the Matrix." As security chief for NovaTech, the situation was incredibly anxiety-rife for Lanier. These were the instances Villiers paid him for, and the ones he lived to handle. His mind was already flying, figuring out angles to get around Ironaxe's presence. "We're going to lose our secured link with the teams you've got in Pueblo. Before we do, I'll contact my captain there and tell him that if he sees Nakatomi's people move in, or if Sencio is identified and captured by Ironaxe's people, or if the vid-feed is interrupted, he's to move in at once."

"I want Sencio secured or terminated. Anything else isn't acceptable."

Lanier agreed with a nod and punched the code into the telecom, counting down the seconds. He still had a really bad feeling about the whole situation. Going in bold as brass wasn't Argent's way. Not unless the shadow-runner was holding a hell of a hole card.

57

"We're not going to get the sat-link back. A scout team I ordered over there just confirmed that it's been totally fragged. We're down to the Phillips Tacticom communications system, which is going to limit us to local aud-links only because we don't have sat-link capabilities with those units."

Seated in the air-conditioned and bulletproofed Command and Control Ares Mobmaster, Clay Ironaxe glanced at Aaron Bearstalker. "I've just placed a call to Richard Villiers," he said, controlling the anger he felt. "He's agreed to let us use the sat-links he has in the area."

The Command and Control vehicle housed computer equipment that linked them with the individual ground and air units, leaving precious little space left over for the tech ops who marshaled those capabilities. Four techs worked feverishly around Ironaxe, trying to set up another in-country sat-link from his corporation, and going on-line through Villiers's systems through the secondary comm-link.

"Villiers admitted they were there?" Bearstalker asked.

"Yes. He told me they'd been put into place to watch Nakatomi. There's another Asian Fuchi sec team outside of Pueblo."

Bearstalker glared at the eight small monitor screens in front of him. All of them showed different views of the action taking place outside. "So who's backing this play?" he growled. "Villiers or Nakatomi? Who's covering up ownership of these posers we've ran to ground?"

Ironaxe shook his head. "I don't know. I've also called Nakatomi and requested access to his sat-link. In case Villiers's techs try feeding us false information, we can check the two feeds."

"Unless they're in it together."

"Worst case scenario," Ironaxe said, "and I can't believe that's possible after everything that's transpired between them." He glanced at the monitors Bearstalker was watching. "Let's find the people responsible for this, and flatline them. Then we'll get all the answers we need."

Bearstalker nodded in agreement.

"And make sure our people know we're not working off of a secure line anymore. The world is listening in."

58

Archangel tripped the light fantastic inside the Matrix, flowing along the lines of data that suddenly rerouted through the direct satellite feed she'd managed through the comm-link. Once inside the Matrix, accessing from the LTG in Pueblo, she watched the cyber landscape spread out around her in all directions.

In all those directions were strands of rainbow colored lights, threading through the black sky above her and the black firmament below her. Most of the ones streaming from the Pueblo Corporate Council appeared as southwest turquoises and blacks, shot through with reds and streams of silver. Between those strands of light that actually represented encrypted communications and data-transfers along the LTG were colorful nodes in thousands of hues and shapes.

Concentrating on the datastream jetting out of the Pueblo LTG she'd identified, Archangel forced herself to concentrate on the job ahead of her. She was a professional, fraggit, and despite the confusion Argent had created within her during the last few days, she was going to do a professional job. She wasn't going to think about Jack or Emma or Quint or Elvis or Wheeler or Cullen.

She reached out in front of her, imagining that the datastream coming from Ironaxe's location in Pueblo had gravity till she felt the pull of it. A private sat-link felt much different than normal LTG, and the sleazing took a whole new level of skill.

The fact that the datastream wasn't a true exchange, but rather a vampiric relationship as the Pueblo site drank down all the incoming vid-feed from the sat-link boosting images from the drone NovaTech had over the area, made tackling it even harder. Still, Archangel was decker enough to know that Villiers's dataslaves would be trying to swipe as much data from Ironaxe's on-site decks as they could.

Getting into NovaTech's outer cybernetic perimeters wouldn't be easy, but she knew she could do it. Provided she masked herself and her surprise packages as something that looked both intriguing and passive.

With access to the same vid-feed as Ironaxe was getting by virtue of the fact that Villiers was feeding it to the VaulTek CEO, Archangel knew even before Argent had suggested it, that Villiers and Lanier would try to access the aud-feeds coming from the VaulTek sec forces. She disguised herself in a string of audible communication data from one of the verbal reports a field op was giving of the sat-link's destruction and the ensuing chase of the person or persons responsible, compressing herself till she blended in. As the communication went along, she went with it, hurtling through the Matrix.

The hard part was keeping herself and the compressed data together as they bounced through the sat-link systems back toward Boston.

The first line of security was the Boston System Access Node. The datastream Archangel was part of surged toward the SAN. As she got closer, she recognized the white IC surrounding the SAN. It was represented in the Matrix as a huge, disembodied hand wrapped tightly around a phone booth.

Sleazing her way through the Boston SAN was simple. Any serious decker had a dozen different passcodes to any LTG SAN on any given hour. She flashed the passcode and went into the Boston LTG as a matter of course, sliding right between the huge fingers.

Without warning, the datastream she'd made herself part of jaunted into a huge cylinder of light wrapped around the heart of a collapsed star. Suddenly, Archangel felt as though she was ten times heavier than what she was accustomed to. She fought against the panic that filled her, making herself stay masked and encrypted.

All light went away in the tunnel and the datastream's speed picked up dramatically. Archangel stayed aware, knowing she could still jack out at this point any time she wanted to.

The tunnel ended abruptly in front of her, slamming into the exploding star construct that represented Nova-Tech in a rushing torrent of color. The barrier IC ahead of her took the shape of a plastiglass gargoyle rendered in tri-D against a wall of plastiglass bricks. The datastreams on the other side looked tantalizingly within reach.

Archangel kept herself relaxed as she hurtled toward the open mouth of the plastiglass gargoyle. Barrier IC wouldn't accept the deception program she was using to slide by in the datastream. She had no choice but to attack it and hope for the best.

As she rose from the datastream, stretching out into her full persona, movement to her right drew her attention. She turned to look, spotting a neon blue kimodo dragon hurtling across the intervening cyberspace. She knew instinctively that it was another decker launching an attack on the barrier IC.

The kimodo dragon slammed into the plastiglass gargoyle at full speed, grinding to a halt as the barrier IC held up. Before the dragon lizard could pull back to safety, the plastiglass gargoyle wrapped its arms around it.

From the way the system was set up, after traveling through the light tunnel, Archangel knew she wasn't at a readily accessed path to the NovaTech construct. Her ruse had gained some ground.

Flipping through her attack utilities, she pulled out one she'd only started working with, thinking under the circumstances it might work fine. She flew closer enough to the barrier IC to see her own reflection in the plastiglass gargoyle's eyes. In the Matrix, her icon was a green, winged woman.

She extended a hand and released the attack utility. Instantly a frost formed over the barrier IC, blurring the plastiglass gargoyle's features. When the attack utility completed its job, the elven decker slapped her hands against the barrier IC in a deliberate off-rhythm.

The barrier IC shattered into a million gleaming shards, leaving the path open ahead of her.

"Who are you?" the freed kimodo dragon demanded, turning to face her. Its great, snapping jaws were open, revealing plastimetal teeth with serrated edges.

"For the moment," Archangel said, "I'm an ally."

The kimodo dragon's eyes narrowed in angry distrust, but it kicked its feet and swam through the area where the barrier IC had been, following the same datastream that Archangel had come in on. Apparently it had a time problem too.

Archangel believed she already knew who the kimodo dragon represented, but she tagged it with a track utility in the form of a gold ring around one of its feet.

"You son of a slitch!" the dragon lizard exploded, turning in on itself immediately. Its clawed feet pried at the gold ring, trying desperately to pull it free.

Suddenly, a lightning blaze of blue-white seared through

the space between Archangel and the dragon lizard. Immediately, the other decker forgot about the track utility locked around its leg and got set to deal with the black IC coming up in the form of an Ares sentry drone.

Archangel saved the information coming back through the track utility, trying to ferret out who the other decker was and where he or she had come from. She flapped her wings, gaining speed, using up one of the slow utilities she had at the ready on the black IC. The slow utility went to work immediately, taking shape as a large fishing net that wrapped around its target, dropping the sentry drone's speed by half. But the intelligent movements, not quite as smooth as a real program's, let the elven decker know the sentry drone wasn't black IC after all, but a NovaTech decker taking the field.

Already on the attack again, dodging the blue-white electrical beam that burned past her, Archangel unleashed a black hammer utility that smashed into the NovaTech decker. The results were immediate. The utility traced the decker back to the real world and rendered him or her unconscious. The sentry drone persona faded, leaving only a few electrical sparkles floating in its wake.

Moving swiftly, Archangel seized the floating specks in one hand and used another track utility on the residual connection. Though the decker was off-line, his jackpoint into the Matrix was still open.

Archangel followed the track utility, sleazing her way into NovaTech's outer perimeter with ease. The kimodo dragon was on her heels, gnashing at her wingtips with its huge jaws as it tried to close the distance.

She only stayed for a quick trip through the decker's CPU, then used the route open to her to lock in on the sat-link interface through the LTG. The construct for the sat-link interface was a shimmering emerald triangle filled with a single glowing yellow eye.

By the time she reached the sat-link, the kimodo dragon

had been identified to her by the track utility as an Asian Fuchi decker.

In the datastream outputting to the sat-link over Pueblo again, Archangel unloaded the surprises she'd packaged into her deck. The hog utility was candy-coated in a Trojan Horse package that scanned like perimeter definition requests from the NovaTech computer.

As soon as the sat-link programming gulped the hog utility down, the triangle blinking the utility into its eye, the programs Archangel had designed for the deck virus went ballistic and nasty. In nano-seconds, the hog utility filled the sat-link program up with a self-replicating code that overtaxed the deck's active memory and started the collapse of running utilities.

The kimodo dragon swam up out of nowhere, its giant jaws distended as it tried to gulp Archangel down. The long pink tongue in its mouth suddenly shot out, coiling around one of Archangel's wrists, letting her know she'd been tagged with a track utility herself.

Instead of attacking the track utility, the elven decker used a relocate utility. As she'd hoped, the dragon's tongue stuck to the sat-link construct as her relocate utility shoved it off onto the closest target. The track utility the Asian Fuchi decker was using would ensure that the hog utility spread in that direction as well. As an added incentive, she slaved the hog utility to the track utility already attached to the kimodo dragon.

Stepping back from the Asian Fuchi decker struggling with the NovaTech sat-link construct, Archangel put her hands together, accessed her deck, and jacked out of the Matrix as black IC from Villiers's cybernetic defenses swarmed the position.

59

[Chip file: Argent
Security access:******—23:06:19/10-14-60]

UPLOAD CONTINUED

Location: Seattle Safehouse (recorded at a later time)

I kept watch out the window, standing guard over Archangel's prone body while Harrison Dane and the Travers twins unleashed a drekstorm over the warehouse district. The twins had been busy since they'd hit Pueblo armed with packs filled with boomjelly. I'd forgotten how truly destructive they could be when properly motivated. Dane's sniper skills added to the bodycount and the general confusion.

Even though the Ingrams weren't long-range weapons, the smart-link and move-by-wire systems I had helped me account for more of Ironaxe's stormtroopers. And they did have a vested interest in the building where Archangel and I were.

Peg kept up a steady conversation inside my head, wanting to know what was going on although she was as privy to the conversations as I was and had a clearer picture due to the sat-link she monitored from the drone Wakiza Summertrees controlled above us. My answers were short and distracted. I was too conscious of the retina chron counting down the time. The schedule was too tight to allow any lost time.

"Argent." Archangel's voice sounded weak, hoarse.

I turned to face her, seeing her slip the fiberoptic cable from the datajack at her temple. I looked the question at her, not bothering to put it into words.

"Their systems are down," she said. "I took out Villiers's and I believe I got Nakatomi's at the same time. He had a decker in the system who was trying to break through into NovaTech." She let the fiberoptic cable retract into the deck's housing, then stored it in the protective case. She draped the case across her back.

I accessed the commlink and called for Summertrees. "We've got a green light at your end."

"I read you," Summertrees answered back. "Give me the go."

Looking back out at the streets winding between the warehouses, I saw the area where the Travers twins would have to put the truck they'd commandeered. "Jesse," I said over the telecom.

"Here."

"Showtime," I said.

Bullets drove me back from the window, but I remained close enough to watch as Jesse pulled the big GMC Bulldog Step-Van into position in the middle of the street. He and his brother had stolen it earlier in the day, then set it up for the op now. The motion attracted only a handful of Ironaxe's sec guards. Jesse and Jason caught the secmen in a crossfire as Jesse cleared the Bulldog. Jason covered his brother from the shadows of a nearby building.

A heartbeat after they reached relative safety, the Bulldog became ground zero for the biggest explosion of the night. They'd used most of the boomjelly they'd brought for the shaped charge they'd put under the truck, placing it so that the blast would be directed downward. Evidently they'd tapped some of the VaulTek security teams' ammo stores during the last couple minutes and added to what they had on hand.

The blast sent a minor earthquake through the immediate vicinity.

When the smoke cleared, a gaping hole cut through the street. I didn't have any doubts that it had broken through to the mine tunnel below. Using the maps Peg had found in her data searches, I'd located the mining tunnel closest to the surface that would be big enough to do what we needed it to do.

"Summertrees," I said over the telecom, "you have your go." I didn't bother looking up. I wouldn't have been able to see the Skytruck or the Devil Rat that came tumbling out of the cargo hold. Laveau and Summertrees would accompany it down.

Turning to Archangel, I took the lead and we beat feet out of the room. Before we made the second landing, one of Ironaxe's secmen put a grenade through the window, firebombing the room. The heat of the blast crawled down over us.

A small knot of men met us at the door, assault rifles naked in their fists. I covered Archangel with my own body right before they opened fire on us, knowing that her reflexes weren't quite back on-line. Whatever she'd faced in the Matrix had taken a lot out of her.

Bullets smacked against the Espirit armor, but only two of them cored through to flesh beneath. One of them did a through-and-through on my right thigh, and the other penetrated but didn't pass through my back somewhere over my right kidney.

I ignored the pain, dropping the Ingram from my free hand and snagging an armor-piercing grenade from my equipment vest. Yanking the pin and slipping the spoon, I arced the grenade into the middle of the men.

"Grenade!" someone yelled, but his voice was lost in the ensuing explosion that robbed the warehouse of any other sound.

Dead men blew in all directions. Even before the dust settled, I had the Ingram back in hand. I went on down the stairs, firing into two men I saw still moving before they had a chance to bring their weapons up.

Blood leaked down my back and my leg under the armor, forming a sticky barrier. I paid attention to both areas, testing for any weakness that might throw me off later, but both of them were numbimg up well and stayed responsive to the demands I was putting on them.

"The Devil Rat is on target," Peg said into my head. "ETA is a minute seven seconds."

Striding over the dead men, I glanced out into the street and spotted the Chrysler-Nissan Patrol-One security vehicle parked in front of the warehouse, the engine idling. The driver saw me coming, bringing up the Colt assault rifle at his side. The ruby aiming laser skated across the faceplate of my helmet.

UPLOAD TO CONTINUE

60

[Chip file: Argent
Security access: ******—23:08:22/10-14-60]

UPLOAD CONTINUED

Location: Seattle Safehouse (recorded at a later time)

I put a pair of rounds between the driver's eyes, then reached in through the open door of the Patrol-One and spilled his corpse out onto the street. I reached back for Archangel, helped her climb inside the Patrol-One's forward cab. If there were still men in the rear compartment, we were separated from them and they couldn't get to us.

A quick scan of the controls familiarized me with the vehicle's handling. Patrol-Ones weren't just Lone Star or law enforcement vehicles; they were used in security and military ops around the world. I'd used them myself on occasion.

Shoving the stick into gear, I put my foot on the accelerator and surged forward. The four-wheel-drive caused all four tires to bite into the street with banshee shrieks. I accessed the commlink. "Laveau."

Her voice came back, filled with the sound of wind whipping by her helmet as she fell to the earth. "Yes, cher." As a voudoun priestess, she didn't go in for cyberware because it took away from her Art. But the Espirit helmet and BattleTac gear brought her on-line with the rest of us.

"I need to know where those DNA samples are being kept." I took the next corner hard left, downshifting and pegging the accelerator again to fight for traction. The Patrol-Ones had beefed-up suspension and handling, but they still behaved like ungainly beasts if they weren't treated properly. And I wasn't treating this one close to proper.

The DNA samples were important to the exfiltration. With them, Ironaxe's mages could still track Sencio and her group. Even if we escaped now, it would only be a stay of execution.

"I have worker loa out looking for them now, cher. We should know in moments."

"Get back to me," I said. "Andi?"

"I'm here," she answered, her voice sounding more hopeful than it had before. "What the drek are you doing? That hole just marked our position for Ironaxe's fragging sec teams!"

I heard the suspicion in her voice, and was only mildly surprised. Andi had called me because there'd been no one else she could believe in more. She just couldn't believe the way she used to. "Transport's on the way," I told her. "Keep your people back until it arrives."

"There's no way we're going to make it back through the plex. If Ironaxe's people don't get us, there are others."

"Stay put." I cut the wheel hard right, avoiding a van full of sec guards who figured out that I didn't belong on the team. Then I called out to Dane and the Travers Twins, telling them to get set for the rendezvous. It was Jesse and Jason's job to keep the street pit clear.

The van pursued me, closing the distance. I watched it in the side mirror.

"Give me a machine pistol." Archangel reached out to me.

I slipped off my right Ingram and passed it over. She wasn't chipped for the weapon, but with the autofire it was capable of and as close as the target was, she didn't need to be.

The Ingram chattered in her hands as she hung out the open door, one foot on the running board. Even though the van was armored and carried bulletproof glass, the driver pulled over to my side of the street. We roared through the vacant warehouses.

Plucking a high-explosive grenade from my vest, I pulled the pin and slipped the spoon, then ticked off two seconds from the four-second delay fuse on the retina clock. I released the grenade and watched it bounce from the street behind me. Before it could bounce again, the van was on top of it.

The resulting explosion ripped the van's chassis to pieces, taking one tire off completely and squirting it across the street. The van slewed, then rolled and turn over, skidding to a spinning stop on its roof.

I closed on the pit area. If there was no other choice, we'd abandon the idea of getting the DNA samples and try for them at another time.

Then I spotted the Devil Rat sliding through the air in

front of me, a few blocks from my position but still airborne. The huge black cargo parachute belled above it. Tracer-fire lit up the night, tracking the APC's descent.

"Argent, cher," Laveau called.

I saw her in the air above the Devil Rat, following it down expertly with a paraglider. "Yes."

"I have found de DNA samples, cher. My worker loa have only just gotten back to me."

"Where?"

"I do not know de location, cher," she told me in a strained voice.

I lost sight of her as she plunged below the roofline of a warehouse in front of him. I had to turn left to avoid the sudden dead end. A glance down at the BattleTac assured me that she was still mobile. The purple blip with the number 7 beside it that represented Laveau moved across the BattleTac monitor screen.

"You know how dese things work," Laveau went on.

I didn't know for sure how magic worked, though I'd studied a number of the concepts. While in the astral, a mage or voudoun houngan can whip around incredible distances and see any number of things, but reading is impossible and it's hard to know an exact location without a familiarity with the terrain. "Give me something to work with."

"I was in a round room, cher, on top of dis warehouse. But dere are so many warehouse, I couldn't tell you which one."

"Peg," I said. Ahead of me, another sec van slammed crossways in the street, blocking any further progress in that direction. A quick glance in the rear view mirror let me know another VaulTek sec vehicle was behind me, cutting me off.

"I'm searching," Peg replied.

I pinned the Patrol-One's accelerator to the floor, listening to the engine roar in protest. The throb in my wounded leg picked up the pace along with the acceleration. "Get down," I growled at Archangel as I pulled on the wheel and aimed it at the warehouse in front of us.

UPLOAD TO CONTINUE

61

[Chip file: Argent
Security access: ******—23:07:59/10-14-60]

UPLOAD CONTINUED ·

Location: Seattle Safehouse (recorded at a later time)

The plastisteel sheet metal wall of the warehouse caved in when the Patrol-One's reinforced bumper slammed into it. The vehicle was built to be a four-wheel-drive powered battering ram when it needed to be. Twisted sheets buckled around the vehicle, and a support strut gave a moment's pause before tearing away.

I sheared through two more supports on my way to the other side of the empty warehouse. The Patrol-One's headlights reflected a sickly green from the eyes of a rat horde clustered around the remains of a fresh corpse in the corner. They started to scurry away as I raced through.

The Patrol-One's reinforced window starred under the repeated impacts as it battered its way through the wall on the other side. A fine webwork of cracks covered the panes, blurring vision.

Once we were safely through, I pulled hard right, my mind racing as I tried to keep everything straight. By now the Devil Rat would be on the ground, hopefully in one piece.

"I found the location," Peg called over the commlink. "At least, I believe I did. It's the only building in the area with the architecture Laveau described."

"Light it up for me." I glanced at the BattleTac monitor on my wrist. The Patrol-One handled sluggishly for a moment till it cleared the jumbled plastisteel sheets from under its tires.

A gold hexagon formed on the BattleTac monitor, marking the location Peg had uncovered. I tapped a key, bringing up all the street markings. I also scanned the positions of the other members of the team, checking the life signs indicators. Everyone was still alive, still moving.

But I knew Ironaxe was out there waiting to change that. I accessed the commlink again, knowing we were about out of time there, too. "Summertrees, what kind of shape is that Rat in?"

The rigger's voice came on-line almost immediately, sounding resonant and distant, letting me know he'd jacked into the APC's cybersystems. "The gear here is all wiz. We missed the hole, but I'm getting there now." The sound of autofire rattled in the background of the commlink, punctuating the roar of the Rat's engine.

"We're also attracting a lot of attention," Dane added.

I consulted the retina clock, knowing we were going to lose the sat-link in minutes. "Where are you?"

"Making my way to the exfiltration point. We're running hot on this one, Argent. It's time to slot it and go, chummer. If we don't have everything, call it a burn and let's buzz turbo anyway. Live to fight another day."

But I couldn't and I knew it. Those DNA samples spelled death for Sencio and her team. And maybe they could lead back to the team I'd put together for the run. That was a responsibility I couldn't ignore.

I put my foot on the brake and pulled into an alley. "Can you make it from here?" I asked Archangel.

The elven decker gave me a hard look. "What are you doing?"

"I'm going for DNA samples."

She hesitated, one hand on the door. "I—"

"No," I told her. "You'd only be in the way. It's a one person job if it works at all. And it's my responsibility."

Color drained from her face as the anger took her. I'd had no right saying that, and we both knew it. But I wasn't going to be responsible for getting her flatlined. "Damn you, Argent." She dropped my Ingram on the seat.

"Later," I said.

She got out of the Patrol-One and jogged into the shadows, following the directions given by the BattleTac.

I started the Patrol-One rolling, picking up a VaulTek security vehicle and three motorcycles that pulled onto my back trail. None of them appeared to have seen Archangel getting out. I pulled across the street so that the passengerside window looked back the way I'd come. Then I thumbed the window down with the electronic keypad and unleashed a burst at the lead motorcyclist to make sure I kept their attention.

The bullets knocked dust from the bike's front wheel, but it was a runflat tire and didn't deflate. I brought the cross hairs up and targeted the slag's helmet. The bullet-proofing kept the rounds from penetrating, but didn't take away all the impact. His head danced to the ballistic mambo and he went out of control.

I didn't wait to see what happened. I put my foot down hard and streaked for the site Peg had lit up. The sec vehicle behind me managed to overtake me and ram me, but the Patrol-One shrugged the effort off, hardly shuddering at all.

Since tracing DNA samples was mage work, it was a wiz bet that there'd be one or more spellworms at the site. I also knew Laveau hadn't come into the run alone.

She'd spent most of the last few days creating govis to hold the worker loas who were making the run with her. I accessed the commlink. "Laveau, there are going to be mageslaves at the site. Could you run interference for me?"

"Dis already be done, cher. Just you keep your head down, and Ogoun be dere in two shakes of a dead lamb's tail."

I didn't respond to that bit of advice. With the sec vehicles on my tail and VaulTek every bit as capable of outfitting their people with armor piercing rounds as anyone else, I had no margin for error.

Then there was nothing left because the sky lit up with arriving helos. My low-light vision marked the aiming lasers of several weapons. I counted at least five of them before I had to bring my attention back to the road. Even then, the Patrol-One slammed into the side of a warehouse and nearly jerked out of my control. "Peg, who the frag are these people?" The sure touch and the strength of my cyberarms helped me keep the Patrol-One shiny-side up.

"I'm checking, but I can't verify. It looks like Nakatomi's and Villiers's people."

I'd been wondering when they were going to make it in. With Archangel taking out their sat-links, they'd had no choice but to chance an on-site visual recon. Both of them were fighting for the same secret, the same edge over Ironaxe. The arriving helos drew groundfire as soon as they were within range, and they weren't shy about returning it either.

A glance at the BattleTac confirmed that I was on top of my destination. Checking ahead, I spotted the warehouse ahead and to the left, the second floor round instead of rectangular.

I reached for the weapons control pad to the left of the wheel, keying up the control menu for the turret gun I'd spotted when I checked out the console. Machinery whirred behind me, pushing the turret up to bare the Vigilant rotary cannon mounted there. Cross hairs pulsed through the Patrol-One's webbed windshield and I used the thumb toggle to line up the shot on the target. When it was there, I fired.

The cannon round smashed against the warehouse's front wall. I'd expected it to be blown apart. Instead, it held up under the explosion, the incendiary force spending itself in a flaming wave meters from the wall. I almost pulled my foot from the accelerator and hit the brake, thinking I'd pile the Patrol-One up against that wall as well.

Then I heard Laveau over the commlink, her voice sounding strange and distant. "It's okay, cher. You ain't alone, you."

Without warning, Laveau levitated in front of me, approaching the building faster than the Patrol-One. I barely made her out as she moved, but noted the strange stiffness to her movements that told me she'd been mounted by one of the loas.

She drew back a hand and a huge fireball made up of massed coals formed in her palm. She threw the fireball against the front of the building. Green sparks raced like lightning. For a moment, the fireball hung in the air several centimeters from the building. Then, all at once, the fireball crunched into the building and punched on through.

"Dere, cher," Laveau said over the commlink. "Now de way is made clear. You be—"

Her voice cut off and the silence inside my head told me we'd just lost the sat-link Peg had arranged. I was alone, with only the living or dying to do.

END UPLOAD

62

Argent drove the Patrol-One into the weakened side of the building, exploding through the wall and skidding across the open expanse of plasticrete floor. His move-by-wire systems caused reaction problems because his body kept trying to move independently of the vehicle. He maintained control with difficulty, fighting the Patrol-One as well as his own body. He scanned the interior of the building.

Stairs to his left led up to the second floor. Laid out in a half-moon cut-out, the second floor overlooked the first, leaving a lot of open space. A dozen men occupied the second floor, surrounding tactical decks and equipment.

Argent slipped the transmission into first gear again and powered toward the stairs. Before he reached them, one of the sec vehicles and two of the surviving motorcycles roared through the opening he'd torn in the building's side. Autofire rattled the rear of the Patrol-One, and some of the armor-piercing rounds cored through.

Less than three meters away from the stairs, the plasticrete floor and a section of it surged up as a mound of earth broke through to the surface. It was proof enough that some of the people present were mages. Argent had no time for evasion.

The Patrol-One shuddered to a stop when it hit the earthen barrier. The front end collapsed and the engine dropped out onto the ground as the collision safety features took over. In the next heartbeat, the pursuing sec vehicle slammed into Argent, barring escape in that direction even if the Patrol-One had still remained operational.

The Vigilance rotary cannon, though, was still working. Argent thumbed the keypad, watching the gunsight trying to manifest itself on the shattered remnants of the windshield. The cross hairs never locked in. Flipping another toggle, Argent shifted the cannon over to manual control.

He lined up the shot from sight judgment. The distance made the target even more accessible. A few of the men on the second floor noticed the cannon turret turning in their direction and yelled out warnings to the others. They started to clear from the tables.

Without hesitation, Argent thumbed the FIRE button. The Patrol-One shuddered as the cannon belched out a deadly round. The resulting explosion was almost instantaneous, whipping across the second floor and dropping flaming sections of it free. Before he could fire again, an incendiary force hammered the turret, twisting it out of shape.

The crash against the earthen wall had jammed the door and Argent wasn't able to open it easily. Ramming his shoulder into the door, he knocked it off its hinges and dropped out onto the plasticrete floor with the Ingrams in his hands.

A semicircle of secmen fanned out behind the Patrol-One, firing at him. Argent squeezed the triggers of his weapons, rattling off short, telling bursts that knocked his opponents off their feet. Their return fire smacked against the light military armor, gouging it and slapping pieces from it. He felt another armor piercing round core through the flesh and blood part of his shoulder where his right cyberarm was connected, dangerously close to the control module that kept it working. Another pair of bullets cut through his cyberarm, leaving a buzzing sensation that signaled damage in their wake.

He aimed for feet and hands, areas where the secguards'

armor didn't fully cover. And he geeked them when he could. In seconds, he was out of ammo for the Ingrams, and had broken the advancing line of VaulTek secguards.

Turning, gliding on legs powered by the move-by-wire systems and his own adrenaline, he let the Ingrams drop to the ends of the Whipit slings. As he started up the stairs behind him, he drew the Savalette Guardian and a Cougar Fine Blade fighting knife with a 30-centimeter blade.

A secman ran to the top of the stairs in front of the big shadowrunner, thinking to cut him off.

Argent raised the Guardian and put a pair of armor-piercing rounds into the man's face. The corpse fell backward.

By the time Argent reached the top of the stairs, smoke from the pools of fire left behind by the cannon round obscured some of the area. He scanned the floor, taking in the damage, listening to the gunfire coming from below as the secguards on the first floor tried to mount an offensive.

A mage stepped out of the smoke, hands working frantically in front of him.

Argent tried to bring the Guardian up, but suddenly it felt too fragging heavy at the end of his arm. Then he stopped moving entirely as the spell paralyzed him.

The mage slave grinned, then slammed across the room with crushing force and dropped to the floor.

The paralysis left Argent immediately. Turning, he spotted Laveau levitating on a level with the second floor. Her posture was ramrod stiff, letting him know that she'd been mounted by one of the loa she'd called in to help during the run. She carried a short sword in one hand. Her eyes looked like they were rolled up in her head, but he had no doubts that she could see him.

"You are free again, human," a deep, cold voice said from Laveau's lips. "Mambo Laveau says you are to come immediately. They await you."

The address let Argent know Laveau had been fully possessed by the loa she had named as Ogoun. He reloaded the Ingrams, staying out of sight from the gunners below. The slap of leather against plastisteel warned him of secguards racing up the stairs. "Can you get a message back to her?" he asked the towering loa.

"She hears you now."

"Laveau, get back to the team and get them moving," Argent said. "I'll catch up."

"That is not acceptable." Laveau's loa suddenly blazed flames, creating a fiery halo. It threw an arm toward the group of men racing up the stairs. A huge fireball formed in the air, growing five meters across before it slammed into the secguards and scattered their flaming bodies.

"It's going to have to be," Argent growled. "Even if I started back now, it would hold them up too long. They need to buzz turbo now."

The loa-mounted mambo reached for him, levitating closer. "Not acceptable."

Knowing he could fight the loa on a physical level since it had manifested itself, the big shadowrunner slapped the hand way. Even then, the force only moved the hand a few centimeters. "Fight me and you may get me geeked because I'm not going till I'm ready. And if you fail to get Laveau back soon enough, you may get her geeked as well."

The loa snarled in anger, then levitated for the nearest window filled with broken panes of plastiglass.

Lungs burning from sucking down the smoke-laden air, trying to meet the need for oxygen in his system, Argent scanned the floor. The loa's fireball had not only taken out the secguards, but it had slagged the stairs as well. Moving forward, he found a wagemage, knowing the man for what he was by the fetishes he wore and the cut of his clothing.

Argent pressed the snout of an Ingram into the wagemage's face. "Tell me where the DNA samples of the runners are or I'll geek you right here."

The wagemage was young and scared. A trickle of blood wormed from his nose and across his lips. "Portable freezer unit."

"Where?"

The wagemage pointed.

Glancing through the smoke, Argent spotted the wheeled portable freezer. It canted back against the wall, obviously blown there from the cannon round, the door not fully closed anymore. He left the wagemage laying on the floor and crossed the room.

Before he reached it, the window nearby exploded inward, shattered by withering machine gun fire.

63

Argent dove to safety, narrowly avoiding the stream of machine gun fire that tore chunks from the plasticrete floor. Vibrations moved throughout the floor with the crescendo of impacts. He came up with the Ingrams firing, both of them locked onto the helo hovering outside the window.

His initial bursts cut holes in the helo's tail, then swept across the door gunner mounted in the cargo hold. The gunner's body shivered as the bullets hit him, and he sprawled in the grip of the door gunner safety rig.

Then the ceiling window above Argent's head came apart. The big shadowrunner whirled, still lying on the ground, and raised the machine pistols to the latest threat. His mind raced, seeking the possibilities, selecting the greatest likelihood as a cybered man from the helo had leaped onto the top of the building and come crashing through the plastiglass.

He recognized the armored form in front of him, the face barely discernible through the helmet. Aaron Bearstalker was the number two man in Ironaxe's corporation, and was almost as heavily cybered as the VaulTek CEO.

Moving inhumanly fast, Bearstalker chopped at Argent with a short sword. Argent caught a glimmer of light as the sword streaked for his hands, realizing that the sword carried a monofilament edge that could shear through his cyberlimbs like butter. There was no time to shoot and save his hands at the same time. He tried to pull his hands back, but the sword whistled through the Ingrams, lopping them off just short of his knuckles.

Argent dropped the useless machine pistols and rolled to one side as the sword came at him again. The monofilament edge bit deeply into the floor.

"Hola, motherfragger!" Bearstalker yelled. "I'm going to cut your slotting arms and legs off." He swung again as Argent pushed up to his feet, cleaving the air less than a centimeter from Argent's left shoulder. "Then I'm going to find out who you're working for." The blade picked up speed as the Amerind samurai launched himself into his kata.

Argent reacted to the martial arts moves, not bothering with trying for the Guardian in its thigh holster. Going for the pistol would have thrown his reactions off, split his attention. And Bearstalker was too good with the sword to allow that to happen.

Bobbing and weaving, keeping his hands out in front of himself and looking for an opening, Argent stayed almost toe-to-toe with the bigger man. Trying to run, trying to open up more space between them, would have only gotten him flat-lined. Staying in close eliminated some of the moves Bearstalker had open to him.

"You're good, browncone," the Amerind said. "I'll

give you that. Never figured on you dropping a vehicle down inside the mine shafts to use to bug out of here."

Argent didn't respond to the conversation. He kept his mind loose, relaxed, concentrating on the give and take of the sword. The latest blow came at his shoulder again, but this time he'd anticipated it well enough that he was able to slap it along the flat of the blade and push it further away.

Bearstalker brought the weapon back around even more fiercely, but the damage at been done. His kata style was looser now, in danger of deteriorating. "But now they're gone, Argent, and there's no way out for you."

The blade licked in at Argent's throat. He dodged it, then put his hands together and pulled his left thumb out of his hand with a slight twist. A monofilament garrote followed the thumb out, glowing slightly.

A monofilament whip and garrote were dangerous usually even to the joker who used them, Argent knew. A chummer had to be slotting good to use one effectively because even a loose swipe of the whip around a limb would amputate it in a heartbeat.

Argent kept his arms apart, out of harm's way, expanding the monofilament garrote between them. Before Bearstalker could pull his sword back around in another slash, Argent trapped it in the coil of the garrote. The monofilament edges, molecule thin, canceled each other out in a haze of sparks.

Setting himself, knowing Bearstalker was caught off-guard, Argent yanked on the garrote and tugged the sword free. He flipped it away, out of reach, then tugged on the garrote and sent his thumb zipping back into place.

Recovering, Bearstalker launched a roundhouse kick at Argent. The big shadowrunner blocked the effort with an arm, but the impact rocked him back on his heels. Bearstalker brought a heavy hand against Argent's helmet. Meant to withstand gunfire and light explosions, the helmet came apart under the cyberarm's attack.

Bare-headed, Argent backed off a half-step to recover his balance. He went into his defensive kata automatically, blocking most of Bearstalker's blows and connecting with a few of his own. He tasted his own blood when Bearstalker hit him a glancing blow in the mouth. Even reinforced as his skull was, it wouldn't have handled the punishment the Amerind samurai was handing out.

Argent blocked another blow, pushing his opponent's arm up, leaving him open for the short jab to the face. Bearstalker's skin split under the impact, showing the white flash of bone and cesium underplating that had been used to reinforce his skull.

The Amerind staggered back, bleeding profusely. Mercilessly, Argent took the fight to him, blocking a weakly returned blow and smashing a hard right to Bearstalker's temple. Bone and subdermal plating crushed inward, cutting into the vulnerable brain tissue beneath. Instinct alone made Bearstalker bring the attack to Argent again. Executing a spinning back fist, taking full advantage of his cyberarms, Argent slammed his knuckles into Bearstalker's cheek.

Bearstalker's head turned violently to the side, and the crack of his spine shattering at the base of his skull filled the room. Dead on his feet, his cyberware systems finally catching up to what his meat body already knew, Bearstalker collapsed face down on the floor.

Staggering, winded from the pain of his wounds and the beating he'd taken, Argent crossed the room to the portable freezer. He looked inside long enough to ascertain the existence of the DNA samples, then plucked a high-explosive grenade from his combat vest. He armed it and dropped it into the freezer.

Then he ran toward the edge of the second floor looking down over the first. He didn't pause when he reached it, leaping downward. The HE grenade went off before he touched the floor, destroying the DNA samples and throwing a gust of super-heated air over him.

He landed off-balance and tucked himself into a paratrooper's roll. As he came back up to his feet, he spotted movement ahead of him. His hand swept down for the Savalette Guardian in the counter-terrorist drop holster on his thigh. Pulling it up in front of him, the smartlink flaring through his synapses and putting the cross hairs in his vision, he leveled it and killed the two secguards firing at him from the shadows.

Nothing else appeared to be moving inside the building.

Knowing that there was no way he'd make it out of Pueblo on foot, and that there was no way he'd be able to catch the Rat without wheels, he spotted one of the motorcycles laying abandoned on the building's floor. He crossed over to it and lifted it, not noticing any damage that would keep it from running.

The motorcycle was a Harley Electraglide-1000, a model that he was familiar with. He straddled it, then thumbed the engine to vibrant life. More of the VaulTek security people closed in from outside, their lights slashing through the shadows and smoke that filled the warehouse.

Argent gunned the engine and popped the clutch, squirting the big bike through the hole he'd made entering the building. He stayed low over the handlebars as gunfire slashed through the air around him. The BattleTac monitor was blank on his wrist, cut off from the sat-link Peg had provided earlier.

But he knew where he was.

Riding squealing tires around the next corner, avoiding the glaring headlights of the sec vehicle coming at him, Argent headed for the street where the Travers twins had blown through to the mine shafts below. There was only one way to attempt to catch the Rat running through the plex's underbelly.

64

"Sir, I have a confirmation on that report: Aaron Bearstalker has been geeked."

Clay Ironaxe stood at the edge of the pit that had been blown into one of the mining shafts under the plex, glaring down into the darkness. A few of his men moved below, hanging from ropes and playing lights around. The news of Bearstalker's death hit him like a hammerblow. The loss was more than just a valued and trusted employee; he'd been the best friend Ironaxe had ever had. "Who did it?"

"Argent, sir," the sec guard answered over the limited radio contact they had established after the sat-link had been blasted out of existence.

"Where is he now?" Ironaxe demanded.

The sec guard answered hesitantly. "He got away, sir."

"I want that man found, and I want him flat-lined," Ironaxe shouted. "Do you understand me?"

"Yes, sir."

Ironaxe let his breath out through his nose, hoping to expel all the anger and fear trapped inside him as well. Failing to trap the runners, watching them virtually slip through his fingers in the last few minutes had been intolerable. The helpless feeling surging through him reminded him too much of the way he'd felt while in the hospital waiting to have his body cybered so he could move again.

Ray Hawksclaw came up beside him with a coyote skin

over his head and shoulders and wearing true leathers, dressed in the more traditional clothing of the People. Fetishes hung from a rawhide necklace, his belt, bands around his biceps, elbows, and wrists.

Ironaxe pointed into the hole. "Get a road built leading down into there now. It doesn't have to be fancy, just something I can get some vehicles down."

The shaman nodded, then selected a fetish and began to sing.

Ironaxe watched as the earth below rose and breathed, cracking and splitting as it formed a steep incline that linked the broken street to the mine shaft floor below. He accessed the radio. "Where are those fragging vehicles?"

"Here now, sir."

Lights from the approaching GMC Multi-Purpose Utility Vehicle played over the area, chasing away the night with their foglights and searchlights. The MPUVs held a favored world opinion as the most popular combat vehicle. Armored and fast, on road and off, they stood the test of working as personnel transport to light scout. Tonight, Ironaxe intended to use them as attack craft.

The Devil Rat the shadowrunners had dropped from the sky had been a fragging surprise. And taking his sat-link out the way they had allowed the APC to get to ground intact. When the rigger handling it had driven it off into the hole, dropping nearly twelve meters, the Devil Rat had even survived that when Ironaxe felt certain it wouldn't.

Still, the APC only had a few minutes' headstart. The Devil Rat's top speed off-road was 45 kph. Ironaxe knew because he'd had a dataslave check out the specs when he'd first learned of it. The MPUVs could do almost twice that. They wouldn't get away.

When the shaman stumbled away, finished with the task given him, Ironaxe waved the MPUVs forward. He ousted the man in the shotgun seat of the lead vehicle, then belted himself in and ordered the driver down the newly erected incline.

Before they'd rolled more than a few meters, multiple hits from an airborne autocannon left pits in the street and blew chunks out of the nearby buildings. The MPUV driver froze into place.

Ironaxe looked up to see the unmarked helos in the sky above him. It didn't take much skull-sweat to figure that mercs working for Villiers and for Nakatomi occupied those machines. If they'd belonged to the team of shadow-runners there to take Andi Sencio and her group from the Underground Awakened, they'd have put in an appearance much earlier.

But they were there now.

Slapping the console in front of him, Ironaxe said, "Go."

The driver engaged the transmission again and started down into the yawning mouth of the cavern below. Jerking and bouncing, the suspension taking a beating, the MPUV made the incline and pulled onto the uneven mine shaft floor.

The headlights and foglights lit up the cracked walls of the mine shaft. Mounds of debris, some of it decades old or older, some of it freshly dropped from the ruined street above, lay scattered over the tunnel. The shaft was nearly ten meters wide, allowing plenty of room for the APC to maneuver.

They had room to move, Ironaxe silently agreed as he freed a Colt assault rifle from between the seat, but the people aboard that APC weren't going anywhere. He was going to see to it personally.

65

Argent cut the Harley Electraglide hard right to avoid the sudden blistering hail of heavy machine gun fire that tracked across the street toward him. The motorcycle's front tire hit the curb leading up to the sidewalk at less than optimum incline, causing the handlebars to shiver and almost tear free from the big shadowrunner's grip. If his hands and arms had been normal flesh and blood and unaugmented, he would have lost the Harley. As it was, he had to make sure he didn't pull the handlebars free in his attempt to maintain control of the bike.

On top of the curb, he rode in close to the building, staying with the sidewalk. The stream of bullets from the attack helo overhead swept the sidewalk, chipping huge holes in the plasticrete surface, then raking up onto the buildings only centimeters behind Argent.

Shifting up again, Argent twisted the accelerator tighter. The Harley's high-performance engine responded without fail, making him feel like he was holding onto a rocket running a nape-of-the-earth course. He pulled ahead of the helo, pushing past the pilot's estimation of his speed.

He flashed past three streets, ramping over the curbs on the opposite side. By now the helo pilot would have had time to call in for reinforcements. Argent didn't have a clue whether the helo belonged to Nakatomi or Villiers. In the end it didn't matter because he was sure either CEO wanted him geeked.

Headlights gleamed at the other end of the street, letting him know the search pattern had grown tighter. A glance in his side mirror showed more ground vehicles racing up behind him. Without warning, the two groups opened up on each other. Heavy machine gun fire and cannonfire from firmpoints on the vehicles slagged the center of the street, the buildings around it, and each other.

A flying piece of plasticrete debris smashed into Argent's side with bruising force despite the Espirit armor, nearly toppling him from the Harley. He fought for control and remained upright, then geared down as he approached Naylor Street.

The motorcycle still carried enough momentum and weight that it slewed widely around the corner. Argent leaned deeply into the turn, dragging his knee twice against the street. Stubbornly, the runflat tires held traction, shrilling in protest.

Lights from an approaching van blazed across Argent, momentarily blinding him till his cybereyes adjusted. He fought the motorcycle, careening out of the way of the van. The van's bumper missed his head by centimeters, whisking hot air across his face. The curb came up suddenly and the Harley's back tire smashed into it.

The motorcycle bucked violently, plunging up into the air and fishtailing as Argent threw his weight back to pull the front end up. He came down hard, but he came down on the Harley, still rolling. Gearing down, he got the transmission tight again, then twisted the accelerator to pull it more under control. The van wrenched around behind him, the driver trying to follow. Instead, a sudden salvo of cannonfire reduced it to a flaming heap that smashed against a nearby wall.

Argent raced through the streets, winding the Harley's engine out. He scanned the band of vehicles and secmen ahead of him ringing the pit in the street, digging into their positions as they were attacked by a pair of helos in the sky. Some of them started to turn toward him, realizing he wasn't stopping. He aimed the Harley at the flesh-and-blood spectators.

Bullets ripped into the broken street, tracers smashing like fireworks against the plasticrete surface and leaving pitted areas behind. Most of the secmen scattered before the approaching motorcycle, but a big man in armor with obvious cyberware reached out with big synthferrous hands hooked like claws.

Argent didn't hesitate, letting off on the accelerator for a moment while he downshifted. Bullets struck his armor and the motorcycle, leaving vibrations in their wake. The big shadowrunner downshifted again, losing a little speed, then red-lined the acceleration and popped the clutch. The Harley's gears protested the mistreatment with a metallic howling and racheting that made Argent certain he was going to leave engine parts scattered behind him.

Instead, the front end of the Harley came up in a wheelie. The heavy metal boy before him reached out, confident of his cyberware systems.

It was one thing, Argent knew from personal experience, to be braced properly and have the strength to lift a motorcycle. It was another to have that motorcycle in motion. The Harley slammed into the secman, driving him backward even as his hands seized the front tire.

They went over the edge of the pit, airborne, the engine screaming as the rear tire tore free of traction. The secman's weight pulled the front of the Harley down. In the brief time he was airborne, Argent spotted the inclined trail that someone had built to allow vehicles into the mine shaft. The Devil Rat was running, but pursuit was closing in on it somewhere. Even if the pursuers weren't able to take the Rat down, Argent knew, they might be able to track it.

Then the Harley started falling, the heavy metal boy

pulling at the wheel and slamming a big hand up to grab the center of the handlebars. The secman smiled, baring augmented teeth that he'd chosen to deliberately leave looking like edged steel.

66

Arm burning with the effort, Argent drew the Guardian from its holster and fired pointblank into the secman's face. He didn't stop until the pistol was empty. Even then, the corpse didn't drop away before the motorcycle slammed into the mine shaft floor.

Argent came off the motorcycle with the impact, feeling it roll forward under him. He twisted in the air, struggling to find his balance and go limp at the same time. His augmented balance, improved by the move-by-wire systems, allowed him to start coming around. If there'd been enough time, he'd have been able to land on his feet.

Instead, he came down hard on his side, losing his breath to the impact. He moved immediately, using the cyberware that kept him ambulatory in spite of the shock to his flesh and blood nervous system. On his feet, using the low-light capabilities of his cybereyes, he spotted the motorcycle draped across the nearly headless corpse of his opponent.

Autofire ripped into being from above, chiseling rock from the mine shaft walls and ricocheting from the stone surfaces. A couple slammed into the Espirit armor.

Argent had lost the Guardian during the fall, his hands opening automatically to try to save himself. Unable to find it in the time allowed him, he grabbed the Harley and righted it, satisfied that the motorcycle had only accumulated a few more dings. He straddled it and thumbed the ignition, listening as the big engine turned over a few times before catching.

Dropping his foot on the gear shift, he put it in low and shot across the mine shaft in the direction he'd known Summertrees would head. Bullets erupted into the spot he'd just left, tearing into the dead man.

He switched off the motorcycle's headbeam and depended on his low-light vision to guide him through the shaft. The light would have announced his presence behind Ironaxe's pursuit crew before he wanted them to know he was there.

He drove hard, manhandling the Harley. His team was up ahead, riding guard on Sencio and her people, laying their hoops on the line, trapped between the secrets of three corps at war with each other. As long as he breathed, his place was with the team.

The mine shaft walls flashed by, a constant panorama of cracked stone scarred by machines and pickaxes. Rubble littered the mine shaft floor, some of it big enough to be dangerous. He accelerated in the long runs of the shaft, then tapped the brakes when he had to go around a corner. Dust and grit clung to his face, masking it. He tasted blood and earth, felt the heat of his wounds pounding through him, the buzz of the holes in his arm.

His commlink twitched for attention and he knew he'd pulled back within the range offered by the on-armor units used by the BattleTac systems. The sat-link was no longer operable, so he didn't have the mapping utilities and locations of his team, but communications were a definite improvement.

He accessed the commlink. "Summertrees, this is Argent."

"I hear you." Summertrees still sounded distant and far away.

"You've got a pursuit team on your hoop." Argent rocked to the side to avoid a patch of loose rock that would have been treacherous under the Harley's tires.

"I don't see them."

"Have you got a drone out?" The rigger had outfitted the Devil Rat with two Sikorsky-Bell Microskimmer IIs capable of transmitting aud and vid back to the LAV-98. He was also able to control the drones from the APC.

"I've got one out front to vid and transmit everything back to me so we don't run into any nasty surprises," Summertrees said. "I was saving the other one in case the first one got fragged."

"You need it," Argent said.

"The drone's been popped," the rigger said a moment later. "Frag, but keeping track of two drones and the Rat isn't fun at all in this enclosed space."

Riggers accomplished miracles, Argent knew, but the run through the mine shaft was pushing the envelope. They were speeding through the tunnels faster than a south-of-the-border inspired enema.

"Got them," Summertrees said. "Looks like two, no, three units. MPUVs. I've don't have any whammies packed on-board the Microskimmers."

"Dane," Argent said, "if you've got some armor-piercing rounds left for the Barrett, you can shake them up."

"Can do," Dane replied tightly.

"And I have yet one more trick up dis old sleeve," Laveau said.

"Where are you, Argent?" Archangel asked.

"Coming up fast. I've liberated a Harley as my transport." Argent accelerated again, this time picking up a ghost of a dust haze from the vehicles ahead of him. In another heart beat, he saw the red lights of the MPUVs. He reached to his vest and removed an HE grenade, pulling the pin and slipping the spoon. He kept a thumb locked over the plunger to keep the fuse from igniting and twisted the accelerator again.

The first MPUV had a heavy machine gun mounted on its rear deck, the tarp pulled down so the weapon pointed across the vehicle's hard top. The gunner blasted the frag out of the Devil Rat. A Vanquisher mini-cannon mounted on the last MPUV's rear deck belched flame as it fired a round at the APC. The cannon round slammed against the Rat's ablative armor in a crescendo of flame. The wrecked section of armor peeled away from the APC and whizzed through the air to collide with the tunnel wall.

The Rat's tracks dug into the stone floor with renewed zeal, tearing drek out of the floor as Summertrees weaved back and forth in the room available to become a harder target.

Argent roared up beside the last MPUV before the driver or the crew knew he was there. He tossed the HE grenade into the MPUV's interior and accelerated again, jockeying around the vehicle.

They saw him for a split second, and the machine gunner twisted his weapon toward the speeding Harley. Then the grenade went off, unleashing a fireball of orange and black flames inside the MPUV. The vehicle swerved left suddenly and impacted against the wall. In the next moment it flipped end over end, the flames continuing to cling to it.

The Rat cut to the right without warning, blocking off the lead MPUV's attempt to come up along side. Then Argent got a brief glimpse of Harrison Dane popping up from the Rat's rear hatch. The Barrett sniping rifle was in his hands.

The lead MPUV slewed out of control and went turtle, flipping upside down.

The second MPUV sped around it, swerving to barely miss it.

Leaning into the Harley, controlling it as much with his weight distribution as the controls, Argent whipped around the wreck as well.

Heavy machine gun fire lanced from the second MPUV, streaking across Dane's position in the open hatch. Dane jerked back, bleeding profusely from the head. His body draped loosely across the Rat's back, starting a downward slide toward the ground.

One of the Travers twins reached out of the APC and seized Dane by the vest with a big hand. Straining, he managed to get Dane back inside just as the heavy machine gun fire cut through the space where the elven sniper had been.

"Dane?" Argent said, and felt as cold inside as he had the day Toshi and Hawk had died.

"He's breathing," Jesse Travers replied over the commlink. "Hurt bad, but he's breathing."

Argent closed on the remaining MPUV, spotting Ironaxe in the passenger seat at the same time the VaulTek CEO saw him. Ironaxe waved, yelling to the driver. Immediately, the MPUV came across to the right, cutting off Argent's path to the Rat. The gunner on the rear deck brought the machine gun around.

67

Knowing that if he attempted to back off he'd only remain a target, and that getting around the MPUV in the narrow confines of the tunnel was impossible, Argent sped toward the rear of the vehicle. The machine gun blasted flame and rounds over his head, filling his cyberears with the thunderous roar.

Before the gunner could shoot again, Argent grabbed the weapon by the barrel and stepped onto the rear of the MPUV. The Harley dropped away, out of control, turning quickly into a pile of twisted wreckage.

The sensor feedback in Argent's cyberhand let him know the weapon's barrel was hot enough to burn normal flesh and blood. He kept it away from the rest of his body and straight-armed the gunner with his free hand, hitting the man in the chest.

The secman flew from the MPUV's rear deck with a yowl of pain.

Bullets chopped into Argent's armor as he turned his attention back to Ironaxe. He couldn't bring the captured machine gun up because the area was too confined. Reaching out before Ironaxe could train the assault rifle on his unprotected head, the big shadowrunner bent the barrel.

Trapped, the next half-dozen rounds exploded, turning the rifle barrel into a collection of shrapnel that thudded into Argent's armor and razored his face. Blood streamed down over his left eye, partially blinding him.

Ironaxe erupted from his seat, using his cyberware to rip through the MPUV's hardtop and knock it away. Panicked, the driver swerved to the left and right, striking both sides of the mine shaft, seeking desperately to dislodge Argent.

Setting himself as best as he could, Argent met Ironaxe's fist with a blocking arm. It wasn't enough to completely shrug off the blow, though, and the VaulTek CEO's fist grazed Argent's chin.

The big shadowrunner drew back, staggered, his senses reeling. Instinctively, he blocked Ironaxe's next attempt to crush his head with a punch.

"Who are you working for?" the VaulTek CEO roared.

Argent slapped another blow away, his vision and senses clearing.

"Who sent you here?" Ironaxe grabbed the remaining support struts for the MPUV's missing hardtop and braced himself to kick at Argent's chest.

The man had been trained in the martial arts as well, or chipped for it, Argent knew from the skill displayed. Ironaxe's foot slammed into the center of his chest, enough strength and weight behind it to knock the big shadowrunner off his feet. He fell backward, rolling over the edge of the MPUV's deck, dropping toward the ground.

He flailed with a hand and caught the edge of the vehicle's rear deck. His legs slammed against the ground, dragging hard along the rough stone. Pain flooded his synapses as the armor buckled in spots. He knew from experience when his shinbone broke over a large rock. His leg started going numb and swelling almost immediately. Blood started filling his boot.

Ironaxe stepped into the MPUV's rear deck as Argent tried to crawl back onto the vehicle. The VaulTek CEO leered down at the big shadowrunner. "Did your hands lock up on you?" Ironaxe shouted over the noise of the racing combat vehicle. "Are they going to hang on while the rest of your body falls to pieces?"

Argent struggled to keep his body limp, to keep from taking any more damage than he had to. But the beating he was being given shuddered through his whole body. Thankfully, the pain had already progressed past the point of cognizance. He was operating on adrenaline and stubbornness.

But a part of him briefly considered giving in. His body was battered and torn more than at any time he could remember. Escape seemed a million klicks away. And the light blossoming behind him revealed that more of Ironaxe's people had driven down into the mine shaft.

Death had been such a constant companion for so long, and he'd kept his life so small since Toshi and Hawk had been flat-lined, that it wasn't unsettling to think about at all. And to die, all he had to do was let go or hang on. It would be simple.

"Who betrayed me?" Ironaxe demanded. "Tell me who hired you and I'll let you live."

Death would be easy. Only Argent knew he couldn't take the easy way out. He'd never been given anything easy. Working for Brynnmawr, being brought up with all the lies, finding the few truths he actually knew to be deep within himself and recognizing that he'd never be able to walk away from them without losing himself had been hard. So had walking away from Brynnmawr and Sencio when that had become impossible to avoid.

But those were the fundamentals that had built him.

Argent was a crucible, and he'd been in fires that had shaped him to be more than a man. He couldn't take the easy way out; he would never be able to. He'd been born to go down fighting, his battle or someone else's. Maybe that was one of the things Brynnmawr had seen in him all those years ago as well: that inability to give up or admit defeat.

"Mr. Johnson hired me," Argent said, shouting to be heard over the MPUV. Moving swiftly, wringing everything out of his cybersystems that he could muster, he grabbed the front of Ironaxe's protective vest and yanked.

68

Off-balance from the swaying combat vehicle, the Vaul-Tek CEO tumbled from the rear deck. Argent released his hold on the combat vehicle and fell on top of Ironaxe. He guessed the MPUV was doing somewhere near sixty or seventy kph, fast enough to do a lot of damage even to someone who'd been as heavily cybered as Ironaxe.

Argent stayed on top of his opponent, using the man as a buffer against the harsh surface of the mine shaft floor, riding him like a sled. Ironaxe screamed in agony as the rocks smashed against him and ripped his flesh.

They came to a stop in a tangle of arms and legs, smashing up hard against a boulder. Dust plumed up around them in a cloud, interfering somewhat with Argent's low-light vision.

The shadowrunner rolled from his opponent and took a deep breath, amazed at all the places that hurt. It was suddenly incredibly easy to tell where the cybersystems began and ended.

Silent, moving quicker than Argent would have given the man credit for, Ironaxe rose to his feet. He cocked and twisted both hands, unleashing forearm blades that jutted well out from his wrists.

Favoring his broken leg, aware of the headlights closing from the other end of the mine shaft, Argent forced himself to his feet, ignoring the explosion of pain that accompanied the movement.

Blood ran down Ironaxe's neck. His face on the right side had been torn away, revealing the dermal plating and synthferrous reconstruction work that had been done. His cybereye peered pure hatred, moving in the bared orbital compartment that housed it. "Going to die, you son of a slitch." Even his voice had been damaged, coming out hollow and inhuman.

Unable to move well because of the injured leg, Argent stood his ground as the man attacked. He twisted, avoiding Ironaxe's left-hand thrust, then blocked the right-hand-thrust, knowing he was only going to get one shot. His left hand smashed into Ironaxe's torn and bloodied face, caving it in to the back of his skull.

Even with the cyberware, Ironaxe's neural systems shut down, sending his corpse into spasms. The dead man dropped at Argent's feet.

Breath rasping hard, burning against the back of his throat in spite of the improved circulatory respiration provided by not needing to provide for the flesh replacements, Argent limped to one side. The MPUV Ironaxe had been riding in streaked back toward him. Beyond it, the Devil Rat had come to a stop a hundred meters away, dust boiling around the tracks.

"What the frag are you doing?" Argent demanded over the commlink. "Get out of here."

As he watched, the Travers twins bolted from the rear hatch and raced toward him. "Not leaving without you, omae," Jesse said.

"Depending on you to help us finance the bar with some more wiz work in the future," Jason said. "That would be hard—"

"—if you were dead or got noosed tonight."

Argent looked around as the MPUV bore down on him at 30 kph at least and rising, but there was no place to run. He braced himself, depending on his cyberware and move-by-wire systems. As the combat vehicle closed, he took a couple limping steps directly at it. Senses alert, the move-by-wire thrumming inside him, he placed both hands palm down on the MPUV's front end and vaulted over it.

There was a moment of vertigo as even his cyber-systems struggled to keep the pace. Argent flipped, barely clearing the top of the vehicle. He came down fast, the MPUV already past him. If he hadn't been injured as badly as he had, he could have landed on his feet. He'd managed it before at other times. But he knew the broken leg wouldn't support him, and any serious attempt at a standing landing would have aggravated the injury even more.

He came down in an undignified sprawl, but managed to control the fall well enough to roll and come up on his good leg. As he limped around to look back at the opposite end of the tunnel, he saw a phalanx of approaching vehicles. Ruby laser sights were starting to lock onto his position as well as the Rat's.

"Fraggit, Summertrees, clear the Rat from the LZ," Argent ordered.

"A moment more, cher," Laveau said calmly over the commlink, "and we shall all be on our way."

"I can't make that far quick enough even with help from the Twins," Argent said. He tore a grenade free from his vest, knowing he was too close to Ironaxe's MPUV to use it safely, but knowing too there was no choice. "Get clear."

"Patience, cher," the mambo said. "You forget dat you are not alone in dis. You chose good people. Believe in dem."

As Argent watched, Laveau levitated up from the darkness around the Devil Rat. Her body ramrod stiff and showing signs of the Ogoun loa possessing her, she made a series of intricate gestures.

The MPUV in front of Argent came around, gaining speed. The driver lifted an assault rifle this time, the laser aiming sight glowing ruby.

Before Argent could use the grenade, the ground opened up in front of the MPUV and swallowed it down whole. In seconds, only a weak glow shone through the thin layer of mud covering the red taillights. Then that was gone.

Autofire opened up from the approaching line of Vaul-Tek sec forces. But they were quickly erased by the avalanche from the roof of the cavern that pulled a wall of rock and earth down in front of Argent. A few pebbles and a handful of dirt spilled across the shadowrunner's boots.

"Come on, cher," Laveau called weakly. "It is time to go."

Bending quickly, the sound of cannonfire echoing from the other side of the earthen wall, Argent rigged a quick leg brace out of his combat vest using straps. The leg still hurt like bloody frag, but he used it long enough to jog back to the Rat.

Sencio stood in the rear hatch, looking worriedly at him. She offered him a hand up and he took it. Her strength wasn't enough to aid that much in getting his heavily cybered body onto the Rat, but the gesture meant a lot.

Once on top, he peered down into the Rat and saw the rest of his team and Sencio's people. And Harrison Dane, bloody and small, lay sprawled on several of them. Crimson pooled from a wound at his temple, but Archangel placed a fresh compress on it from the APC's medkit.

"He's wiz," Archangel told Argent.

"Like fragging hell," the elven sniper snarled. "My head's pounding like a sybaritic troll's whanger in rutting season. And I've got sweeps coming up during the shows I'm going to be making in the next few weeks. You owe me, Argent."

"I'll be there," Argent promised. "I always pay my debts." He laid back across the rear deck of the Rat and tried in vain to find a comfortable position for his broken leg. He left the boot on so it would contain the swelling spreading down to his foot. It was still a long ride to where Summertrees had stashed the T-bird that would take them back to Denver.

"I'm glad you came," Sencio said low enough that only they could hear.

Argent remained seated on the outside of the APC along with the Travers Twins. "Null sweat," he told her. And he reached out to take her hand, surprised to see the tears that gleamed in her eyes.

"Argent," she said softly. "I had to call. I didn't have a choice. I just don't want you—" Then her voice failed.

"It's okay," he told her. "I understand." And with his gaze, based on all the years they'd had together, he let her know that his understanding wasn't just about the exfiltration. She wanted him to know that calling out to him didn't mean she was changing her mind about why they were apart. But he was comfortable with that. This way, his life remained intact as well, without compromise. It was the only way he could live it.

Epilogue

[Chip file: Argent
Security access: ******—12:16:57/10-20-60]

BEGIN UPLOAD

Location: Denver Safehouse

"So what happened?"

I looked at Archangel sitting across the table from me in the UCAS district in Denver. We were having lunch at the Cafe Giovanni on Market Street. The restaurant was small, dark, and intimate, which fit my mood at the moment because I was worn out and feeling empty and wanted quiet around me.

She was the last one of the team remaining in Denver. Laveau had shipped out first, headed back for New Orleans. Summertrees headed back into the T-bird crowd after we negotiated the sale of the Banshee. The Travers Twins had gone back to Atlanta three days ago, and Harrison Dane, patched up at a street doc who specialized in plastic surgery reconstruction, went back to Dallas. I knew Archangel had stuck around for her own reasons.

She looked classy, like she had just walked out of the pages of a glamour screamsheet. I was still carrying a lot of bruises even six days after the run, and I wore a hideaway cast on my shin, holding the break together.

Normally, I wouldn't have answered the questions Archangel was asking me unless Peg had asked them.

Which Peg had asked, and I had answered, so I was already somewhat practiced. It had helped that Peg had stayed out of my biz until after I put Andi on the jet to Boston that morning.

"Villiers offered her a chance to come back into the corp," I said. I'd put a white noise generator on the table to keep our conversation private.

"And she did?"

"Yes. She had some paydata that Villiers hadn't gotten in an earlier download."

Archangel's eyes remained hidden behind the White-laws sunglasses she wore. "And you just let her go?"

"I couldn't hold her."

"She might have stayed if you'd asked."

I looked at her then, knowing the questions she was asking me were coming out of her own situation, three years unsettled and still fresh in her mind. "I didn't want to ask."

"All the love was gone?" She sounded sarcastic or bitter. I didn't know which and I didn't try to figure it out because I knew both emotions came out of the same place.

"No. That's what made putting her on the plane this morning so hard."

"Then why let her go?"

"Because she couldn't stay," I replied.

She understood then. "Because of you, or because of her?"

I started to say both, because it was in me to protect Andi if I could. I'd protected her somewhat that morning by calling Villiers after I'd put her on the plane. The conversation was short. He'd offered me a job with NovaTech at an obscene salary. I'd turned it down, then offered him advice to the effect that I didn't want to hear of anything bad happening to Andi at his hands while she was in his employ. Or anything that might be construed as happening at his hands. He'd told me he'd take that under advisement. But my advice had rankled, as well as my turning down the offer. Villiers was a man who was used to getting what he wanted. For the moment, I knew I had a powerful enemy if he chose to handle it that way.

With Archangel and the prying I'd already done, I remained honest. "Because of me," I said.

"You didn't want her to stay?" She looked surprised. "But the two of you stayed in a hotel room together for the last five nights."

"I slept on the couch," I said. Sencio had needed me there while she put herself back together, reassembled that tough armor that she needed to make Villiers come around to her way of thinking. I'd made her feel safe, and I'd taken some comfort in that as I worked on healing myself.

"Why?"

"Because I think more clearly when sex isn't involved."

"Sex doesn't necessarily have to mean love."

"No. I'm not a prude. But with someone like Andi, with the history we'd shared together, it would have been too confusing."

"For her or you?"

"For me," I answered. "I can't say how she'd feel."

Archangel sipped her soykaf, thinking. I could see it in the way she held herself. "Do you think she would have stayed if you'd asked?"

"I don't know."

Archangel fixed me with her stare, her eyes and deeper emotions still invisible to me. "I think she would have."

"Why?" I asked. "Would you have stayed if you'd been asked?"

She gazed at me, and for a moment I thought I'd gone too far. She'd been treading around the real issues at hand and I'd deliberately stepped on them. "I don't know," she said finally.

"You bailed before the issue even came up," I pointed out.

"It would have interfered with my work. After everything I've been through, I don't need all the insecurity that comes with a relationship. All I've got in this life is me. I had to work hard to get that. And I don't want to lose it."

I heard the brittleness in her voice, saw the glimmer of moisture on one of her cheeks. She was hurting and we both knew it. "Sometimes," I told her, "you have to face your greatest fears by looking them in the eye, not just beating them into submission. You didn't look your situation in the eye. You picked up and moved on, beat it on one hand, and that may have been harder on you than staying and dealing with any potential problems on your team." I thought about Toshi and Hawk. "People in the shadows that you can trust, they're far and few between. And the ones you can love? They're priceless."

She looked away from me. "I've got to be going."

"If you really want my advice," I told her, "go see this guy Jack that you've been thinking about. Face him and face yourself, then let the chips fall wherever they may. It's been three years for you, and it's still like yesterday."

"It's not that easy."

"I didn't say anything about it being easy. I've got some issues of my own I have to face." I was thinking about Brynnmawr, remembering that dead planet construct in the Matrix what was left of him was stuck on, surrounded by graves that he'd helped fill. "Even this thing with Andi might not be over with. But I know what it is right now. You can't say the same thing."

She stood up from the table and smiled down at me. "I'll think about it, Argent. I appreciate your time. I know you didn't have to answer these questions." She offered her hand and I took it. "If you ever need a decker for another run and Peg can't cover for you, give me a call."

"I will," I said.

She turned and walked away. I watched her for awhile, wondering how she was going to handle her situation, knowing she was going to have to deal with it because it wasn't going to go away. The feelings ran too deep. But so did the fear that I saw inside her.

Back in the hotel that afternoon, I had Peg jack me back into the Matrix and take me to Brynnmawr.

"Are you sure this is something you want to do?" she asked as we stepped down into the desolate world where he'd been confined. The eternal night draped shadows over the cemetery around us.

I gazed around at the row of tombstones, looking for him. "It's something I have to do," I told Peg. I spotted him walking toward us. Peg had changed her persona to look like me. In the Matrix I couldn't feel the pain from the broken leg or the bullet wounds quite so bad.

"Argent, my boy, what are you doing here? Is something wrong?" He sounded genuinely concerned, his eyes raking me from head to toe.

"No sir," I responded. "Everything is fine."

"You're moving different."

I guessed that some of the gingerly way I'd been moving while recovering from the run had bled over into my mannerisms. Peg had looped a feedback into the program to allow her to read my stored body language. "I was wounded, sir."

"Of course you were. But are you well now?"

"I'm getting there, sir. Thank you for asking."

Brynnmawr reached into his pocket and pulled out one of the pecans that he gathered from the trees over the graves. He cracked it between his fingers, dropping bits of the hull onto the ground.

"I brought you something, sir." I held up a plain white box with Peg's help. She was still in control of the persona.

A wary look entered his eyes and he drew away slightly. That was the first time I'd ever seen him appear frightened, and seeing that reaction hurt me.

"What is it?" he asked.

"A gift, sir." I flipped open the top, revealing the dozen bagels inside. "Something to offer a change to the palate." I'd asked Peg to design a program that would replace the pecans the construct Brynnmawr had been imprisoned in forced him to eat. She'd told me that she guessed the pecan data was a small support program designed to help keep the integrity of the construct attuned to Brynnmawr's needs.

"I've always had a fondness for bagels." He tossed the pecan away and reached in for one.

Peg's programming was good. The bagels still gave off heat, and I could tell how soft they were from the way Brynnmawr tore them in his hands. "There's something special about the box too, sir." I closed the lid, then opened it again. Once more, there were twelve bagels inside. "As long as you don't completely empty the box, it will refill." The program was also designed to replicate itself if it wasn't totally used up.

"Ingenious." Brynnmawr graciously took the box. "I thank you for the gift, my boy, but why?" His face got suddenly stern. "If this is given out of pity, I'll have none of it."

"No sir," I said. "It's just a gift. Maybe you can even consider it as a down payment."

"A down payment for what?"

"I've come to realize something lately, sir," I said. "You taught me everything I knew in the beginning. And I've gone on to teach myself several other things. But you've never once taught me everything you know."

Brynnmawr smiled. "So the prodigal *has* returned."

"There are some things I'd like to talk over with you sir. Some things I need to understand."

"Sencio didn't stay with you?"

I shook my head.

"I'm not surprised," Brynnmawr said. "She was never as disciplined as you were."

"I don't feel very disciplined, sir. Frankly, these past few years, I've kind of felt all over the place."

"Because of your lost team mates?"

"I think that brought things to a head, sir," I told him. "There's more left over from my time with you than I'd thought. I need a clearer understanding of you to put it all into perspective."

"Introspection is never a good thing for a field agent," he told me. "But as for becoming a man, truly becoming the man you were born to be, there's no harsher teacher than one's own self. And it's the only thing that will allow you to be what you most need to be." He smiled and clutched my upper arm, pulling me into motion, guiding me again like he had all those years ago.

I went willingly, following him into the gravekeeper's house in the middle of that virtual cemetery, surrounded by the dead of his life. I wondered what the house would look like on the inside, what kind of comforts or tortures his captors would have dreamed up and programmed for him.

"You and I talking," Brynnmawr said, "it's not going to be the same. We've both grown."

And I wasn't as young or as idealistic, or as sure of myself. He knew that.

"I know how you feel, my boy," he told me in a low, compassionate voice that surprised me. "Broken up and busted inside. It hurts having to look at your own mortality and your own capability for making mistakes."

"Yes sir."

"But those things are truths, my boy, and the truth shall set you free."

I went with him into the house, to learn the things that only an adult son could learn from a father. And I was already feeling freer than I had in a long time.

END UPLOAD

ABOUT THE AUTHOR

Mel Odom is the author of over 60 books in the science fiction, computer gaming, action-adventure, horror, young adult, and juvenile fields and makes his home in Moore, Oklahoma. Besides writing books, he coaches his nine-year-old's and fifteen-year-old's basketball teams, a Little League baseball team, and teaches.

In addition to being a contributor to the Shadowrun® universe, he's writing books for TSR's Forgotten Realms setting, for Sabrina the Teenage Witch and Alex Mack, and a popular on-going adventure series. He's also done the recent *Blade* movie novelization starring Wesley Snipes. His books have been translated into Russian and German, and he is an inductee of Oklahoma's Professional Writers' Hall of Fame. At a young age.

He shares his life with wife, Sherry, and their five children, Matthew Lane, Matthew Dain, Montana, Shiloh, and baby Chandler. And a lot of friends and ball teams.

He can be reached by e-mail at denimbyte@aol.com and welcomes comments.

SHADOWRUN

Dragon Heart Saga

☐ **#1 STRANGER SOULS**

0-451-45610-6/$5.99

☐ **#2 CLOCKWORK ASYLUM**

0-451-45620-3/$5.99

☐ **#3 BEYOND THE PALE**

0-451-45674-2/$5.99